I0619341

TARRAGON WORLD

Book Six of the Tarragon Series

Elizabeth James

Thrall of Darkness

THE TARRAGON SERIES

CONTENTS

PROLOGUE

Margot fumed as she stalked the length of the Queen's chamber. That damned Queen. Jamie had acted so quickly she hadn't been able to complete her attack. Now she was exposed as she hadn't been in centuries. Yasmina, her beloved dragon, wouldn't even tell her where Jamie and Scott – and those kittens – had gone, other than to tell her that they were safe. They had to be at the nesting grounds again with Marisol, where they would lure the council away from her to try to defeat her just like Ashton. Well, she wasn't a fool like him. She broke no rules.

"Margot?"

She turned. Gerald, the head of the men's council, was standing in the open doorway. Time to see how much power she really had. She smiled and approached him. He flinched. Her smile faded a little. So he knew what had happened. That meant the ranking dragons had likely told all their partners. Unfortunate, but it would ensure their obedience.

"A council meeting needs to be called," she announced. "Both campuses. Immediately."

He agreed and started to leave when she grabbed his arm. He paled.

"We'll be able to work together, won't we?" she asked, still smiling.

"Of course," he said. "The council respects its leaders, and you've always been my superior. That will never change."

She nodded and let him go. She took one more look around at Jamie and Scott's room, tempted to destroy everything, but Gerald's answer was reassuring. She reached out to Yasmina and received a confirmation. None of the ranking dragons on campus planned on acting against her because they were protecting their humans.

Margot began heading to the council chambers and fingered the bump on her head. She again cursed Jamie. If only Jamie and Scott had just given her the kittens. But they resisted. She knew she couldn't really hurt Jamie, only erase his memories for long enough to forget the conversation, but she could strike at Scott. She felt a little pleased about that. No matter what else happened, at least Jamie would be in agony having lost Scott.

Oh, Narné would be able to tell Scott about his forgotten memories, his forgotten life, since nothing could erase a dragon's memory, and she suspected Scott would fall in love with Jamie again. But it would be torture for Jamie and it was the only solace she had now that the kittens had escaped.

Her eyes narrowed. She never should have let Jamie adopt the cat in the first place but she had never suspected that she would need to use her powers on him. She still wasn't sure if he realized she had used her powers on him once already. If he had, he hadn't told Scott because when she confronted Scott about it during one of his classes, he had been furious and without fear. She had erased that confrontation, of course, and knew for a fact that he had no lingering memory of it.

She reached the council room and immediately went to the dais. She glanced at the Queen's chair. Once, she would have given anything for that chair. But then she learned the strength of the council and now she would never give up her current role. Ashton had been foolish thinking he could become the Queen's mate. He was far more powerful as head of the council. And now he was dead. She had to remember that, and walk carefully. Jamie was a child, but a powerful one. She would not let him kill her as well.

Those cats. This was her year, the year she had finally rounded all of them up and gotten all of them spayed or neutered. All of the female students had been studying the cats for years, tracking them, counting them, and she knew that with this sweep, she was eliminating the colony from future generations. Even though they were her weakness and a powerful source of what most humans would call magic, she didn't have the heart to kill an animal, especially not a cat. She never would. But she needed to get those kittens away from Jamie and Scott – and those cats, too – and make sure that none of them could spawn any more dangers to her.

She had no idea how one cat had escaped her net, let alone two. It was always possible, of course, that the male tabby was a regular cat with no power to bring back people's memories from the mist where Yasmina banished them. Either way, though, she had to get them. They had to be stopped. She would not start over, watching those cats escape and spawn out of control for centuries until she finally tracked them all down again. It could not happen.

A few councilmembers lingered at the edges of the chamber but didn't approach until there was a significant group. Strength in numbers, she thought with an inward smirk. They kept noticeably back from the dais and when Gerald entered, he came up next to her slowly. Everyone went silent and looked to her. It was clear that no one, not even Gerald, knew what to say or how to act. They knew they wouldn't act against her, but they didn't know anything else. She let them stew for a moment, then stepped forward.

"Our Queen Jamie and her mate will be away for the foreseeable future," she announced. There was some uneasiness but no surprise. She wondered if they knew where Jamie and Scott had gone, if they could access the nesting grounds like Jamie's allies had been able to do in the battle against Ashton.

"As is usual, power will revert to the heads of the council," she said, nodding at Gerald. "I will take lead in disputes. I expect no communication with the Queen until Jamie and Marisol choose to return."

Another murmur of uneasiness but that would prevent Jamie from luring them away and forming an army. She signaled the end of the meeting but placed a hand on Gerald's arm to keep him in place. He was again slightly pale. Once the room was empty, she turned to him.

"I'm sure you have questions."

Gerald licked his lips. "Are they all right? What happened?"

She considered. So the ranking dragons hadn't told their partners everything. That was good. The dragons knew exactly what had happened thanks to Marisol and Jamie's quick actions and Jamie's damnable ability to speak to all dragons, but there was often a large gap between what dragons knew and what they told their partners.

"Scott was injured, regrettably, but they'll be fine until they return," she said. "There may be a need for a new Queen's mate, but I'm sure you and the council would be willing, won't you?"

Gerald looked shocked, but nodded quickly. Then he hesitated. "Do you know how long they'll be gone? Will Marisol's eggs be prepared for the first year exam? She nearly killed Derek last year when he approached her nest."

"Marisol should be prepared this year," Margot said slowly. She actually hadn't considered that. It was true that Marisol's protective nature had nearly led to the death of another Queen and only Jamie had been able to stop her.

Gerald seemed to be preparing himself for another question and she gestured for him to continue.

"Will Marisol have her mating flight here? There are plenty of us who are willing, but if she flies somewhere else, especially in Spokane, the Elder might find her."

She hadn't considered that, either. She asked her dragon again where Jamie and Scott were, and again Yasmina refused. But even if Marisol were far away from all other dragons when she flew, Margot suspected that the Elder would be monitoring the situation and track her down. He already held one of the Queens; she would not let him take both.

"I will ensure that Marisol knows the dangers of flying anywhere else," she said. Surely Yasmina would send that message at least. Margot wondered how far Jamie would go. His aunt's dragon was in Africa so Jamie knew where that community was, but Jamie hadn't yet learned where the exact communities within each nation were. Marisol would know, she realized. Dragons shared everything. They may have gone to the nearby Canadian community. There were only a dozen dragons, but they had the resources to take care of another. Margot didn't know if Marisol had left the eggs but she doubted it. She still suspected all of them were on the nesting grounds, but she did have to consider other options.

Gerald edged away and she dismissed him, then began the long walk through the mist to the woman's campus. To her surprise, the mist didn't clear the same way it usually did. Normally, it opened enough for her to see the trees on each side of the path and quite a ways ahead. Tonight, the mist crowded in around her and she could only see a few steps in front of her. The mist wasn't stopping her, but it was making it more difficult. Clearly the magic of the mountain didn't approve of her actions, but she grit her teeth and continued. She had been on the bad side of Tarragon society and would be again. And once this was over, no one would ever remember what had happened.

CHAPTER ONE

Council Meeting

Derek had to focus all of his energy on sitting up straight as he waited for the council to gather in the Spokane council chamber. He was exhausted. His Queen dragon Jettie had only finished laying eggs a couple of hours ago and he had barely gotten a nap before his mate, the Elder, had woken him up and coaxed him out of bed. The Elder sat beside him now, not touching him even though Derek wouldn't have minded the extra strength. Still, he had to be careful not to appear weak in front of the council and he couldn't rely on the Elder for anything more than was absolutely necessary.

Jamie stood to his right and slightly behind him and Scott beside him. Scott's arm was around Jamie's waist but they didn't have to worry about people thinking Jamie was weak or that Scott had too much influence; Jamie's role as the first Queen was unquestioned and Scott's role as his mate was established. Derek was a little jealous, but not as much as he would have been even a few days ago.

When he had rescued Scott's memories, he had seen into Scott's soul and seen exactly how much Scott loved him, and how much Scott loved Jamie. And while Scott loved Derek quite a bit, his very soul was built upon his love of Jamie. Jamie was his life. Derek might keep flirting with Scott, and he would always love the man, but now he knew that they could never really be together. Oddly, the thought wasn't as upsetting as it once might have been.

The councilmembers already in the room were looking mostly at Jamie, not at him, and he knew there was plenty of confusion. Marisol had only told this campus that Scott had been attacked. Nothing else. Jettie had laid her eggs a few hours later, adding excitement but not clearing up any of the confusion. He saw Mike slip in the back of the room.

Mike had come to him immediately after Marisol's brief message. Ethan and the Elder had been with him when he returned to his senses after saving Scott, and Mike had been waiting outside for any news. Derek knew that Scott held an important place in Mike's heart and was pleased to be able to let Mike know that he was fine. This meeting was the first time Mike had actually seen Scott and he looked immensely relieved.

Finally, Ethan came up to Derek.

"Everyone is here, Queen."

Derek nodded and gathered his strength to stand with his usual confidence. He couldn't afford weakness, especially not with another Queen on campus. The talking among the councilmembers died down as usual and everyone focused on him. He hadn't been nervous in front of the council in a long time but he was now. He imagined his pride at Jettie's eggs and let a smile cross his face. He would start with that.

"Jettie has laid her eggs," he announced. "There will be room for forty-three students in the fall, plus four extra."

There was excited murmuring throughout the room with an edge of disappointment. He knew the disappointment came from those who had just lost enormous amounts of money in the betting pool the councilmembers had going estimating both the time of Jettie's nesting and the number of eggs. He wondered if anyone had guessed forty-three. He was tempted to ask, but that would validate the betting and he didn't really want to encourage it.

He glanced over at Jamie and Scott. Jamie was beaming as if

he had something to do with the eggs. Well, Marisol was Jettie's mother so he sort of did, but Derek suspected it also had to do with the fact that the university could save the lives of forty-three more people. He caught Jamie's eye and Derek realized that a large portion of his happiness was also just happiness that Derek was happy. He was a little surprised by that, since their relationship, while no longer bad, wasn't exactly good, but then again Derek had saved Scott.

Derek returned his attention to the council. He wasn't exactly sure what to say to the council about Jamie's presence here. He hadn't had a moment to talk to Jamie or even the Elder to figure out what was appropriate to say.

"Queen Jamie and his mate Scott will be staying here for a while, with Narné," he said.

Immediately the council started murmuring and he knew he couldn't leave it at that. He glanced at Jamie, wondering what to say, when Jamie stepped forward. Everything seemed to zoom in on him and everyone went silent. Jamie seemed to fill the room even though nothing had changed but Jamie's posture. Derek could almost sense how he was doing it. It seemed like a way of channeling Marisol's power to focus attention on him. He wondered if he could do it with Jettie. This wasn't the time to try.

Jamie smiled at the room. "An enemy within the Portland council attacked Scott and has made it too dangerous for us to remain," he said calmly. "The rest of the council is safer waiting and doing nothing until we are prepared to return. You are safer not knowing who it was. You are also safer if you do not tell anyone of our location."

He came to Derek's side and took Derek's hand.

"Derek is your Queen, of course, and I will be second to him while we are here. Scott will be second to the Elder while we are here. We will take on as few or as many responsibilities as they desire."

Jamie pressed against Derek's hand and knowledge of how

to bend the room passed between them. As Jamie loosened his control over the room, Derek strengthened his. It was a little unnerving having everyone looking at him in awe, even the Elder to some degree, but channeling Jettie's energy gave him strength.

"Thank you, Queen Jamie," he said, smiling at Jamie. "I will be sure to let you know when you are needed."

He realized too late he had left the Elder out of that comment but maybe that was better. He looked out at the council.

"Thank you for coming, everyone. If you have any further questions, please let Ethan know and he will pass them on to me."

He let go of Jettie's power slowly and the room seemed to return to normal. The council dispersed, all except Jamie, Scott, the Elder, Ethan, and, oddly, Mike, who approached them. Scott stepped forward and smiled, extending his hand to Mike. Mike took it and pulled Scott into an embrace, kissing him. Oddly, neither Scott nor Jamie looked upset. Scott allowed Mike to kiss him and when they broke apart, Scott stroked Mike's cheek and whispered something to him. Mike grinned.

Mike then went to Jamie and hugged him. They exchanged whispers as well, and then Mike nodded to Ethan and Derek and left. Derek knew that Mike was very close to Scott and Jamie, but he hadn't expected that kind of greeting. He thought back to what he had seen of Scott's soul. He had only really noticed his own place in Scott's heart, but there had been several other threads. Mike must have been one of them.

Derek swayed slightly and a hand on his shoulder stabilized him. It was the Elder but he couldn't show how grateful he was for the support because they were in public. He glanced up at the Elder, then back at Jamie and Scott. He had no idea how to handle them being in Spokane. He didn't know what their role would be, or what they would do. It was summer, so they didn't need to go to classes, but what would they do? Jamie seemed to pick up on his distress and took Scott's hand.

"Scott and I were planning on a low-key summer," he said. "I don't know if we can risk returning to Portland until we have Marisol, so we'll be here a while. We'll stay out of the way."

"Thanks, Jamie," Derek said. He still didn't know what they would do with their days, but at least he wouldn't have to entertain them. After all, he would be in classes. A wave of exhaustion swept over him and he leaned against the Elder.

"I think I need more sleep," he said. "Ethan, can you show Jamie and Scott around?"

Ethan agreed and the Elder escorted Derek out. Derek was careful not to lean on him too heavily until they were in the apartment building, but once they were in their apartment, he collapsed into the Elder's arms. The Elder picked him up and carried him to the bed, laying him down and taking off his shoes and socks, then helping him take off his shirt. The Elder kissed his shoulder. He smiled but didn't pull the Elder closer as he would have done if he had the energy for more. He loved sex with the Elder, but not now.

"You must really be tired," the Elder said with a laugh. Derek laughed, too, and curled up around him as he sat on the bed. The Elder stroked his hair.

"Jamie shouldn't be doing that with his dragon so far away," the Elder mused. "And he shouldn't have shown you how to do that. He knows Jettie is as exhausted as you."

"What was he doing?" Derek murmured.

"Mesmerizing the room," the Elder said. "I know you noticed it, since you managed it yourself."

"It was odd," Derek said. "But why shouldn't we have done it?"

"It draws on your Queens' strength. Normally that's not a problem but with Marisol so far away and Jettie with so little strength, neither of you should have done it."

"I don't think Jamie knows that," Derek said sleepily. "He

wouldn't put Marisol or Jettie at risk."

The Elder stroked his hair again. Derek reached his arms around the Elder and pulled him down until they were laying together, facing each other. There was a gentle expression on the Elder's face.

"Was there a Queen egg?" the Elder asked.

"No," Derek said, a little disappointed that he couldn't share the truth with his mate. But Jettie wanted the first nest secret so he would obey. Hopefully the Elder thought his disappointment was because of the lack of a Queen egg.

"Perhaps that's for the best," the Elder said. "We couldn't handle a third Queen."

"Maybe someday," Derek murmured, shutting his eyes. Thinking of another Queen dragon brought the cats to mind, for some reason. Maybe because Jettie had emphasized them so much. The Elder seemed to know everything. Maybe he understood why they were important.

"What do you know about the cats?" Derek asked, opening his eyes again and trying to look determined so the Elder would know not to avoid the question.

"I would have to see them up close and preferably hold them to see if my suspicions are true," the Elder said thoughtfully. "I doubt Jamie or Scott would allow me."

"Why not? They let me handle both cats and the kittens."

"They trust you," the Elder pointed out. "If Margot came after the kittens, they might be afraid I was coming after them, too."

"Why does Margot care about them? And why is the council afraid of her?"

The Elder kissed his forehead. "I have to see the cats to be sure why Margot cares. As for the council, well, you don't know what Margot's dragon's ability is, do you?"

Derek shook his head. Although he had spent time on the Portland campus, it had been so chaotic and he had been so focused on impressing his father Ashton that he hadn't bothered to learn other dragons' abilities. Jettie hadn't shown her ability yet and that had been one of his main concerns. He knew Margot was head of the women's council, but that was all he knew about her.

"Her dragon Yasmina can erase people's memories," the Elder said. "Margot has to be close enough to touch the person. She can choose how much they forget and if they fall asleep after."

Derek gasped as Jamie's words suddenly made sense. Margot had tried to erase all of Scott's memories. When Jamie had said it last night it hadn't really made sense but nothing had made sense so he let it pass. Now he understood Jamie's panic when summoning Derek and he realized what the mist was that threatened to choke Scott. He had known that he was saving Scott, that Scott would die without his help. He hadn't realized that Scott wouldn't physically die but instead be drained of everything that made him who he was.

"So you see why the Portland council won't act," the Elder continued. "They're afraid she'll attack them as well. Of course, if they all acted together and were willing to sacrifice one or two of them, they could take her out, but they're far too selfish for that and Jamie clearly knows it. He seems to have some plan to retake the campus, but hasn't shared it yet."

"How did Jamie escape?" Derek asked.

"I don't know," the Elder said. "Perhaps he'll tell you. He's stronger than he appears."

Derek huffed a little, his usual resentment returning for a moment. He knew everyone thought of Jamie as the first Queen, but his mate at least should side with him. The Elder laughed and kissed him.

"He's no comparison to you, my darling. The difference is that he looks weak but is strong, whereas you look strong and are strong. I prefer strength."

Derek snuggled against him, mollified. He and Jamie were

different that way. He never would have survived in Jamie's place, and Jamie never would have survived in his. They were too different, but they shared their love of Scott and their loyalty to their Queens. He would ask Jamie about Margot, and about the cats.

"Sleep, my Queen," the Elder whispered. "I'll keep you safe."

The Elder held him tight and he relaxed. He would worry about Jamie and Scott and Margot and the cats later. He could sense Jettie sleeping sounding by her eggs and he sent her a beam of love, hoping to give her good dreams. Then he let himself drift into his own dreams.

CHAPTER TWO

Settling In

J amie wandered the campus with Scott as Ethan took them on a winding tour of the academic buildings and the sports complex. Although they were probably as exhausted as Derek had looked, neither of them wanted to sleep. Jamie was a little worried about the cats but Scott had assured him that as long as their door was locked, no one – including the Elder – would break in. Jamie suspected that the Elder had snuck in when Scott was here, since Scott had only recently started locking the door.

The campus was beautiful and it was a sunny day. It was almost always drizzly on the main Tarragon campus and combined with the ever-present mist, sunny days were a rarity. The last time he had experienced the sun for extended periods of time was the summer spent in the hatching grounds while they prepared for war with Ashton. They were preparing this summer, too, but hopefully not for war. He didn't think many dragons would side with Margot, but their humans might.

They reached the theatre and started heading back to the apartments, where he could see dragons circling. There had been dragons perching on several of the buildings during the tour and Jamie wondered where the dragons would go in the fall when the freshmen came and the dragons had to stay out of view. It was easy on the main campus with dragon canyon nearby; perhaps there was a similar area for the dragons to fly and play and stay away from the students.

Scott chatted with Ethan as Jamie walked in silence, and Jamie was glad they were on good terms. While Scott wasn't the Queen's mate in charge of this council, he still ranked above Ethan and Jamie didn't want that to cause friction. He knew that Scott hadn't exactly been friendly with the council after his previous trip here because of something they had made Derek do, but over the past few months as reports of Derek doing well with the council came in, Scott had seemed friendlier. They seemed to be talking about Mike now, and Jamie smiled.

He knew Scott and Mike had finally made peace on Scott's last trip and wondered if that had to do with Mike's recovery. Mike had been in pain for too long and now seemed completely himself again. Even stealing a kiss from Scott was something he once might have done, though he had never done it while Jamie and Scott were together that Jamie knew of. Jamie didn't mind, though; he was just glad that Mike was back and he knew Scott felt the same.

Jamie zoned out of their conversation again and reached to Marisol. She was happy with her eggs. Actually, she was flying lazy circles around her nest to stretch her wings at the moment. The nesting site was completely hidden and could only be accessed during the first year exam or by people who knew the tune to enter, and Jamie and Marisol had told no one the tune.

Marisol informed him that Jettie had been quizzing her about caring for the eggs and they had been sharing their experiences. Jettie, she informed Jamie, would be an excellent mother. Jamie was pleased. Hopefully with Marisol's guidance they could avoid some of Marisol's mistakes, too, such as when she had attacked Derek. Derek had been the first student in the first year exam and he had been destined for her most prized egg: the Queen egg. Panicked and threatened, Marisol had attacked and only Jamie had managed to coax her into leaving. Derek had survived, of course, and Marisol had saved his life later when one of Ashton's hitmen tried to kill him so she and Derek had no hard feelings, but if Marisol could help Jettie leave before the first year exam then hopefully they could avoid injuries like that.

It wouldn't be an issue for Marisol this year because she was leaving her eggs at the start of the fall semester to join him. He had insisted. It was far too lonely without her. Jamie looked around and considered. Would they still be here in the fall? No, he reassured himself. It wouldn't take that long. He would figure something out. There would be some way to neutralize Margot and Yasmina.

"Jamie," Scott said, taking his hand. Jamie blinked and realized they were at their apartment door and Scott and Ethan were both looking at him. He had been completely absorbed in Marisol and in his thoughts.

"Jettie and Marisol are helping each other," he said, knowing he needed to explain his distraction somehow. Both men looked just as pleased as Jamie had felt.

They said goodbye to Ethan and entered the apartment. As soon as the door was closed, Scott hugged him. Jamie hugged back tightly. He knew how frightened Scott still was after nearly losing his memories. Scott had broken down during the night, sobbing into Jamie's arms. Jamie had never seen Scott like that before, especially since it came on rather suddenly. Jamie had been half-asleep when Scott lost control but there was no room for sleep when his love was in pain. Even Tiger, Scott's cat, had sensed his pain and came to cuddle Scott.

When their hug didn't end, Jamie reached up to stroke Scott's hair. He wasn't sure if Scott needed to cry again, if hugging were enough, or if Scott were so exhausted he just needed to lean on Jamie for a while. Finally, Scott kissed his cheek and the hug ended. Scott was smiling and Jamie was relieved. It hurt to see Scott in pain. Jamie took his hand and led him to the closet where the kittens were. They both crouched in the doorway.

Janna was sitting like a sphinx with six squirming kittens partially under her, partially playing beside her. Their eyes were still tightly closed. Jamie would have to look up how kittens aged. Although they didn't really have fur, they did have fuzz and he could see what their coloring would be. One looked like its mother, grey and white, and one like its father, a brown tabby, but the rest were a blend of grey, white, tabby, and one was a calico cat for some reason. It must have been a recessive gene, Jamie thought, since he didn't think Janna had been going out while in heat. She did go out, though, so it was possible.

Tiger sat beside her, one leg stuck out as he licked his belly. At least it looked like his belly. Jamie blushed and wished cats would be a little more private when cleaning themselves. Scott must have seen his blush because he laughed and poked Tiger, who looked up with a guilty expression and closed his legs.

"Tiger," Scott said in a sweet, teasing voice. "That's not polite."

Tiger just got up and came over to them, purring and rubbing against both of them. Jamie scratched behind his ears, again wondering why the cats were so important. He thought of the Elder. He knew something. He knew Margot; it was obvious from his lack of surprise when Jamie announced that Margot had tried to erase Scott's memories. Derek had been surprised, but also confused, and Ethan had been shocked. The Elder, though, had only been slightly surprised and a little thoughtful. He had to know something, but Jamie didn't know how to approach the Elder.

Jamie's only direct contact with the Elder – as direct as it was – was during Derek's mating flight when Jamie had accidentally gotten caught up and the Elder had deliberately filled him with mating flight lust. Desperate for relief, Jamie had forced Scott into sex without telling Scott who had won Derek's mating flight and the resulting fight had nearly ended their relationship.

In terms of indirect contact, the Elder had kidnapped Scott for weeks. Although he had treated Scott well, Jamie had suffered. And then the Elder had won Derek's mating flight and, worse, Scott had been forced to seduce Derek yet again to free him from the Elder's influence. Things had been quiet since then, but

Jamie had no good experiences with the Elder aside from the neutral greeting last night when the Elder had helped him off Narné and escorted him inside. That was it.

As Jamie showered Tiger with love and cooed at Janna and the kittens, he wondered if he should confront the Elder immediately or wait. And if he should tell Scott or not, and bring Scott or not. Scott would insist on coming. Did he want that, or did he want to speak in private? Scott had extremely negative experiences with the Elder and his experiences were direct, unlike most of Jamie's. Compared to Scott, Jamie's feelings were almost neutral. He didn't want to start a fight with the Elder, so perhaps it would be better if he went alone. Tarragon law prevented the Elder from harming a Queen, so he ought to be safe. But now how to leave without Scott?

"Scott," he began, and Scott sighed. Jamie looked at him in surprise.

"I suppose you want to go talk to the Elder," Scott said, sounding glum. "And you won't let me come."

"How did you know?"

Scott rubbed his shoulder. "I saw his reaction, too, you know. He knows something. And he's not going to talk if I'm there. It's just, you don't know how dangerous he is, even though he might not look it."

"He kills dragons," Jamie said in a hard voice. There was no greater crime. "I know exactly how dangerous he is."

Scott shook his head. "That's abstract. He would never kill Marisol. I mean that he's pure evil. His soul is corrupt. Everything he does benefits him and no one else."

"Then I'll be careful," Jamie said. "I don't want to dismiss your concerns, Scott, you know I don't, but I have to talk to him and I don't really want Derek to be part of the conversation either."

"Can I at least walk you there?" Scott asked.

Jamie leaned into him and smiled. "Of course, love. Then you can come back and love on the cats some more. Maybe Janna will even let you pet her. Janna, do you think you can do that?"

Janna sneezed and there was a stir among the kittens. Jamie and Scott laughed. Janna curled to her side to let the kittens feed but she batted a paw in Scott's direction as if indicating that she would give him permission. After the kittens fed, probably, but it was a good start. Jamie blew her a kiss, petted Tiger, then walked with Scott down the hallway to the Queen's chambers.

The apartments were set up strangely. Most of the apartments on campus were more like townhouses but this one was more like a dorm with the main doors facing an interior hallway. There were only four units, though they were enormous. The largest was the Queen's, of course, and Ethan's apartment was here too since he was head of the council. The other two were empty. One was intended for the female head of the council, but none had been selected so far. The male and female councils were completely integrated, as were the students, so there might never be one. The other empty apartment was intended for visitors, so Jamie and Scott were using it for its purpose, but not for a visiting Queen since the dragon room wasn't big enough for two dragons. If Marisol did come, she would likely get the room and Narné would have to sleep elsewhere.

It did make sense for the head of council to have quick access to the Queen, but the layout was still strange. There was a couch in the hall right next to the Queen's door and Jamie puzzled over it until he remembered that guards had been stationed by the door for months to make sure the Elder wasn't hurting Derek. He wondered when they had stopped.

Scott knocked on the door quietly, so quietly Jamie almost asked him to knock louder. He didn't want to wake Derek but the Elder had to hear them. Luckily, he heard footsteps approaching and the door opened. The Elder looked at them impassively and Scott tensed.

"I would like to speak with you, if I may," Jamie said, placing his hand on Scott's arm to defuse his anger.

"Of course, Queen," the Elder said, then glanced at Scott. "Alone?"

"Yes," Jamie said firmly.

Scott pulled him into a possessive kiss and Jamie let him, knowing he needed to show his claim over Jamie to feel comfortable with this. Scott followed up with a quick peck and then headed back to their apartment. The Elder held the door open for Jamie. He took a deep breath and entered into the Elder's territory.

CHAPTER THREE

Submission

Mike hesitated outside Carys's door and wondered briefly if he should go to the Elder instead. He knew the Elder could give him what he needed, but there was Derek. Derek just wouldn't allow it. So here he was, hoping Carys could give him something he couldn't even express. Kissing Scott had been like lightning, but seeing Jamie had reminded him too strongly of Ashton and the combination of lust and longing for his former master had brought him here. He glanced at the door, trying to gather the courage to knock, when it opened. Carys stood in the doorway looking amused.

"Come in, Mike," he said, extending his hand. "You know you're invited."

Carys took his hand and pulled him in without giving him a chance to refuse. Maybe he did know what Mike needed. As the door closed, he pinned Mike and kissed him. Mike grabbed his arms and nearly tried to resist, but Carys wouldn't let him. Carys's knee slid against his groin as Carys took one of his wrists and forced it over his head. His tongue was dominating Mike's mouth and giving him no chance of air except when he allowed it. Mike resisted a few more moments, then gave in. This was what he needed, after all.

As soon as Carys felt his resistance fade, he let go of Mike's hand. He began kissing along his jawbone and unbuttoning his shirt. Mike knew better than to help. Instead, he leaned his head against the door and luxuriated in the sensations his body was experiencing. As soon as his shirt was unbuttoned, Carys pulled him off the door into his arms and Mike went willingly. Carys led him into the bedroom and pointed to the bed. The familiar gesture was almost too much and before he obeyed, he kissed Carys's cheek.

He stripped as he went to the bed as Ashton always liked, then sat and watched Carys strip. Carys was extremely handsome and while no one could compete with Ashton, he was very impressive. Mike felt a familiar thrill run through him. He wanted Carys. He remembered how Ashton had taken him once before punishing him and he knew he wanted that. As Carys approached, he rolled unto his belly and reached out to Carys, who looked a little puzzled. When Mike took Carys's hand and placed it on his head, giving him control, Carys seemed to understand. Carys drew closer, his cock brushing against Mike's lips. Mike wanted to be ordered, but didn't know how to tell Carys. Luckily, he didn't have to.

"Open your mouth, Mike," he said, pulling Mike's head back to give him better leverage. Mike obeyed and relaxed at the same time. Carys tapped his penis against Mike's lips teasingly before sliding in, taking his time as he slowly entered Mike's throat.

Mike swirled his tongue against the cock filling his mouth. Carys thrust in and out gently, without fully entering him. Mike was eager to feel him deep in his throat, but Carys was clearly teasing him, enjoying Mike's tongue. Ashton sometimes teased him, but more frequently dominated him with force. Mike had always loved it when Ashton teased him, though.

Carys continued for long minutes, then tightened his grip on Mike's hair and, in one smooth motion, slid completely into his throat. Mike nearly gagged because it had been so long since he had taken anyone in his throat, but he knew better than to react with anything but pleasure or risk punishment. And it was pleasure. Mike relaxed further into Carys' hand, letting him take total control over his body.

His cock was pressed against the mattress but he was incredibly hard and hitched his hips to get friction. Carys pulled out suddenly, then helped Mike onto his hands and knees and got behind him. Mike kept his eyes closed and smiled as he felt Carys pressing against his opening. Carys stroked his back, then pushed into him. Mike arched his back and gasped at the painful pleasure of being breached.

Carys begin thrusting against him hard and Mike's body rocked with the force as he gasped in time with the thrusts. The other man stroked his back again, then reached along Mike's side, drifting down and inward until he gripped Mike's cock. Carys' other hand stroked up Mike's back to grip his neck firmly.

Completely at Carys' mercy, Mike allowed the other man to stroke him and control him until he felt that he would burst. But he knew he wasn't allowed to come yet, and he moaned.

"Please," Mike whispered.

"Almost," Carys said, tugging him ruthlessly.

Mike moaned again and struggled to contain the pleasure spiking through him, sparked by Carys' hand on his neck, the hand on his cock, and the powerful thrust of a penis deep inside of him. Carys twisted and struck his prostrate as Mike stifled a scream. Carys leaned over him, thrusting unevenly and increasing in speed.

"With me," Carys managed to say, and Mike whimpered.

Carys thrust against his prostrate again, and then exploded into him just as Mike lost control. An orgasm overwhelmed his senses, wiping through his mind and erasing everything except pleasure. He arched his back and pressed against Carys, seeking every last bit of the experience. After a long, blissful moment, his body relaxed and it felt as if every bit of strength he had vanished. He slumped on the bed, resting his head on his arms with his ass still angled up as Carys leaned over him.

With a light push, Carys knocked him to one side and he rolled obediently. He was spent, and wasn't sure how much more he needed. Being dominated like that was everything he wanted. Should he let Carys continue? He wasn't sure. He stretched out as Carys lay beside him, head next to his. Carys kissed his cheek and wrapped an arm around his shoulders, but didn't make any especially aggressive moves.

"Thank you," Mike said softly. It was both sincere thanks and also an indication to Carys that he was satisfied. Carys grinned and squeezed his shoulder.

"You're a pleasure," Carys said in a velvet voice. "I hope you feel this urge more often. I'll always be here for you."

Mike reached out and ran his hand across Carys' cheek, smiling.

"That was perfect," he said, then looked away. "I miss him so much."

Carys pulled him closer, cradling him. Mike felt a sudden urge to cry, though Ashton didn't deserve any tears. Ashton had manipulated and abused him, tortured him, killed his lover, and been about to kill him and – even worse – his dragon. He deserved nothing. But even after all this time, the longing was still there. He cuddled against Carys, remembering how it felt when Ashton held him like this, back when he still trusted Ashton. He would give anything for that innocence again.

"I don't know what it's like for you," Carys admitted. "I know what it was like for me, for the others, to move from pet to council member. But he was always there if we needed him. Our relationship ended after the mountain sacrifice, after we were freed from our collar, but he never completely left us."

Mike shut his eyes against the prickling that he knew meant tears. How would things have worked out if Ashton were alive? But no. Too much had happened. From the moment Kale entered his life, things with Ashton were doomed. And when Ashton kidnapped Jamie, when it was revealed that Ashton killed dragons and ate their flesh, it was far too late. Ashton deserved death for what he had done and while Mike missed him, he would never undo the man's death even in his thoughts.

Carys held him for several long moments, then brushed the hair off his forehead.

"Why did you betray Ashton?" he asked softly. "I've always wondered. You had reason; we all know what he did to you. But why did you wait to act when you did?"

Mike flushed, remembering the jealous rage that had pushed him past his tipping point. He had put up with the abuse and torture. But he hadn't been able to stand the thought of Ashton with someone else.

"Ashton was sleeping with Jamie," Mike whispered. "And that night, I knew he was going to send Jamie into the mating flight so he could win uncontested. He had the poison ready and Jamie didn't stand a chance. I couldn't let it happen. I couldn't let Ashton be with someone else again."

Carys seemed puzzled. "Are you sure he was sleeping with Jamie?"

"Well, not spending the night with him, if that's what you're asking," Mike amended. Ashton had always let Mike share his bed. "But he had to be doing something."

"I don't think he was," Carys said slowly. "We all assumed he had been having sex with Jamie. Despite having you," Carys said, kissing Mike's forehead. "None of us approved, since you should have been his only partner while you were his pet. But Ashton wanted the mating flight."

"Why wouldn't he have slept with Jamie?" Mike asked, confused. Carys had just listed reasons why Ashton would be sleeping with Jamie, but was claiming that Ashton hadn't.

"Before Jamie killed Ashton, Ashton mentioned their time together. The pleasure he gave Jamie," Carys said.

"Exactly," Mike said. He had been shell-shocked at the time, but those words had shaken him once he was strong enough to process them. Ashton had given Jamie pleasure, and Jamie's reaction had proved that it was true.

"He wouldn't have said that if they were fucking," Carys said. "I don't know what he would have said, but he wouldn't have said that. He probably wouldn't have mentioned it at all. It was a bad strategy bringing it up anyway, but if they had actually had sex, I don't think it would have occurred to him to try to use it to save his life. The other council members who were there agree. Something happened between them, obviously, but they never had sex."

Mike considered Carys' reasoning. He had never thought of that before. It had been a terrible strategy, reminding Jamie of their intimacy in an attempt to convince Jamie to spare his life. Anyone who knew Jamie knew that Jamie would be upset and ashamed at physical contact with anyone other than Scott. Most people in Tarragon society were fairly free with their affection, especially those partnered with female dragons since mating flights were rarely won by the same dragon, but Jamie was strictly monogamous. Even his fling with TK was mostly non-physical, Mike knew from his conversations with TK.

But Carys was right. Ashton knew all of that. If Ashton had actually managed to seduce Jamie and have sex with him, he never would have brought that up. And if it had happened and he did bring it up, Jamie would have killed him a lot faster. But the way Ashton had phrased it and the way Jamie had been shaken but not devastated indicated that whatever had happened between them, it wasn't sex.

That meant that Mike was wrong for betraying Ashton, he realized. He had turned against Ashton when the man took Jamie hostage and Mike believed that they were having sex, and the thought of the mating flight had pushed him over the edge into attacking Ashton. But if none of that were true, then he shouldn't have turned against Ashton. He should have remained loyal, as Ashton was loyal to him.

No, Mike told himself. He was right to turn against Ashton. Maybe his reasoning was false, but it was the right thing to do. There were no other options.

"I think you're right," Mike admitted. "I never thought of that before. I let my emotions get in the way. When I rescued him, and in the days after that before Ashton's death, he didn't act the way he would have acted if there actually were something between them. I just didn't notice."

"You know him better than most," Carys said. "And you know Scott. Are they safe on this campus with the Elder here? They might be safer than in Portland, but there are other places they could hide. Derek's here, TK's here, and the Elder can easily manipulate that to his advantage."

A flash of relief washed over Mike at the concern in Carys' voice. Carys, like many of the council members here, had been loyal to Ashton right until the end. Jamie could sense his loyalties and had decided to let Carys and the others remain on the council and even come to a campus outside of his direct control, but Mike knew he still had serious concerns about their loyalty. This concern, however, indicated that Carys was fully loyal to Jamie, and Scott as well. He accepted their role as first Queen and first Queen's mate. And he wasn't loyal to the Elder, another serious concern that Mike and Jamie shared about the Ashton loyalists in Spokane.

"Jamie's capable of holding his own, for the most part," Mike said slowly. "But he's young. He's not going to make the same mistakes twice, so I don't think the Elder will be able to manipulate him the way Ashton did, but the Elder has centuries of practice manipulating young men."

"Is he safe here?" Carys asked again.

Mike pondered, unable to answer. He didn't know why Jamie and Scott had left, or who had attacked Scott. They were undoubtedly safer here than in Portland, or else they wouldn't be here, but were they safe? Could they protect themselves?

"I'm not going to let anything happen to them," Mike vowed. "No matter what it takes."

Carys was silent for a moment, then kissed Mike's cheek again.

"If they need protection, they have it. The council will protect both of them even if it harms our Queen's mate."

Mike shut his eyes and relaxed fully into Carys' arms. The blissful buzz of sex was gone, but the comfort of Carys' arms was just as necessary. His affair with TK was pleasurable, but Mike preferred to be in charge and didn't let TK cradle him like this. Only Carys would be allowed to hold him. He nestled against the man's chest and took a deep breath. He felt safe, for the first time in a long time.

CHAPTER FOUR

Following Protocol

J amie sat across from the Elder a little nervously. The Elder had followed protocol exactly so far and was politely waiting for Jamie to speak and announce the purpose of his visit, but Jamie couldn't quite get Scott's warnings and his own past experiences out of his head. The Elder didn't seem to mind the wait as he relaxed in his chair, completely confident. As first Queen, Jamie outranked him but Jamie didn't really have any power over him aside from title.

Jamie folded his hands. He had waited enough. Any more would make it too uncomfortable.

"Thank you for speaking with me, Elder," he said, wishing the Elder had a name so it didn't sound so awkward. "I had several questions that I believe you know the answers to."

The Elder smiled. "I suspected you would. What can I help you with?"

"You know Margot," he said. "How do you know her?"

"Surely you realize I've been alive a long time. Margot has also been alive a long time, so naturally I know her."

Jamie considered. He knew Margot, like Ashton, had taken pets and then sacrificed them to the mountain. Ashton had occasionally killed the dragons first and his dragon Arion had drunk their blood, a crime so horrific that when the dragons discovered it, Ashton had been condemned to death. He had never really considered whether Margot did the same but if she were as old as

Ashton, or at least older than most of the councilmembers, and still looked as young as she did, there was a chance.

"Did she kill dragons?" he asked, a little afraid to hear the answer.

The Elder smiled again. "What would reassure you?"

"The truth," Jamie said quietly. The Elder's question had already confirmed the answer, though.

"Of course," the Elder said. "She's nearly as old as me, far older than Ashton. She let him take control because he had the personality to take charge and she prefers to remain in the shadows, but she's just as deadly a foe. No one will side with you against her," he added. "You will always be first Queen and hold the loyalty of all dragons, but you'll have to avoid her the rest of your life. Or rather, your mate will have to avoid her."

"Why are the kittens important?" Jamie asked, hoping he had some insight into that since he had known Margot.

The Elder smirked. "They're her weakness. I would have to see your cats to be sure, but I believe they're descendants of a pair of cats we received from Egypt many centuries ago. The cats were descendants of the Gods and held strong magic, able to prevent any dragon from using its gift when they were nearby. We took care of them, even though they were quite annoying at times, and naturally they multiplied. They bred with domestic cats and their powers faded. Again, I would have to see them, but they might still have enough power to block Yasmina's ability to erase memories."

"They can," Jamie said. "Both of them. So the kittens will too?"

The Elder nodded. "I don't know why she acted against you now, though," he mused. "The cats have been there for so long. Perhaps she didn't know you and Scott had the cats."

"No, she actually encouraged me to adopt Janna," Jamie said.

"Interesting," the Elder said. "Either she only recently realized the danger or she didn't think you would be a threat to her."

"I'm not a threat to her," Jamie pointed out. "Or at least I wasn't. Well, I guess that's not exactly true," he said, thinking of the time she had tried to erase his memory and Janna had saved him. "But we got along."

"She did try to erase your memories, then, and your cat saved you?" he asked.

"Yes," Jamie said. "Not very many memories. Just about fifteen minutes or so. I wouldn't have told anyone except she did it to Scott, too."

"And his cat saved him."

"No," Jamie said, feeling his anger rise. "We didn't have Tiger yet. She erased over an hour and we don't know what happened. Not even Narné knew."

"So you did have reason to act against her," the Elder said.

"Yeah, but that was months ago. We've gotten along since then. And I don't even know if she knows I remember what happened. I've been pretty careful."

"Except now," the Elder said. "You're telling me. What if I were to tell her?"

"If your dragon were to tell Yasmina," Jamie said with a smile, "Then I would be able to read your dragon just like every other dragon. I doubt you'll risk that. And the council will prevent you from sending a normal message. Plus, you're a Queen's mate, I'm a Queen, and you can't break my confidence. Not even with my mate."

The Elder smiled back at him, but his smile was seductive. "You're right, I can't tell your mate. Is there anything else you want from me?"

Jamie was a little flustered, because he did have questions but he didn't want to be seen as flirting with the Elder. The Elder laughed and leaned back in his chair.

"I won't steal you from your mate, don't worry. I could," he added, running his tongue along his upper lip and eyeing Jamie in a way that made Jamie feel naked. "But I won't. Unless you ask," he added further, again eyeing Jamie.

Jamie blushed and stared at the ground, remembering the blast of lust the Elder had sent him during Derek's mating flight. He wondered if the Elder really could seduce him. Maybe. But he didn't want it. He had Scott.

The Elder's hand was suddenly on his and he glanced up in shock. The Elder was kneeling by his chair, holding his hand and reaching up to stroke his cheek. Jamie drew in a sharp breath. The Elder's hand on his cheek was gentle and drew his chin forward as the Elder's face came closer. Jamie hadn't even processed the gesture when the Elder's lips landed on his.

Jamie's eyes went wide and the Elder's hand tightened around his. The Elder leaned into him and he gasped. Instantly, the Elder was inside his mouth and Jamie was overwhelmed with the searing sensations he had experienced during the mating flight. He unconsciously pressed against the Elder and shut his eyes, unable to pull away from the extraordinary kiss. It felt as though he was on fire, starting with the sparks in his lips and tongue and spreading throughout his body until he could barely stand it and longed to strip in an effort to cool himself.

Then the Elder leaned back and he opened his eyes, panting for breath. The Elder winked at him, a knowing smile on his face as Jamie struggled to recover. He snatched his hand away from the Elder's hand and placed it on his lips, longing to wipe away the memory of the kiss. The Elder returned to his chair as Jamie trembled.

"Derek wouldn't approve of that," Jamie said, not knowing what else to say.

"Did you approve of that?"

Jamie felt as if his face were burning up.

"No," he hissed. "Don't ever do that again."

The Elder grinned. "I won't. Unless you ask. I do have a question for you."

Jamie was still struggling to contain the lust flushing through his body. He wasn't hard, but he was almost there. Just from a brief kiss. He could barely believe it. He knew it was because they had shared the mating flight, but still.

"What?"

"May I see the kittens?"

Jamie stared at him in disbelief. First he tried to seduce Jamie, then he expected Jamie to let him near the kittens?

"No way," Jamie said firmly.

"Aren't you curious to see how powerful their strength still is? They could interfere with your power, or your mate's."

"They don't interfere with mine," Jamie said. He thought of Scott. Narné hadn't had any visions since the cats were near him, but he also didn't have visions on a regular basis. It could just be chance. But if they did interfere, then having so many of them together might cause problems for other dragons, not just Narné. It also might mean that when the kittens grew up, they could place them around the Portland campus to prevent Margot from retaliating when they finally acted against her.

Jamie examined the Elder. He just didn't trust him. Scott didn't trust him. But it was the cats who had the final say.

"You can come to my room and see if Tiger accepts you. If he doesn't, you can't see them. If he does but Janna doesn't, you can't see them."

"That sounds reasonable," the Elder said. "Why don't we see what they think of me."

The Elder stood and held out his hand, and Jamie stood and reluctantly took it. The Elder tucked Jamie's hand in his arm as he escorted Jamie into the hall. It was a short walk to their door and the Elder released him as soon as they arrived, but Jamie wondered if he should have allowed the gesture. It followed protocol, and it was important to maintain protocol. Protocol was his main protection against the Elder, after all, and it was one of the few things keeping the Elder in check. He didn't want to reject it, so he had allowed the Elder to touch him. But he didn't want to encourage physical contact from the Elder, not after that kiss.

Jamie glanced at the Elder, licking his lips and tasting the lingering impression of the man's touch. The Elder smiled innocently and gestured at the door. Jamie sighed and opened it. At least Scott wouldn't know about the kiss. Maybe Jamie should tell him, and maybe he would, but not yet. Not until they had everything they needed from the Elder. He couldn't afford having Scott attack the Elder and their relationship was already razor-thin.

Scott was already heading towards them as Jamie opened the door. He must have been listening for them. But he clearly wasn't expecting the Elder to be with Jamie, and his glare would have shaken most people. The Elder just nodded in acknowledgement, and turned to Jamie, waiting for him to speak. Scott wasn't going to like this, but Tiger would make this decision.

CHAPTER FIVE

Acceptance

Scott listened to Jamie's sparse explanation of his meeting with the Elder. He suspected Jamie was leaving things out, but maybe he didn't want to share something in front of the Elder. It was possible that Jamie had reached a conclusion that he didn't want the Elder to know about. Scott shouldn't be so suspicious. But he didn't trust the Elder, and he didn't want the Elder to see the cats.

As Jamie explained, Tiger pranced in. He sat at Scott's feet and seemed to consider the Elder. Scott wondered how intelligent the cats were. Tiger seemed to know that he was supposed to be judging whether or not to let the Elder see the kittens, but was that giving the cat too much credit? Probably. But if Tiger were descended from the gods, maybe it wasn't.

Tiger let out a small meow and went up the Elder, twirling around his legs. Jamie's eyes narrowed and Scott wondered if he hadn't wanted Tiger to approve. Had something happened between them? Or was it just Jamie's natural hatred for the Elder? He had plenty of reasons to hate the man, after all.

"I guess you can come in," Scott said, and led the Elder into the bedroom. There were faint mews coming from the closet and Scott opened the door for him to see. Janna hissed at the interruption, then cocked her head and began licking one of the kittens cuddled against her. She didn't seem to have a problem with the Elder either.

The Elder crouched beside her. He stretched out his hand as if to touch the kittens and Janna growled. He quickly withdrew his hand and Scott was grateful he was respecting her. The Elder straightened and Scott brought him back to the main room, where they sat down. Jamie sat on the couch practically on Scott's lap. Something must have happened because he wasn't usually this possessive in public.

"They're very powerful," the Elder said. "It's dangerous having them all together like this. You'll want to help wean them as soon as possible. All of the nearby dragons will be completely unable to use their abilities. This might even affect the entire campus."

Jamie licked his lips nervously and glanced at Scott. "Kittens can't be weaned until they're six weeks, right? What do we do until then?"

"Four weeks is probably adequate, but that is a long time," the Elder said. "Would you consider relocating them somewhere else? Somewhere safe, but not so close to dragons?"

"I suppose this affects you," Scott inserted. "You want to keep using your ability. Is that your problem?"

The Elder's lips curved into a smile. "My ability won't be affected by a month or two with them present. But other people will be affected, perhaps significantly."

"We do want to avoid that," Jamie said slowly. "But I won't move them. Is there any way to shield them? Surely if you had a bunch of these cats around the academy you had to have solutions."

"When their population grew too large, we restricted them to the woods between campuses. As their strength lessened, some were allowed onto the female campus, but never the male. Did Margot ever see your specific cat?"

"Yes," Jamie said.

The Elder tapped his lips. "That might be why she didn't mind you taking her. Perhaps she thought the cat would weaken you.

31

The mother cat is quite strong."

Scott glared, feeling a little slighted on behalf of Tiger. The Elder smiled slightly and gestured towards the bedroom and the cats.

"All of them are powerful. Too powerful. All of them are stronger than those at the end of my time there. If they had regained their power after I left, I don't know why Margot would have tolerated it for so long. Ashton was far less reliant on his dragon's ability, but it was the source of Margot's power."

"How reliant are you on yours?" Scott asked, trying again to figure out the man's ability. If they could figure it out, they would have an easier time defeating him.

"As I said," the Elder chuckled. "I can easily go a few months without it."

Jamie seemed deep in thought, staring towards the cats. "We could look for safe places nearby, places we could reach," he suggested. "No one will know. They are feral cats, so they know how to survive. We can visit and keep an eye on them, or Narné could stay with them."

Scott glared. He didn't like that Jamie was openly considering the Elder's advice, even if it was a good idea. He didn't want the Elder to know where the cats were. Some of it was just a protective feeling for his family, and for the cat that had saved his memories, but a lot of it was resentment and anger towards the Elder.

"We can talk about it in private," he said sharply. "Do you need anything else?"

The last was directed at the Elder, who still had a smile tugging his lips. The man shook his head and Scott escorted him out, nearly slamming the door. He returned to Jamie, who blushed deeply. So something had happened.

"Well? What did he do?" Scott asked, trying to keep his voice gentle and not succeeding. "What did he say?"

Jamie touched his lips, then reached out to stroke Scott's face.

"He, um, kissed me," Jamie whispered. "I didn't think to stop him."

Scott stared in shock, then leaned forward instinctively and kissed Jamie himself. He wanted Jamie to know that he loved him. Their lips touched and he leaned into Jamie, cradling his head, pulling him closer. Jamie melted into him, opening his mouth cautiously as they explored each other's bodies.

Every touch felt new. Scott's memories had been returned, but he still didn't feel comfortable. There was a slight disconnect when he remembered things. He did remember everything – far more than he had before – but it didn't feel as real as it should. Right now, Jamie felt real. He knew this memory would be absolutely real, and he would never let it be stolen by anyone.

His heart beat faster as Jamie's hand slid through his hair and Jamie curved under him, their lips breaking apart as Jamie kissed his jaw, his neck. Scott inhaled sharply and trailed his hands down Jamie's back, caressing his strong muscles, the firm shape of his shoulderblade.

They hadn't had sex since Scott's memories had returned. There had been no chance and Scott had still been recovery. Was still recovering. But he suddenly knew that he would recover a lot faster if he had Jamie beside him, surrounding him.

"Come with me," he whispered, then led his willing lover into the bedroom. It was possible they were being watched. It was always a danger in Portland and it might be here as well. But he didn't care. He wanted Jamie more than he could ever remember wanting him before.

But he was gentle. He coaxed Jamie to sit on the bed and slid his hands up Jamie's torso, lifting his shirt and pulling it off him. He tossed the shirt away and kissed Jamie's warm shoulder, sucking hard, wanting to mark his lover. Jamie laughed and fell backwards, pulling Scott over him.

"I want you," Jamie said softly, in a husky voice Scott couldn't ever remember hearing before. "Just you."

Scott locked his lips on Jamie's as he stroked his body, then pulled off his own shirt and the rest of his clothes as well. Jamie shuffled out of his shoes and socks and pants with an adorable clumsiness. Scott rested his hand on Jamie's thigh and traced it up the side of his body. Jamie drew in a sharp breath, his cock growing hard at the light, teasing touch. Scott loved how responsive Jamie's body was, how his skin flushed when he was aroused, how beautiful his cock was as he grew aroused. Scott kissed between his belly button and his pubic hair as Jamie moaned helplessly, hitching his hips as if hoping Scott would lower his mouth. Scott obeyed.

Jamie tasted glorious as he ran his tongue along the surface of his cock and precum began to spill from his tip, salt and spice and everything he loved. He let Jamie fill his mouth, fill him, and caressed him with his tongue, enjoying every moment. He had a memory of the first time he had done this, Jamie's first sexual experience. Scott had worried that it wouldn't be enough, but the oral sex had given Jamie the experience he needed to bond with Marisol so he knew Jamie considered this as intimate as more penetrating forms of sex. He was glad, because he loved this.

He wanted to give his lover pleasure but he seemed to be succeeding too quickly as Jamie grabbed his hair desperately, moaning constantly now and hard as a rock in Scott's mouth. Scott wasn't ready and he wanted them together. Always together. So he began kissing his way up Jamie's body until he was nuzzling his lover's neck, his body grinding against Jamie's wet cock.

Jamie wrapped his legs around Scott's waist and arched his back, inviting Scott in. Scott slipped a finger into Jamie's mouth and his lover sucked it ferociously, then Scott took his wet finger and used it to stretch his lover. He couldn't quite remember how long it had been but he didn't want to hurt Jamie, and Jamie was enjoying it, he could tell. But Scott was a little desperate, too, so it wasn't long before he poised himself and gently entered Jamie.

They both gasped and Scott thrust into him without thinking, needing the pressure and tightness and love he felt. Their minds locked and he felt the doubled sensations he only felt with Jamie, the passion that was overwhelming his lover and amplifying his own passion. He felt echoes of Narné and Marsiol as he pushed into Jamie again and again, needing the sensations, needing to feel Jamie around him, to feel the phantom sensation of Scott entering Jamie, needing everything about his lover. They clung to each other in a passion far beyond any mating flight until Scott felt his cock twinge and the climax swamped his senses just as Jamie crashed into an orgasm as well.

Together, they gasped and moaned and stretched the final few thrusts as Scott filled his love and soon they were limp and exhausted, sticky and covered in cum, Jamie's sweaty face smiling at him.

"I love you," Jamie said warmly, in an exhausted voice. "Only you. Only ever you."

"You are the only one for me, Jamie," Scott said without thinking. And it was true, he realized. In the past, other men had filled him with lust. Mike, Derek. Especially Derek. But that need wasn't there anymore. Only Jamie mattered. Only Jamie held his attention. Something about regaining his memories had changed him and he wondered if Derek had done something. Derek had helped with his memories, after all; maybe Derek hadn't restored everything. It didn't matter. There was only Jamie now.

Jamie had tears in his eyes and cradled Scott sweetly.

"I mean it, Jamie," Scott said. "I only need you."

CHAPTER SIX

New Mission

Something was seriously wrong, Chris knew. Jamie and Scott were gone with no explanation and the dragons were furious about something, though Yaris refused to say what. He said it was for Chris's protection. While that was probably true, Chris would have liked some clue as to what was going on. The council undoubtedly knew what was happening and why the Queen and his mate were gone, but the council never shared anything. Chris had never realized how frustrating the council's silence could be because he had always been on the council, and in the inner circle. He had joined the council only a few years after graduating, though unlike most who joined as young as him, he wasn't one of Ashton's pets.

The silence might have to do with Jettie's eggs, though he didn't know how. The council had announced the birth of Jettie's eggs. Gerard, the head of the council and someone Chris had been close to for years, had told him privately. Jettie was probably overjoyed to have eggs, Chris thought, and wondered how Derek felt, if Derek had any friendliness for the Elder by now or if he was steeling his heart and waiting for Chris to return.

He had wondered why Jamie wasn't the one to tell him about the eggs, since he and Jamie had spoken several times over the semester. Since the council was shunning Chris for disturbing a mating flight and allowing the Elder into power, Chris had no friends on the campus. Jamie was the closest he had. When he asked, Gerard had reluctantly explained that Jamie and Scott had left the campus for an undetermined period of time. Gerard had refused to answer any more questions with a sharp reminder that Chris was no longer on the council, but he wondered what could possibly make Jamie leave.

It was summer, so it was possible Jamie and Scott had simply left to enjoy the summer together, possibly even at the nesting grounds again. But last time, the entire campus had known where they were. Most people also knew why, and that Ashton couldn't really be trusted around them anymore. Ashton was gone now, though, and there weren't any threats to them. Why would they leave when it was safe to stay?

No, something was wrong. He knew Yaris was unhappy about something, and he suspected all of the dragons were. But whatever had happened, whatever was happening, only the council knew.

Chris stared out at the dragon canyon and wondered what he should do. Most of the people living in dragon canyon had jobs in nearby Portland if they weren't directly affiliated with the academy. Gerard had offered Chris a teaching job, but Chris had declined. He had no interest in teaching. As far as he was concerned, students were only good as potential bedmates and he hadn't been interested in anyone since losing Derek. He hadn't taken a job in Portland either, though. Sometimes one of the friendly councilmembers would ask him to help with paperwork or other things that his time on the council gave him knowledge of, but there was a thick wall between him and the current council.

He would have fallen through the cracks if it weren't for Jamie checking up on him once or twice a week. Even Scott had been to see him several times. But he had no real job, no real way to occupy his time other than train Yaris to win Derek's next mating flight.

There was a knock at the door and he wondered who it could be. Jamie and Scott were gone, Gerard had already spoken to him today, and no one else made a point of talking to him. He opened the door and was startled to see Margot. He invited her in, puzzled.

"How are you doing, Chris?" she asked, sitting in the chair he offered her. "I should have been by to see you before this."

"I almost went to you, at first," Chris admitted. "I couldn't take it and wanted you to erase everything, but eventually I realized you wouldn't be able to do anything."

"My gift has its limitations," she said, but sounded oddly pleased about it. "I'm glad you found the strength to continue with your memories. Derek would have been devastated if you forgot him."

"I know," Chris said. "I realized that after a while. Can I help you with something?"

"Yes," she said. "I wanted to see you first, but you are doing better than I expected. I think it's about time we reinstated you on the council."

Chris jolted in surprise. "What?"

"You've been out long enough. Are you no longer interested in serving on the council?"

"Of course I'm interested," he said. "But you know why I was removed. The other councilmembers hate me. I ruined Derek's flight."

"They'll get over their anger. The only one with a real stake in this is the Elder, and he won't care now that the eggs are laid."

Chris flinched. It was true. The Elder wouldn't care about him now that his eggs, Jettie's eggs, had been laid. The Elder would always be a part of Tarragon society now. Why would he worry about Derek's former lover when he had such a strong claim as Derek's mate? But even though he understood the timing, it didn't make sense.

"Why do you want me?"

Margot smiled. "You used to be my best informant on the

men's council. Had you forgotten? I don't have anyone like you anymore."

Chris blushed. He had never really thought of himself as her informant. He gave her information, of course, but only when she asked for it and nothing that was truly secret. Well, perhaps he had volunteered information a few times, he realized. And perhaps shared a few secrets. But there was very little that Margot didn't find out about eventually, and most of what was kept secret between the campuses wasn't actually secret, it just didn't apply to the other campus. Besides, she had to know that he had used his occasional access to her to inform the men's council what she was doing. She had to realize that the communications went both ways.

It was clear how reinstating Chris would benefit her. And it was certainly something Chris wanted. But he wasn't sure it was possible and despite her dismissal of the council's hatred of him, he knew that would be an issue. He had violated a principle tenant of Tarragon society. While he didn't like the punishment, it was just. In fact, it had very recent precedent.

"I don't think they'll let me on the council again," Chris said. "What about Jared, who attacked Scott during Jamie's last mating flight? He would never be reinstated. If I were on the council and someone suggested it, I would never accept it."

"The circumstances around your violation were different," Margot said. "Jared had no relationship to Jamie and attacked Scott out of revenge. You were Derek's established partner for quite a while, and you were motivated by love. The council is much more sympathetic to your cause than you think, even though they've no doubt made their disdain known."

Chris snorted softly. Disdain was a mild word for the hate and resentment some of his former friends now showed him. He had never realized how fragile his relationships were, and how bound up in belonging to the council. All of the people he thought he could count on had abandoned him.

"Even if they would agree, I'm not really prepared to do what it would take to get back on," Chris said, thinking of the sexual submission that would undoubtedly be required. There was quite a lot of it involved in getting on the council in the first place – the male council, at least – and he was sure at least one council-member would demand more if he were to be reinstated.

"I doubt they would ask that of you a second time, but something must be done about you in that regard," Margot said. "You've changed."

"Of course I've changed."

"More than is good for you," Margot clarified. "That is why you're so alienated from your former council right now. You haven't taken a single lover since you returned."

"Of course not," Chris said, a little puzzled. "I have to win Derek's mating flight."

"Then you should be sharpening your seduction skills, not letting them wither. The Elder didn't win based on speed and size alone, I heard."

Chris blushed crimson, furious that she knew one of the deep causes of his shame. It was true. The Elder had seduced Jettie, seduced Derek, and made Derek choose him over Chris. It was the reason Chris had fought him in the first place.

Maybe she had a point. He had been so dedicated to Derek and once he knew Derek was his, he had stopped trying as hard. If he were still with Derek, he would never consider another lover but he didn't have Derek. It was still a hard thing to accept. But he needed to accept it so that he could do whatever it took to win Derek back. Maybe he did need to take other lovers.

Bile rose in his throat as he thought of the terror and self-disgust he had felt when Carys had demanded a few minutes alone with him after the failed mating flight. He never wanted to feel that dead inside again and he had thought all sex would be like that until it was Derek again. But maybe it wouldn't. Maybe it was just the shock of losing mixed with the residual lust of the flight that had caused his intensely negative reaction. He did need to win Derek back and he knew the Elder would be sinking his teeth into his love with every minute of every day, so he would need every trick he could think of to win Derek back and that certainly included seduction.

He nodded. "You're right. This has gone on long enough."

Margot grinned. "Once you return to your usual self, the men's council will have no problems reinstating you. I've spoken to most of them, including Gerard. All you have to do is prove yourself the same man who was admitted all those years ago, and nothing more will be asked of you."

"Are you sure?" Chris asked.

"I'm sure," she said. "Are you interested?"

He nodded eagerly, but wondered who he could take to prove his renewed interest. Margot stood to leave and he caught her sleeve as she left, though it was probably too bold a move for a head of council. She didn't seem disturbed, though, and simply looked at him curiously.

"Do you know where Jamie and Scott are? Will I know when I rejoin the council?"

Margot stared at him for such a long time he grew nervous. But he wanted an answer, so he wouldn't take the question back. She was welcome to lie, if she wanted, or tell him to wait and see. But he wanted to know.

"You seem very worried about them," she said. "Why is that?"

"Jamie's been kind to me," Chris said. "And my dragon seems angry about something related to them being gone."

"Has your dragon told you what?"

"If he'd told me, I wouldn't be asking," Chris said, annoyed at his dragon. They shared everything together and he could tell that his dragon knew exactly what was going on and just hadn't told him.

"You'll know more when you rejoin the council, but I must

warn you," she added. "We don't know much either."

Chris blinked in surprise. He hadn't been expecting that type of answer. Were all of the dragons keeping secrets, even the council's dragons? Margot left and he pondered her answer for several moments. Jamie was the only one who could tell the dragons not to share something, so Jamie didn't want anyone knowing whatever had made the dragons upset. How much did the council know? They had to know more than he did now, and perhaps they were just frustrated because they didn't know everything.

He shook his head. He needed to get on the council to learn anything else, and Margot had given him a clear path back. He was a little nervous, since he usually used his position on the council to pressure students into sleeping with him. That was his preferred strategy, but it wouldn't work yet. He would have to charm them, as he had charmed Derek at first. He didn't know any of the new students and they were usually easiest, but he remembered all of the upperclassmen. He knew a couple that would fall for a handsome, charming man despite him not being a student or being on the council. It would be a challenge, but one he was up for if it helped him win back Derek.

CHAPTER SEVEN

New Knowledge

J amie wandered past the boundaries of the campus into the mist. It was dark, but he hadn't gotten a chance to explore during the day and he trusted the mist to protect him. Scott was sound asleep, probably still recovering, but all day, as he and Scott adjusted to the Spokane campus and worked with the council members here to figure out what, if anything, they needed to help with while they were in Spokane, Jamie had been itching to explore beyond the campus and see if he could find a protected place for the kittens.

Already, some of the council members had mentioned an inability to use their abilities. No one understood why, but the fact that it started when Jamie showed up was obvious and they had pointed it out to him. The first time it happened, he wasn't sure what to say, but he had settled on telling everyone that he was aware of the problem and working to fix it. And that was exactly what he was doing now out here in the mist.

He suspected the mist would protect the kittens but he wasn't sure, and they needed to be protected. They weren't just a potential weapon against Margot, they were his family. He would never put them in danger.

As he wandered, he thought of what little he knew of the area. Before the Elder became Derek's mate, he knew no one was allowed to wander for fear that their dragons would be killed. Even after the Elder stopped killing dragons, a general policy of not exploring had been firmly established and Jamie knew no one left the campus except on dragonback. The dragons seemed to want it that way, not wanting people to explore. He had felt a little resistance from them when he left campus and he could almost feel them consulting with each other before his exploration had their blessing.

Marisol probably persuaded them, he figured. She was the only one who knew why he was out here, but she may have shared his reasons. He still wasn't entirely sure what was shared between dragons and what wasn't, and more importantly, what they shared with their human partners. But most dragons couldn't even speak to their partners without verbalizing, he knew, so there was a fairly strong level of security with the average member of Tarragon society. Only the ranking dragons mattered, and he had instructed them not to say anything about his location so he knew they wouldn't share his exploration.

The area was beautiful and the stars sparkled in the clear night sky. It had been sunny during the day, too, without a cloud in the sky. It was strange how the weather was so different even though they were fairly close to Portland still. But there were mountains, he knew, and being near the ocean gave Portland dramatically different weather than the relatively desert-like conditions in Spokane.

When they first built the campus, the dragons had been hesitant about the location. Not Spokane in general, which they had picked partially because it was the closest community to Mount Tarragon and partially also because of Derek's connections to it, but to Mount Spokane. There really weren't any other places to go, however, so the dragons had reluctantly allowed the campus to be built on the mountainside but Jamie knew they had been very fussy about where the buildings could go. The location wasn't ideal, he knew, since the campus would be visible if it weren't for the mist. Given the dragons' reluctance to let him explore, though, he wondered if there weren't something about the area that they didn't like in general, some reason why the mountain was potentially dangerous.

He shivered and took comfort in the mist, which was giving him several options for which way to go but was keeping him protected. The mist didn't seem to have problems with him exploring, though it wasn't pointing him in any specific direction, and he trusted the magic that protected him.

After nearly an hour of searching for something and not even really knowing what he was searching for, he decided it was time to return. He had found a couple of places that could potentially work, fallen logs that were protected from view, a patch of dense undergrowth, but nothing had really stood out to him. He would return in the morning with Scott and they would decide.

Jamie sent his desire to return to the mist and waited for a single path to coalesce. It did, and he followed it. He entered an open area and without warning, the path vanished. He looked around. The mist was surrounding him in a wide circle, but there were no paths indicated. He could push his way through but maybe there was a reason he needed to stay here. He shivered and wondered if something dangerous were nearby and the mist was protecting him.

A branch snapped and he gave a start. That had come from almost directly in front of him, in the direction he had been heading. He took a few steps back and hid behind a tree, peeking out. The mist must have been protecting him. He saw a dark shape appear in the mist and his heart thudded. It was big. Very big. He knew there were cougars in the area; were there bears? Because this was too big to be a cougar.

He felt a tingle along his spine and shivered with fear. The creature emerged through the mist and he frowned. It was a horse. A beautiful, white horse that sparkled in the moonlight. But then it turned its head and he caught its eye and gasped. It was as if something slid away from the horse and he could truly see it, and it was no horse.

Without thinking he took a step towards the magnificent

creature as myths and legends ran through his head. The creature was far more delicate than he had first seen, with thin ankles and cloven hooves, but it was the single silver horn spiraling from its forehead that caught his attention. This was a unicorn. This was undeniably a unicorn. There were tribes that worshipped unicorns, he knew, including some in the United States. Mr. Ferrin's history lessons were flashing through his mind as he took another step towards the beautiful creature, who stared at him with those wide, dark eyes.

But unicorns only appeared to virgins, he remembered with a start. He blushed. He was no virgin. How could he possibly see this? Had he stumbled and hit his head? Was this a vision or a hallucination?

The unicorn neighed and he could almost sense words in the sound. They just escaped his understanding. He reached his hand out to touch the creature.

"Don't," a voice said. A human voice. He whirled to the right, where the voice had come from, and saw a young woman leaning against a tree watching him with amusement.

He stared at her in shock. She was dressed in a white, almost military-like uniform, which sparkled just like the unicorn. Her ebony hair was in an elaborate braid and her dark skin was in stark contrast to the uniform, but the effect was beautiful. She was just as beautiful as the unicorn. He wanted to say something but words were beyond him. She must belong to the unicorn's tribe, but the name of the tribe escaped him, as did any details beyond their existence. But surely they were friendly, if they were associated with unicorns. And the mist would protect him if she were a threat, he reassured himself.

He looked at the unicorn again, and the woman went to the creature's side and stroked its mane.

"What do you see?" she asked curiously.

He opened his mouth to reply but his voice didn't seem to work. He took a deep breath to calm down. His heart was still thudding, but not with fear anymore.

"A unicorn," he managed. "How?"

She laughed and the unicorn neighed. Again, there were words just beyond him.

"What is it saying?" he asked.

The woman looked surprised. "You can hear her, too?"

She. The beautiful unicorn was a she. Jamie wasn't surprised, but he knew nothing of horses or unicorns and hadn't wanted to mentally assign a gender without knowing. But she was gorgeous. He felt Marisol's curiosity, but no surprise from his dragon. Did Marisol know about unicorns? He felt evasion from her.

"Why can't I touch her?" he whispered, longing to touch the unicorn.

"You have a dragon," the woman said, as if it were the most normal thing in the world and it should have been obvious to him. He wondered how she could possibly know, and why she knew about dragons but he didn't know about unicorns.

"I'm surprised you can see her, even though she told me you would be able to," the woman continued, stroking the unicorn again. "I've never met any outsiders who could. But she told me you were looking for something, that we could help you."

He drew in a breath. She could help? Did she know? He reached out to Marisol and demanded an explanation.

Marisol, did you know they were here? Did you ask them for help?

She didn't seem to want to answer but he steeled his mind and demanded it.

We all know they are on the mountain. They gave us permission to build, though. I thought they could help protect the little dragons.

He shook his head. No wonder the dragons had been reluctant to build the academy here, if they knew another tribe was using the area. It was rather sweet that Marisol referred to the cats as little dragons the same way that Narné did, and he wondered if it

47

meant anything. Another thought popped into his mind.

Marisol, are you in contact with other creatures? Besides uni-
corns?

Yes, she answered. *I speak to all of them.*

He was stunned. All? But he felt her politely withdraw from the conversation and knew he wouldn't get any other answers out of her. How many creatures were there?

"Is something wrong?" the woman asked. He realized she was at his side, looking at him in concern.

"No," he reassured her. He remembered how vacant people looked while talking to their dragons and knew she didn't understand what he had been doing. "I was just, um, talking to, uh, my dragon."

He wasn't sure what to say, how much to share. She wasn't part of the Tarragon tribe but she knew about dragons. What could he tell her?

She laughed and touched his shoulder gently. "Where is she? I would love to see a dragon up close. I've seen them flying before, of course, but never up close."

"She's not here," he said. "She's in Portland."

The woman looked shocked. "But you were talking to her. How can you talk to her if she isn't here?"

Again he didn't know what to share. Clearly unicorns didn't have telepathy, but should he tell her about it? How many of their secrets could he safely share? He tried to reach Marisol but she wasn't interested anymore. He reached out to the dragons in general and realized many of them were watching him closely. The woman could be trusted, they decided, so he could talk to her freely.

"Telepathy," he said.

"You were talking to her again, weren't you?" the woman asked. "So you can talk to her in your mind? That's- that's amazing."

She sounded almost jealous. He looked at the unicorn again, glittering in the rays of the setting moon. The stars were brilliant and sparkled in her eyes. She pawed the ground and took several steps closer to him.

"I'm Jamie," he said, still in awe of the creature but looking at the woman now. "I guess I didn't introduce myself."

She looked embarrassed. "Oh, I guess I haven't either. I'm Zari, and this is Rayne."

"My dragon is Marisol," Jamie said. "She might come in a few months, if I'm still here. I'll make sure you meet her. She's curious about you. Both of you."

Zari grinned. He wondered how old she was. Maybe a couple of years older than him, probably out of college, but she couldn't be too old. Jamie looked at the unicorn again.

"We don't learn about other creatures," he said. "I didn't know unicorns were real."

"We prefer it that way," Zari said. "Dragons are the only creatures who don't mind if others know about them, probably because there are so many of you and you're so involved in the world. I don't actually know if there are other creatures, but there have to be, right? It can't just be unicorns and dragons."

"That seems reasonable," Jamie said. If the other creatures didn't want to be known, then he should respect that and not tell her that Marisol had basically told him others did in fact exist. He felt a wave of gratitude from Marisol and realized she hadn't meant to share that with him. "But why can't I touch her? Why does having a dragon matter?"

"Well, anyone from our tribe can touch unicorns, but," she blushed, barely visible in the darkness. "Outside of us, only virgins can touch a unicorn and not be harmed. I've heard that you can't be a virgin to have a dragon."

"That's true," Jamie said, disappointed that he wouldn't be able to touch the gorgeous creature. But at least he could see her.

"So what are you looking for?" Zari asked. "Rayne said we can help."

Jamie hesitated. Even though the dragons had said she could be trusted, this was different. This was his family. His secret. The dragons might be fine sharing it, but was he?

"I'm looking for somewhere safe," he said cautiously.

"You aren't safe on your campus?"

"Not for me," he said. "For others."

The unicorn neighed and again he heard words. He struggled to understand, reached out to her the way he reached to Marisol and the other dragons. Suddenly the words made sense and he gasped in amazement. The words were like bells in his mind, though they were audible as well.

"We know about the kittens, little human," she said.

Zari looked between them. "You understand her?" she asked in awe. "Wow. No outsider has ever understood a unicorn."

"He is not an outsider, not really," the unicorn said in those golden notes.

"I'm not?" Jamie asked, still in awe. He was also considering his options. If they knew about the kittens, then they could help him.

"Your blood is Tarragon," the unicorn said. "But you were raised by one of ours."

Jamie frowned, the kittens fading in his mind. His aunt had a dragon. His mother had a dragon, though a deformed one. His father, he realized. His father wasn't part of Tarragon society. But his father didn't know about unicorns, he was positive. Of course, he hadn't known his father knew about dragons either, so maybe his father did know. But if it were his father, then he should have their blood too, not just Tarragon blood. Did Tarragon blood neutralize the unicorn tribe's blood?

"My father?" he asked cautiously. The unicorn dipped her head in confirmation.

"He did not sire you, but he raised you and you are close to us now," she continued.

"What?" Jamie said, shocked. "He's my father. What do you mean, he didn't sire me?"

The unicorn pinned him with her shining eye. "Your father was one of ours, but he fell in love with a woman from your tribe who already carried a child."

Alan's story rushed back into his mind and he stared in shock. Alan had told him a myth when he asked about his parents, a myth about a pregnant woman who fell in love with someone outside of the tribe. Because it was a myth, and a fairly well-known one within their community, he had assumed the details just didn't fit his mother's situation completely. But what if they did? What if his mother had already been pregnant when she met his father? But then who was his father?

The answer flashed into his mind but he refused to accept it. He remembered how, the first time he had met Alan, he had seen himself in the man's eyes. Alan had the same hair, the same eyes. Jamie knew he strongly resembled his mother, since everyone had always told him so. No one had ever said that he looked like his father and to be honest, he didn't. But he did look like Alan, he realized.

When Alan talked about his mother, he had spoken with love. When Alan talked about his father, there had been clear hate and resentment. Had his father stolen his mother from Alan? Was that possible?

Jamie swayed slightly and Zari wrapped an arm around him as she glared at the unicorn.

"Rayne," she hissed. "How can you just tell him something like that?"

She stroked Jamie's cheek and he stared at her, still stunned.

"Are you all right, Jamie?"

"Yeah," he whispered. He took a deep breath. It made sense.

Perfect sense. And when his father, in desperation, had started searching for the nesting grounds and Ashton had finally ordered his death, Alan had probably been eager to kill him. The situation made sense, but that meant that Alan was his father. His biological father, not his true father, but how could he possibly come from someone so evil?

"Um, I think I need to leave," he said, pushing Zari away gently.

"Don't you need help?" she asked.

He looked around. "I'll come back. Can you help me later?"

"No one can know about us," she said hesitantly. "I don't know if any other time will work."

The unicorn neighed. "We will return here, at the same time tomorrow night. You will come alone."

Jamie nodded. He felt like he was in a daze. How was he going to explain this to Scott without mentioning the unicorn? He needed to talk to Scott, though. He needed Scott's reassurance.

He said goodnight and didn't even glance at the unicorn as he stumbled into the mist. After a moment, the mist cleared into a path in front of him. He didn't even look at where they were, and didn't pay attention to the path as he returned. Either the mist would lead him to the same spot tomorrow night or it wouldn't. He would trust it, as he always did. His mind was too full of knowledge, knowledge that he needed to share but didn't know how.

CHAPTER EIGHT

Night Terrors

Derek stared at the stars out the window. It was late, but he wasn't tired. And he wasn't interested in sex, though the Elder had already tried to entice him. When he had responded with a kiss but nothing else, the Elder had chuckled. But he left him alone and didn't push it. Derek was grateful. He just needed some time alone and the Elder seemed to sense it. It seemed like every minute he wasn't at class, he was with the Elder, and while it had never bothered him before, he needed time alone right now.

It was partially because of Jamie and Scott, he knew. The day had gone well. All of the council members had seemed to want to talk to Jamie, probably to try to glean information about why he was here. Derek had allowed it, since every single one of them had also managed to approach him at some point during the day to confirm their loyalty to him. As long as they still respected him as Queen, he didn't mind if they saw Jamie without him. He knew how curious they must be.

He had seen Jamie heading out to the campus alone a couple of hours ago and wondered where he was going, but maybe he needed time alone as well. It was strange he wouldn't want to be with Scott after what Scott had been through, but Derek had never really understood their relationship. Jamie had given Scott permission to sleep with Derek, after all, but they seemed so incredibly close. He had spent an entire semester trying to pry them apart before he bonded with Jettie and now that he had seen Scott's soul, seen how tightly Jamie was wound up in his very sense of self, he understood why he had failed. But it was still a strange relationship.

With a sigh, he leaned his head on his crossed arms and gazed out the window. He was also in this mood because of the request that had arrived today, a request he had been dreading the entire time he'd been in Spokane. His mother wanted to visit.

She had waited until the school year was over and of course she had no way of knowing that Jamie had just arrived and he was distracted. She probably didn't even realize who his mate was, and how dangerous the situation was. It was hard to think of the Elder as a threat, though, Derek considered. He was always on guard around the man but he hadn't tried anything. Their relationship was good. Not ideal, but good. He still thought of Chris a lot, but Chris was gone and the Elder was here, and he had to survive.

He didn't want to see his mother. He loved her, but he didn't want to see her. She was his past, and she would undoubtedly bring up his father. He was trying to build a new life and forget about his past. He was becoming Ashton's son and didn't need her to tell him he was failing. That was the part of his fear, he knew, but his real fear was different. Everything he did, all of the actions he was taking, he always tried to base off what he thought his father would do. Ashton was in his mind a lot, and the council responded. The Elder responded. They viewed him as Ashton's son. If his mother showed up, they might see him as her son, not Ashton's son. They might see her, and see his weaknesses, and stop respecting him. He couldn't let that happen. But he also couldn't deny her visit.

She was coming in a day or two. She hadn't been exact and if he expressed a preference, he knew she would respect it. But she would visit. There was no way out of it. Would he be able to remain the man that he was, or would he instinctively revert to the boy he had been when he was with her? He couldn't return to who he had been before. He needed to be his new self. Ashton's son. Not her son. Could she accept that? He didn't want to hurt her, he realized, and seeing him like this might hurt her. It was an impossible situation and he didn't like it at all.

He noticed Jamie returning, but Jamie didn't enter the apartments. He sat outside, in view of Derek's window though he probably didn't realize it. He was staring at the stars too.

Derek barely hesitated before heading to the door. He wanted to join Jamie. He didn't want to be alone looking at the stars. The Elder rose and nearly stopped him, but then allowed him to leave without a word. He might watch them through the window, Derek thought. But it didn't matter.

He called Jamie's name softly as he approached. Jamie turned in surprise, but gestured him over. Good. He sat beside Jamie and was surprised to see that Jamie looked deeply upset by something.

"Is Scott okay?" Derek asked. Was that why Jamie had left?

"He's fine," Jamie said. He laughed and covered his face. "I just learned something I'd rather not think about, but I can't think about anything else now."

"What's wrong?" Derek asked, reaching out to Jettie to see if Marisol was upset. Marisol was fine, he sensed, and Jettie wanted to sleep. He wished her sweet dreams and knew he wouldn't be contacting her again until the morning. It was odd, though, that Marisol was fine but Jamie seemed so upset.

Jamie studied him for a long moment as if considering whether or not to talk to him, then sighed.

"All my life, I thought I knew my family," he said. "My mom died when I was a kid, and my dad died after that, but I thought I knew them."

Derek watched him, puzzled. He had heard the rumors about Jamie's family, of course. Everyone had.

"The council killed my father," Jamie said, and Derek gasped. He hadn't known that. "Not my mother. But they killed my father. Alan killed my father."

Derek's eyes narrowed in rage even as his stomach flipped at the memory of slitting Alan's throat. He remembered the way Alan's body had flailed even after his throat was slit, moving for far too long after he should have been dead, and the blood that had sprayed on Derek's face and hands. But while normally that image was accompanied by horror and disgust, now his rage was numbing the horror. He knew Alan killed. Alan had admitted to the council that he led other dragons to their deaths and killed their partners. But Derek had never suspected he killed others.

He must have killed at the council's command, if Jamie's words were true, and Derek's stomach flipped again. The council had been so cavalier about killing Alan, he remembered, and Ethan had known exactly how to kill someone. Had Ethan killed before? He didn't like to think about it.

"I'm sorry, Jamie," he said, not knowing what else to say. "I'm glad he's dead," he added fiercely.

"I don't know if I am," Jamie whispered. "I found out- I realized- my father wasn't my father. Alan was my father."

Derek stared at him in confusion. He did look a lot like Alan, to be honest, but why would he think Alan was his father? And if it were true, then why had Jamie suddenly realized it now, tonight? Derek didn't want it to be true, and not just because he didn't want Jamie related to that man. If it were true, then it meant that Derek had killed Jamie's father. The body flashed before his eyes again but this time the horror was stronger than the rage, and shame tinted it. He pressed a hand against his stomach and shut his eyes.

"You did the right thing," Jamie said softly. "They shouldn't have asked you to do it, but it was the right decision. He killed dragons. He deserved death. But..."

His voice trailed off and Derek awkwardly wrapped his arm around Jamie's shoulders.

"What made you realize it?"

Jamie was silent for a long time and Derek wondered if he had even heard the question or if he were too wrapped up in his own thoughts. It didn't really matter, he decided. It was probably personal. But then Jamie answered.

"I saw something," he said. "It made me rethink things."

Derek considered asking for more details but didn't. This clearly wasn't an easy topic for Jamie and it was understandable. It wasn't very easy for him, either, despite Jamie's reassurance.

"They must know," Jamie said in a musing voice. "The council must know. If my mom was pregnant when she met my father, then the council knows he wasn't my real father. They probably know who my father is, too. Why haven't they ever said anything?"

"He wasn't your father, not really," Derek said. He thought of Ashton. Ashton had been absent all of his life, just as Alan had been absent in Jamie's. But while Jamie had someone to fill that role, someone to care for him, Derek had had no one. Derek had always been obsessed with his missing father, but Jamie had no reason to even miss his biological father.

"You had a father," Derek continued. "You loved him, and he loved you. Biology doesn't matter. He was your real father."

Jamie nodded slowly. "You're right," he said. "I guess it doesn't matter. He wasn't in my life. But he must have known. How could he hurt me when he knew?"

Derek wasn't sure what he meant, but Jamie was lost in his memories. He must be talking about how Alan killed his father, Derek decided. But Alan was heartless. He could easily see Alan killing a man for taking his place, but not having the paternal abilities to take over for that man. His heart went out to Jamie and he hugged Jamie, wishing he could share some of his pain. Jamie hugged back. Strange to think that not too long ago they were enemies fighting over Scott's affection. Derek hated what Margot had done to Scott, but seeing inside Scott's soul had allowed him to see how important Jamie was to the man and because of that, he could put aside his jealousy. He might still flirt with Scott – he probably would – but he knew his place in Scott's heart and he knew Jamie's and he would protect Jamie in order to protect Scott.

"Thank you, Derek," Jamie whispered. "I think I need to see Scott."

"Of course," Derek said. He squeezed Jamie as they stood up. "I'm here for you if you need me."

Jamie beamed at him, then they headed into the apartments and split up. The Elder greeted him with a hug as he entered, but only a light kiss.

"Are you okay?" he asked, stroking Derek's cheek.

"Yeah," Derek said.

"And the Queen? Is he all right?"

"He's just got a lot going on," Derek said, not wanting to share Jamie's secrets.

He eyed the Elder, remembering again the Elder's desire to get revenge on Jamie for Ashton's death. He needed to warn Jamie about it but hadn't had a chance. Still, the Elder didn't seem to have any plans for revenge yet. The Elder also didn't like Scott, Derek remembered. Would the Elder try to attack Scott in order to get to Jamie? Would he side with Margot against them?

The Elder stroked his cheek again and kissed him. Derek pulled out of the kiss nervously. Not only was he in the wrong mood for intimacy, he was scared now. It was easy to get lulled by the Elder, to forget his crimes. Easy to blame Alan for the deaths of the dragons when in reality the Elder had been the one to kill them. He knew the Elder would bide his time and wait for his chance to strike. His teachers reminded him of it constantly. Was this his chance? Would he strike while Jamie and Scott were so vulnerable?

They shouldn't be here. Portland might be dangerous but there had to be other places. He would have to warn Jamie immediately, help them find some other safe place. Any of the Tarragon communities would take in their Queen, he knew, and the Queen's mate as well. It was too dangerous here with the Elder.

"I think I want to just go to sleep," Derek said, wondering if the Elder would push. The Elder controlled his bed, after all, and could demand anything of him at any time when they weren't in public. But the Elder just nodded and hugged him tightly.

"I'll be up a little longer," he said. "I'll try not to wake you up."

Derek nodded and went to his room, changing into his pajamas slowly. Was the Elder going to strike? He reached out to Jettie and gently eased her awake. She was annoyed but as soon as she felt his fear, she turned sweet. He sent her his fears, and asked her to tell Marisol so Jamie could have warning. He listened for the Elder and heard him in the other room. He heard pages flipping. The Elder must be reading. He read a lot. He said he needed to catch up on a hundred years of culture and spent a lot of time reading. They hadn't connected the campus to the internet but Derek knew he was curious about everything related to technology. It didn't seem like he was going to leave and try to hurt Jamie or Scott, but even so Derek lay in bed, tense, listening to the pages and trying to figure out if the Elder were really there or if he had rigged something to just make it sound like he were there.

Jettie tried to calm him and reassured him that Jamie was aware of the danger, but he couldn't be calmed. Finally the sound of the pages stopped and he tensed even more. Then the door to their room opened softly and the Elder slipped in. He undressed quietly, no doubt trying not to wake Derek. Derek tried to pretend he was asleep and he did relax considerably. Nothing had happened. Jamie was fine.

The Elder got into bed gently, as if trying to make as small an impression as possible in the mattress, and didn't try to cuddle. Derek nearly laughed in relief. Not only had the Elder just wanted more time to read, he was being so sweet and considerate. Derek didn't laugh but he must have moved because the Elder reached over and did cuddle him.

"I didn't mean to wake you up," he said softly.

"It's fine," Derek said. It was more than fine, and he felt foolish for doubting the Elder's intentions. "I wanted to cuddle."

The Elder's arms tightened around him and he felt the Elder's lips press against his forehead.

"Anything you want," he said in a husky voice, and Derek's body stirred. Now that he wasn't afraid, now that he was reassured about the Elder's intentions, he wasn't sure he was ready for bed after all.

He turned in the Elder's arms and kissed him. It started slow, and the Elder didn't push for more, but Derek rolled onto his back and pulled the Elder over him. They broke apart and the Elder chuckled.

"You are awake," he whispered, letting his hand trail down Derek's body. "Let's see if we can't tire you out."

Derek leaned into the caress and let out a soft moan. He pulled the Elder into a long kiss, then obediently put his hands over his head and let the Elder take control.

CHAPTER NINE

Tense Undertones

It wasn't hard for Mike to find Jamie and Scott that morning. Several of the councilmembers had already spoken to him and pointed Mike in the right direction. Jamie and Scott were probably attempting to stay out of sight and lay low on the campus. Construction had just finished on one building and they were on a field just outside, but even though it was out of the way, people seemed to be finding them. Since every dragon could easily locate Jamie and so many people were curious about his presence, it wasn't a wonder he was getting swarmed and Mike hoped they didn't mind if he came and talked to them as well.

There were a few groups of students sitting at a distance from Jamie and Scott, watching them without going up and actually talking to them, but one student was talking to them as Mike approached. Scott was chatting with her in a friendly way but Jamie looked grateful when Mike interrupted and asked the student if he could speak with the Queen alone. She nodded and waved as she left.

"Good morning, Mike," Jamie said. "Do you need something?"

Mike eyed him. Jamie looked like he hadn't slept all night. Scott only looked a little better. He would have thought the opposite would be true, that Scott were having trouble sleeping but Jamie was staying awake as much as possible to be with him, but maybe not.

"I wanted to talk to Scott for a moment, if I could," he said, glancing at Scott.

When he had seen Scott yesterday he had kissed the man without thinking. Neither Scott nor Jamie had seemed to mind and both had been pleased by his recovery, but he wanted to apologize and figure out what his relationship with Scott should be. He still cared for Scott deeply and Scott had forgiven him. They hadn't really gotten along since Mike had broken up with him and he wasn't sure how to act around Scott now. Scott and Jamie looked at each other and nodded, then Scott got up and walked a few feet away to talk to Mike.

"I wanted to apologize for yesterday," Mike began, but Scott laughed and stopped him with a hand on his arm. The touch was so casual, so accepting, and Mike needed it.

"Ethan warned me you had recovered," Scott said. "I'm glad. You seem much happier. You seem like yourself again."

"I am. I guess I'm not completely myself yet," Mike added, thinking of Carys and the intense desire for Ashton he still felt sometimes. "But I'm getting there."

"You have no idea how happy that makes me," Scott said warmly. "And Jamie, too. We've been so worried about you."

"Jamie!" a voice shouted behind them. Scott's face went dark.

TK was approaching them and had spotted Jamie but not Scott and Mike grabbed Scott to prevent the man from rushing the student and shoving him away. Scott tried to break free of Mike's grip but Mike refused to let him. They watched as Jamie stood up cautiously and TK came to a stop a few feet from him. Jamie looked shocked.

"Oh," he said. "TK. You're here."

"Of course I'm here," TK said with a rich laugh. "Why are you here? How long have you been here?"

"Um, a day? Maybe two?"

Jamie looked to Scott nervously and TK noticed them for the

first time. He noticed Scott first and his face darkened just like Scott's had, but then he noticed Mike and he looked just as nervous as Jamie. Mike wasn't entirely sure how he felt about TK seeing Jamie again. He knew TK still loved Jamie and still wanted to win Jamie's heart, but he was with TK now. Not exclusively, really, and there was nothing formal between them, but he and TK saw each other almost every day and had sex several times a week.

"Hi Mike," TK said. "And Scott. How are you doing?"

Mike tightened his grip on Scott before he could respond and pushed in front of him, coming to TK's side and wrapping an arm around his waist. He wondered if TK would allow it. TK didn't often allow public displays of affection and this was one in front of a man he hoped to seduce. But TK did allow it, to Mike's relief, and Scott relaxed considerably as he went to Jamie's side and held his waist in a similar fashion.

"I'm great," Mike said in answer to his question. "Why are you on this part of campus? Your dorm is nowhere near here."

"Devon said something was going on," TK said. "I didn't realize you were here, Jamie. How long are you visiting?"

"I'm not sure yet," Jamie said. "A while."

TK smiled beautifully. "Have you seen the campus? I would love to show you around."

"We've seen it," Scott interrupted.

Suddenly Mike noticed three other students approaching. They were ones who had been sitting and watching Jamie and he wondered why they were here now. The tallest of them, a burly student who had to be a senior, glared at TK.

"Do you need any help, Queen?" he asked.

"No," Jamie said, puzzled. "We're just talking."

Mike narrowed his eyes. "Why are you trying to protect him from TK when you were fine with him talking to the other students?"

"He's threatening the Queen," one of the other boys said aggressively. "We'll protect our Queen."

"He's not threatening me," Jamie said. "Why would you think that?"

But Mike knew the answer, and so did TK. The racism that so many tribe members held wasn't expressed towards TK directly most of the time. It was subtle aggressions like this. They viewed him talking to Jamie as more threatening than a white student talking to Jamie, and were prepared to intervene to stop it. They might not even realize what they were doing, though based on the hate in their eyes that was unlikely with these particular three. TK shrunk against Mike and Mike squared off with the largest boy, who seemed a bit intimidated. Not only was Mike older and more physically fit, he was also on the council now and though he didn't wear robes like most of the council, he did have the dragon sigil on his chest.

"You'll leave TK alone," Mike threatened. "If anything ever happens to him or any of the students who arrive from Africa, I will look for the three of you and you will pay."

The boys paled and backed up, then turned and practically ran towards the main campus. Jamie and Scott looked confused.

"What do the African students have to do with this?" Jamie asked.

"I apologize for reacting to you the way I did," Scott said a little stiffly. "I didn't realize others were watching and might misinterpret it."

"No one misinterpreted anything," Mike said. "The council is already trying to find students who might have a problem with the African students. We'll probably request that they return to Portland. I guess I have three more now."

"I don't understand what Africa has to do with anything," Jamie said. "Is it because you haven't been a student before and you think the other students from Africa already know about dragons?"

"No," TK said. His voice was a mixture of frustration and relief. He was probably frustrated that Jamie didn't understand the racism in the situation but probably relieved that skin color never even occurred to Jamie as something to discriminate against. Jamie had lived in a very white world here in Oregon, Mike knew, but Mike had grown up in Texas and had much more experience with the ways people dehumanized each other. Ignorance was charming in some ways, but living a colorblind existence led to people allowing racism to happen because they honestly didn't see it. Scott seemed to slowly realize the problem, but then again, as someone with clear Native American heritage, he had probably been the target of discrimination himself.

Scott whispered something in Jamie's ear and the boy's eyes widened and he looked appalled.

"Has that happened a lot here?" Jamie asked. "I knew it would be a problem with some, but the students are usually so well-screen to check for intolerance like that."

"No one has been outright rude to me," TK said. "They just treat me differently than everyone else. It's not always a problem. I think, maybe, once the other students are here from Africa and once we mix with all the students and share classes and common experiences, the problems will lessen."

"You're keeping an eye on it?" Jamie asked Mike, and he nodded. "Good. If you have any problems before the exam, kick them out. There are plenty of others with a potential to link."

"Jamie, that's a little harsh," Mike said gently. "I'm not defending them, but when you kick someone out here, you're sentencing them to death. Expelling the student is a last case scenario."

"There are thousands and thousands of applicants every year," Jamie said icily. "Tens of thousands. Almost all of them will die because I can't let them all in. Why would I save the ones who deserve it least?"

Mike didn't have a good answer for that except that often

students changed after the exam and became more tolerant. It didn't often happen, but it happened enough that it wasn't something to be expelled over. Outright racism had been screened for decades, of course, but it was the subtler forms that made their way in and it had grown stronger ever since Africa had withdrawn and the remaining pool of students was predominantly Asian, white, or Native. Those three groups were universally accepted in Tarragon society, even though Asians and Native Americans still faced discrimination in the wider world. And there were black students, often the ones selected from America. They faced a tough battle, though, and the African students would have it worse.

He sympathized with Jamie's view, though he hadn't realized Jamie took the student selections so personally. He had heard that Jamie had held a prospective students weekend to screen a cousin and she had failed. Something had happened but Eraxes had never been clear and while the council certainly knew about it and Mike was informed of everything happening now, his council privilege didn't seem to extend backwards. They told him everything he needed to know and as new information came up he learned it, but they rarely explained things that had happened in the past. It was extremely frustrating at times. Perhaps whatever had happened with Jamie's cousin was the reason he took the student selection so seriously, or perhaps it was that neither of his parents had been accepted and had been doomed to early deaths.

Jamie was going to be far more selective about this and far more involved than Ashton ever had been, Mike could tell, and he wasn't sure how the recruitment committee felt about it. Even though they didn't tell him past information, he still knew that some of the changes Jamie had made in committee structures had frustrated the council and the changes he had made to that committee in particular had nearly set off an insurrection. The council was still bitter about it even though they accepted the leads of their Queens. Maybe they hoped Derek would undo the changes Jamie had made. He doubted Derek would, though. The Queens seemed to be getting along quite well, to everyone's surprise.

TK smiled hesitantly at Jamie and Scott.

"It's good to see you, Jamie," he said. "I just wanted to say hi. That's all."

"It's good to see you too, TK," Jamie said. "You can say hi whenever you like."

That didn't seem to sit well with Scott but the man didn't voice an objection. As Jamie's mate, he could force the two apart. TK had told him that Scott had done exactly that earlier, and it was what had driven TK to seek out the egg outside of the exam. Scott had insisted that he prove his worth and he had. Now it seemed Scott would allow contact between them, so Scott was acknowledging that TK had indeed proved his worth. But Mike doubted Scott would tolerate Jamie and TK being alone together. Even though their relationship had rarely been physical, there was still a danger and Scott wouldn't risk it. Would Mike? He wondered.

He adored TK and enjoyed him thoroughly, but didn't feel the same type of emotional connection to him that he had felt with Scott, Ashton, or Kale. Those three were unique and special and he loved them deeply in their own way. Of course he also hated Ashton to some degree, but the love was still there. But most of Mike's other lovers over the years were passing things. He took a lover, perhaps they were together for a day, a week, a month, a year, but they both knew it wasn't permanent. TK knew he was in that kind of relationship with Mike. It was clear that neither of them were looking for emotional support, though TK did provide that and Mike did his best to support TK as well. It was a physical relationship and a friendship, and wouldn't ever be more. He might be a little jealous if TK dropped him to go after Jamie, but not much. He would be more worried because doing that would hurt Scott, and Scott was someone Mike cared about.

Mike glanced at Scott and could tell that the man wanted TK gone but wouldn't say it in front of Jamie. He would tolerate TK as long as he didn't appear a threat, but if TK started making any progress, Mike was sure Scott would risk alienating Jamie and would forbid the two of them from seeing each other. Well, Mike could help with that. He could keep TK distracted while they were on campus. TK would still pursue Jamie but with Mike there, it wouldn't be the type of aggressive pursuit that might threaten Scott.

Mike kissed TK's cheek, eliciting a blush from him as he pushed away slightly. Mike had never kissed him in public before.

"We should get going," he said.

To his relief, TK nodded. They said goodbye to Jamie and Scott, who settled back down even though they were likely to keep getting people asking them questions. Mike led TK towards the boy's dorm. Once they were in private, he smiled at TK.

"Be patient," he said.

"I'm sorry," TK said. "I didn't know Jamie was there. Devon didn't tell me. And I didn't see you or Scott. I wasn't trying to rush things with him. I know it'll be different with his boyfriend here."

TK hesitated, then looked up at Mike through his lashes. He was absolutely beautiful.

"Do you think I still have a chance with Jamie?"

Mike wondered. His heart said no, but Jamie and Scott had fought frequently throughout their relationship. Derek was a huge wedge between them and Derek was now in the picture again. If their relationship did fall apart, it was very likely that Jamie would turn to TK. If he gave TK that hope, would it spur him to pursue Jamie more aggressively? If he didn't give TK that hope, would TK turn to the Elder for help?

"I honestly don't know, TK," Mike said. "But I know you won't if you push. You have to go slow."

TK nodded and seemed deep in thought as Mike pulled him close and cradled him. He wondered what TK was thinking and if he had given the right answer, the answer that would steer TK in the direction he wanted him to go. Only time would tell.

CHAPTER TEN

Intrusive Visitor

Derek stared into the distance for several minutes before hauling himself to his feet and heading to the main campus. His mother had arrived. He had been hoping against hope that she would change her mind, or at least put it off. But she was probably eager to see him. Her dragon had let Jettie know that she had arrived and was waiting in the knoll.

The Elder had spent the morning with him, cooking him breakfast and pampering him since he still felt exhausted. Part of it was Jettie's exhaustion leaking through to him, but he hadn't slept the night before, first from fear and then from pleasure. He hadn't told the Elder about his mother yet, though he wasn't exactly keeping it a secret. He just didn't want to talk about it to anyone, let alone someone who might view him differently because of her. He would have to say something now, though; otherwise the Elder would probably go with him.

Derek put a hand on the Elder's chest.

"I'm going out," he said. "Alone."

"Is something wrong? You've been acting strange. It's not just your dragon; something's wrong."

"My mom just arrived," Derek said, ducking his head with a blush. "I have to go see her."

The Elder stroked his arm. "You're the queen. If you don't want to see her, you don't have to."

"She's my mom," Derek said. "I do have to. She shouldn't stay long though. I hope."

"Has she ever hurt you?"

His question was deceptively calm but Derek could hear an edge of angry possession in it and he hastened to reassure him.

"No, of course not, it's just, I haven't seen her since I left," he explained. "So much has happened since then and she doesn't – can't – know most of it."

"You think she'll treat you as a child, and you don't want that," the Elder observed. "Any woman would be honored to have you as a son. Act like the adult you are, and she'll respect that."

Derek sighed. He was probably right. But would he be able to act like an adult when he had always acted like a child around her? Still, the Elder was sweet to give him advice like this and he kissed the Elder's cheek.

"I just need to spend an hour or two with her and then she'll go. You don't mind?"

"No," the Elder said. "But if you need anything, have Jettie tell my dragon and I'll be there. Remember that you are queen now, and take pride in your accomplishments."

Derek nodded and the Elder squeezed his hand before playfully pushing him out the door. He laughed and started heading to the knoll. He was glad that she hadn't come to find him. It was less likely that the council would find out she was here. They might realize it, as they seemed to keep close track of him, but he could control the introductions. As he started across campus, he reached out to Jettie. She was busy with her eggs. She was staying mostly at her second nest because she didn't want anyone to know about the first, but she was flying there at least once a day to check on them.

Apparently caring for the eggs was quite intensive for the first couple of weeks, and then it was more a matter of keeping them warm enough. The nesting grounds were always warm so that was rarely a problem, and it was why Marisol would be leaving months before the eggs hatched. Jettie wanted to stay until her eggs hatched and Derek agreed, with a heavy heart. He didn't like the thought of being alone so long, but maybe he could persuade her to leave early in later hatchings.

He passed several groups of students picnicking on the grounds and waved at them. Everyone was friendly to him here, since he had gotten to hand-pick all of the students. None were originally from Spokane and while most of the upperclassmen didn't know him, they all respected him. The students in his class were the ones who had been friendly, stood up for him, or, in a couple of cases, ignored him. No one who had bullied or harassed him was here and it was a huge relief. He could be himself and everyone seemed to like him. Normally he was extremely popular until people got used to him, and then they turned against him. He didn't know why but it always seemed to happen. Not here, though. He wouldn't let it happen here.

There were several people standing and talking and he saw Jamie's red hair and Scott's muscular shape as they talked to someone. He hadn't realized they were here. Perhaps they were avoiding the Elder after Derek's warning the night before. He needed to explain everything to them, but not now. He approached and recognized the woman Jamie was talking to. His heart stuttered. It was his mom.

She was talking to Jamie in an animated fashion, as she always did, and he and Scott were smiling. Derek's feet slowed but Jamie caught sight of him and waved, and his mother turned to him. Her face lit up and she rushed at him, sweeping him in a hug before he could stop her. He extricated himself as quickly as possible, not wanting to be seen hugging his mom like this. She didn't seem to mind.

"Derek! You look so handsome," she said. "Jamie was just telling me what a good job you're doing here. I didn't realize you were in charge of this campus. Is your dragon here? I'd love to meet her. I've never met a queen."

"Hi mom," he said awkwardly. "Jettie's at the hatching

grounds. She won't be back until the first year exam. I didn't expect you today."

"Is this too soon?" she asked. "You didn't specify and I was so eager to see you. How have you been? Tell me everything."

Derek looked at Jamie and Scott, who were nearby but not directly in the conversation. He didn't want to talk about anything. Too much had happened. Pursuing Scott, bonding with Jettie, Alan's attack, Ashton's death, his mating flight, the Elder, there was nothing he wanted to tell her. Jamie seemed to sense his distress and came to his side, even putting a hand on his arm for support.

"Derek, we were about to get lunch. Would you and your mom like to join us?"

"Oh, yes!" his mother cried, then turned to him and took his other arm, batting her lashes at Jamie. "I can't believe you know the queen, Derek."

"I'm a queen too," Derek said, irritated and wondering if having Jamie there might actually make things worse.

"You know it's not the same. Everyone felt his mating flight. I'm glad, of course," she added. "I wouldn't want to see my son like that."

Both he and Jamie were bright red, him from anger and Jamie from embarrassment. Derek had forgotten that Jamie's first flight had been broadcast worldwide. He hadn't realized that even his mother had felt lust for Jamie, and Jamie clearly hadn't realized it either. Scott cleared his throat.

"Derek's mating flight was just as significant, and our society is honored to have two wonderful queens," Scott said. "Jettie is the only queen on this campus and every student admitted to this campus next fall will bond with one of her eggs."

"Oh, of course," his mom said, and turned to Derek. "You're sure she can't come meet me?"

"I'm sure," Derek said sharply. "Her eggs take priority."

Jamie looked at him uncertainly as if wondering if he still wanted them to stay, but his mom smiled brightly.

"Is there a cafeteria on campus? Is that where everyone eats? I haven't been on a campus since I graduated."

"Why don't I bring us something?" Scott said quickly, and Derek nearly sighed in relief. He did not want to go anywhere with his mom. Especially not somewhere the council might be. "Derek, you and your mom can catch up and Jamie and I will bring some meals. Is there anything you'd like? There's usually sandwiches and pizza, and salad."

His mother described what she wanted and Derek tried to figure out how he could regain control of this situation. He needed to get her talking about something besides him, besides Jamie... he needed her to stop talking, really, but he didn't know how. He certainly didn't want to talk. Scott and Jamie headed towards the cafeteria and Derek led his mom to a bench along the newly-completed building where they would be out of the way. He hoped. She beamed at him and reached out to stroke his cheek.

"You really do look good, honey," she said. "You look just like your father."

Derek smiled hesitantly. He didn't think there was any criticism in that.

"I can't believe he's gone," she continued, and Derek's mood soured. "Can you believe it? He barely got to know how wonderful you were. You did get to know him, didn't you? I'm sure he was so proud of you for bonding with a queen. Not that you'd do anything less, of course. You were always destined for great things. I could tell."

She paused and Derek wondered if he were supposed to say something. She had tossed a couple of questions in there but it didn't seem like she wanted the answers. He had forgotten how annoying it could be when she just started talking without paying attention to anything he said. But she did love him, he reminded himself. She must be lonely without him, and he could put up with her chatter for an hour or two. Still, maybe he could redirect the conversation a little.

"What is your dragon like?" he asked. "You can talk about her now, right?"

"Of course!" she exclaimed. "Why, it's hard to believe you've never met her. She's a pretty little green. You almost found her a few times when you were younger," she said indulgently. "You were always so curious. I wish I could have let you play with her. She wanted to play with you so much, but rules are rules and I would never break Tarragon law."

Derek thought about the students from Africa who would know about dragons. They didn't have any experience with dragons, though. But when they graduated and returned to Africa, they would bring their dragons. Would their children play with dragons? Were dragons even good with children? It seemed distinctly dangerous to let a dragon near a child, even a mother dragon like Jettie.

"I was one of Ashton's favorites, you know," she continued. "He was in almost all of my mating flights when I was a student. I became pregnant right after graduating and moved here, but there are good men here too. No one like him, but they're good. Who is allowed in your flights?"

Derek shrugged uncomfortably. "The council here and in Portland decide."

"Who won your flight? I haven't heard anything about your mate," she said. "Of course, I know nothing of the other queen's mate either, though he seems nice enough."

"He's fine," Derek said. "It wasn't the person I wanted."

His heart clenched as he thought of Chris. He tried not to think about Chris too much because it hurt, but he missed Chris deeply. He and the Elder got along quite well and he enjoyed the Elder a lot, but he still wanted Chris. He worried that when he did see Chris again it wouldn't be like he remembered, because he knew he was idolizing Chris in his thoughts. But he needed it.

He needed something to remember and hold onto and cherish, so he clung to the good memories and forgot the negatives that existed in every relationship.

His mother put her hand on his shoulder and for a moment he felt comforted by her presence. Her smile was sad and she hadn't picked up her chatter. Instead, she made a clucking noise.

"You deserve the man you want," she said. "But you'll have plenty of flights in your life. There's time."

"Thanks," Derek said, but he wondered. Time was on the Elder's side, not his. Still, he appreciated the words and her kindness. She was always kind to him, though he rarely told her his problems. He had hidden the bullying from her as much as possible, and hid his sense of abandonment when he thought of his father. She was vaguely aware of it, he knew, but she had no idea how unhappy he often was growing up.

"I would still like to meet him," she said. "I'm sure I'll have the chance. I can stay for a couple of days. You have guest rooms on campus, right? Of course you do. Who do I ask about that?"

"You can't stay here," Derek said, aghast.

"Don't be silly," she said with a laugh. "I want to see you."

"But you are seeing me, right now," he said, his mind whirling. "Why do you need to see me more?"

"I want to make sure you're happy here," she said. "You were always such an odd child. I want to make sure everyone loves you."

Derek shook his head. He remembered the Elder's advice to be firm. He was a queen and if he didn't want her here, he could tell her. Even if she was his mom.

"Look, mom, I'm happy you came to visit but you can't stay more than an hour or two. I'm sorry."

"Don't be silly," she repeated. "Who do I ask about the guest room?"

"Me," he said sharply. "You ask me. I'm in charge of this campus. I decide who comes here, and how long they stay. This is my campus."

"You're just a child," she said dismissively. "They might let you think you're in control, but I'm sure someone on the council is really in charge."

"No," he said. "I'm not a child anymore. I control the council. You could ask them but they'll just ask me. This campus is mine, mom. All of it."

She stared at him in surprise, then her eyes filled with tears. "You're so much like him," she sniffed. "And you don't want to see me again either."

Derek sighed. "I do want to see you again," he said. "You can come visit again in the future. But you can't stay. I'm sorry."

"Well, I'm happy to have lunch with you at least," she said slowly. "And it's so nice to meet the queen in person. You've made some good friends. I'm glad. Will I have a chance to meet your mate?"

"No," Derek said. "I think it's best if you leave after lunch."

"If that's what you want."

There was a silence and he was tempted to fill the silence with an apology, with an invitation to stay, and he knew that was exactly why she was silent. She wanted to guilt him into an invitation but he wouldn't give it. He did not want her here and he had the right to choose. Luckily, he spotted Jamie and Scott approaching and waved them over. His mother would no doubt gush over Jamie the entire meal but at least she wouldn't be focused on him, and then she would leave. He was almost certain of it. He would not invite her to stay and he would just have to make sure Jamie or Scott didn't accidentally invite her. He had known this would be unpleasant and his fears were well-founded for once. She viewed him as a child and if the council talked to her, they might view him that way, too. He needed to be strong, in himself and in decisions. She would leave after lunch.

CHAPTER ELEVEN

Supporting the Queen

Scott held Jamie's hand as they waited at the cafeteria for their picnic to be packed. Jamie was still blushing and Scott pulled him into a quick hug. He felt sorry for Derek, who clearly didn't want his mom there, and wondered how he would react if his own parents were still alive and tried to treat him like that. They would, too. They would be impressed by everyone except him and try to diminish his role, and treat him like they always had: a child. But they were his parents and he missed them. He would put up with anything for the chance to see them again and he wondered if Derek knew how incredibly lucky he was to have a mom who could treat him like that.

"We need to talk to him in private," Jamie said, his blush fading. "We have to know what the danger was last night."

"You said it passed, though," Scott said. Last night had been difficult. If the threat of the Elder weren't so real, he might have thought Jamie made up the sudden threat just to keep them from talking about his new-found heritage. Scott had barely been able to react to it. Jamie had quietly told him about going out in the mist and remembering the story Alan had told of his mother going into the mist and finding the nesting grounds, and how the story had made him think about things more deeply and realize the truth. As much as Scott wanted to deny it and reassure Jamie, Jamie was absolutely certain. And unfortunately, it did seem likely.

But before Scott could even properly comfort Jamie, Jamie had stiffened and warned that they might be in danger from the Elder. They had decided against fleeing, since it seemed to only be a possibility and not a certainty, but Scott had grabbed a heavy pan from the kitchen and waited by the door. There wasn't much he could do if the Elder attacked but he would protect Jamie at any cost. Time had inched forward as they both waited nervously. Jamie was in constant contact with Jettie, Scott knew, and Derek continued to be fearful. And then abruptly Jamie had relaxed and said the danger had passed, that Derek had misjudged the situation and there wouldn't be an attack. The Elder was now occupied, Jamie had said with a blush and Scott had grimaced at the thought of how the Elder must have been occupied. Still, it meant they were safe for now.

Jamie had looked for Derek in the morning but he was sleeping in and they didn't want to knock and see the Elder. So they had gone out to wander campus and try to avoid people. It hadn't worked. Students had found them, Mike had found them, TK had found them, Derek's mom had found them, and then Derek had found them. They did need to talk to Derek about the Elder, though. If there was even the slightest risk to Jamie, Scott was willing to leave. He didn't want to run. He wanted to stay here until they returned to Portland. But if they needed to leave to keep Jamie safe, then he would ignore his own comfort and take his boyfriend as far away as necessary.

"His mom said she was staying a while," Scott said. "Maybe we can borrow him. He didn't seem worried about last night, though. He was just worried about his mom."

"I talked to him when I went out last night and he was worried," Jamie said. "But he would have warned me if he was worried about him. Maybe he really was just worried about his mom. I hadn't thought of that."

As they waited, Ethan approached them, nodding to Jamie and smiling at Scott. As the head of the council here, he was technically the same rank as Scott, and might even be higher since Scott was acting as second to the Elder. A decision that still rankled even though he knew it was necessary to maintain Derek's control. It seemed they really were running into everyone today.

"Have you seen Derek?" Ethan asked. At their nods, he sighed in relief. "Is he safe?"

"Physically," Jamie said dryly. He had seemed to get along with Derek's mom until she mentioned Jamie's mating flight and now he seemed to dislike her quite strongly.

"He'll be fine," Scott said. "We're about to have lunch with them."

"Is he with someone?"

"You don't know who he's with? Then why are you asking?" Jamie asked suspiciously.

"The Elder indicated that he might need support, and Jettie just gave my dragon the same message," Ethan said. "Are you sure he's all right?"

"His mom is here," Jamie said distastefully. "She's harassing him but he'll be fine."

Ethan blinked in surprise. "His mom? Who is his mom? When did she arrive? All visitors are supposed to come through me."

"Her dragon indicated that they just showed up," Jamie said with a shrug. "She must have let Derek know, but he didn't expect her today. Her name is Angela. She didn't give a last name."

"Oh, Angela," Ethan said, still sounding surprised. "I had no idea Derek was her son."

"How many kids does Ashton have?" Scott asked, wondering how many other children Ashton had neglected. He had seen how desperate Derek had been for Ashton's approval and didn't like to think of other children in the same position.

"Three who have been to the academy while I've been there," Ethan said. "He probably has more. None have been anything like him, except Derek."

A worker handed them a large basket and Ethan eyed it. "I might join you. I've eaten, but if Jettie is upset then I need to confirm that everything is going well, and he may need help getting rid of her if that's what he wants. I remember she was quite aggressive in getting what she wanted."

"Is that why Ashton sent her away?" Scott asked, again thinking of Derek's neglect and hoping that his mom hadn't been the cause.

"No. Anytime he impregnated someone, he sent them away. Usually further away but he was fond of Angela. He wanted to keep her close."

"You can come with us," Jamie said as Scott took the basket from him and they turned to leave. "He might need help. I don't want Jettie's care disrupted and I didn't realize how upset she is."

The three of them walked back towards the knoll and Scott hoped bringing Ethan with them was all right with Derek. He suspected Derek didn't want anyone to meet his mother, especially not the people he needed to impress. And he did still need to impress Ethan. The Spokane council seemed quite content with Derek leading, but there was always a chance their loyalty would waver. He doubted they would turn to the Elder, but Ethan might gain too much power. Already he had noticed that the council here was trying to undo many of the changes Jamie had implemented. They were waiting on Derek to approve the changes and he hadn't so far, probably knowing that Jamie would object, but if Derek lost his influence then Ethan might make the changes on his own.

Derek and his mom turned as they approached and Derek's face darkened as he saw Ethan. Well, too late now. Derek would just have to deal with it. His mom, however, lit up as she saw Ethan and she hugged him with a laugh.

"I didn't know you were on the council," she said. "I knew you were going places."

Scott looked at Ethan, surprised. He had thought that because

Ethan had been confirmed as head of Spokane's council with no objections that the man would be one of the oldest members, but he couldn't be that old if Derek's mom had known him before he was on the council.

"Head of the council here," Ethan said. "And the person you're supposed to ask for permission to visit campus."

"Would I need your permission to stay a few days?" she asked.

"Mom," Derek snapped.

"I'm not going to ask, I'm just curious," she said.

Ethan looked at Derek uneasily and Scott wondered what the correct answer was. She had indicated earlier that she was staying a few days; would Ethan give her permission when Derek clearly opposed it?

"You do have to go through me, but I check all visitors with Derek before granting permission," Ethan said slowly. "His word is final."

Derek looked pleased until his mother patted his arm. "I guess you do have some power here."

"He's our queen," Ethan said sharply. "He has all the power here."

She rolled her eyes and didn't seem to believe it, and Ethan's eyes narrowed. He was offended on Derek's behalf and that was good. If Derek had thought that the council would listen to his mother and view him as less powerful, then he didn't have to worry. Even if they weren't as firmly behind Derek as they were, they likely would have been offended on behalf of any queen. Custom and protocol was highly prized in the council even if regular members of Tarragon society didn't always pay attention to it. Scott hadn't realized it would help in this situation and clearly Derek hadn't expected the support. He looked extremely grateful.

"Here's our lunch," Jamie said. "Do you want to sit at the picnic table? It's in the sun but it's not too hot."

"That sounds great," Derek said, and they went to the picnic tables that scattered the knoll. Most were occupied by the students who had been surreptitiously watching Scott and Jamie earlier but one was empty and they sat around it. Jamie passed out their lunches and offered his chips to Ethan, since he didn't have anything. Ethan graciously accepted a small portion of the chips. They ate in silence, for the most part, and Derek seemed less tense than he had before. Scott wondered how Jettie was feeling. She had to be feeling better since Derek seemed better. He didn't want anything to happen to Jettie's first batch of eggs.

He was worried about Marisol's eggs, though Jamie assured him that Marisol was taking care of the eggs just as well as she would if Jamie were safe and not on the run. Hopefully the Elder didn't pose enough of a risk that they had to run even further. Derek seemed entirely focused on his mother, not worried about the Elder, so maybe he really had misjudged the situation. But something had happened, and they needed to know what.

They finished eating and Jamie eyed Derek's mom.

"How long are you staying?" he asked. "I need to talk to Derek in private."

She looked at Derek. "I was planning on staying a couple of days, but I suppose that's up to my son, isn't it?"

"She's leaving today," Derek said shortly. "But I can take a minute to talk to you, Jamie."

Jamie and Derek stood and headed into the shadow of the building. Scott would have liked to hear what Derek had to say but if he was needed to distract Derek's mother, he would. Ethan watched them leave curiously. Did he know about the danger? Probably not. He would have warned them if he knew anything beyond the obvious threat posed by the Elder.

"So tell me about my son's mate," Derek's mom said. "He won't tell me anything except he didn't get the guy he wanted. Was that you?" she asked Scott, smiling flirtatiously. "Didn't it used to be common for queens to share mates?"

Scott blushed and Ethan stifled a laugh. "Did he say that?" Scott said, trying to hide his embarrassment. It was very true that Derek would have loved him as a mate. The only reason Derek had even considered Chris was because Scott had turned him down.

"He didn't give any specifics, but it was you, wasn't it?"

"No," Scott said, trying to contain his blush. "He had a boyfriend and I already have a mate."

Ethan was smirking and Scott knew he was thinking about the times Scott had come to Spokane with the sole purpose of sleeping with Derek. He had used his body to lure Derek too many times, and his feelings for Derek were too strong. He remembered Derek dominating him in front of the council to prove himself and earn their support. Ethan knew how fragile Scott's romantic allegiances were. But that was the past. Something had happened when his mind had been nearly erased and rebuilt, and now there was only room for Jamie.

"Well, I'd still like to meet his mate," she said.

"If Derek gives you permission to meet him, then I'm sure you will," Scott said.

She pouted, but Derek and Jamie were returning. Jamie looked grim and Scott wondered what Derek had said, and what the threat was. It had to be a real threat if Jamie looked like this, but since Jamie didn't seem panicked or worried, it wasn't immediate. Jamie sat beside him and took his hand, smiling and seeming to want to push aside whatever Derek had said.

There was a moment of silence and then Derek's mom opened her mouth. Derek flinched, no doubt expecting more of the patronizing, intrusive questions and comments she had been showering him with, when Ethan interrupted.

"Angela, why don't I show you around before you leave? Derek is taking summer classes that he needs to prepare for and a lot of business to complete. He is queen, after all."

They stood up and Derek hugged his mom. She was extending the goodbye, probably trying to get him to change his mind about her leaving, and finally Scott took Jamie's hand and led him off after waving. Derek did have classes and Scott wanted to talk to Jamie.

"Do you want to go back to our room?" he asked Jamie softly. It wasn't a simple question. Their room was next to where the Elder likely was, and if the Elder was a threat, then returning there would put them in danger.

"Yeah," Jamie said, and Scott sighed in relief. "It's not a big deal, but it is something to watch out for."

They headed back to the room and Jamie kept his hand in his. Scott glanced over at his boyfriend, wondering what new worries Jamie now had. He wanted to ease Jamie's mind but there were so many things going on he didn't know how. As they entered the apartment building, he pulled Jamie into a quick hug and was rewarded by a kiss.

"We'll get through this, Jamie," Scott promised, hoping it was a promise he could keep.

"I know," Jamie said. "Let's check on the kittens first."

Scott smiled and they headed to the closet where the squirming little kittens were mewing around Janna. Tiger threaded around Scott's legs with a robust purr and Scott wrapped his arm around Jamie's waist. This was his family and as long as they were together, it would work out.

CHAPTER TWELVE

Enhanced Senses

As he explained to Scott what Derek had told him, Jamie wondered how serious a threat it posed. The Elder wanted revenge for killing Ashton but wasn't making any overt threats. He had been polite so far, following protocol exactly. Protocol prohibited hurting a Queen but would the Elder risk his position in Tarragon society in order to hurt or kill Jamie? He wasn't sure, and as he and Scott talked it became clear that Scott wasn't sure either. It was a danger, definitely, but the Elder had established himself here. He had a great deal of power and wouldn't throw that power away without good cause. Was revenge a good enough cause, or would something else have to tip the scales? And was the threat of Margot enough to tip the Elder against him?

Derek had apologized for the misunderstanding last night, and also for not telling Jamie sooner. Jamie wondered how long he had known about the Elder's desire for revenge and why the Elder had told Derek in the first place. He must have known for a while, since Derek hadn't mentioned recently learning it. They had been on such bad terms for so long, though, he probably had known and just hadn't bothered telling Jamie. But with Jamie here, in direct danger, and after what Derek had done for Scott, things were different. They trusted each other now. Or at least Jamie trusted Derek, and Derek seemed to trust him.

His jealousy of Derek had toned down considerably since

Scott had recovered. There was something subtly different about Scott since then. He was the same, but a little more removed than usual. Perhaps he was still recovering; nearly losing one's memories had to be a devastating blow that would take longer than a few days to recover from. But when Scott had talked to Derek today, and in all their interactions since then, Jamie hadn't seen the usual interest in Scott's eyes. He still cared about Derek, that was clear, but the tension wasn't there anymore. Normally when Scott talked about Derek there was a hint of guilt in his voice, a hesitation because he knew Jamie knew what he and Derek had done together. But right now, as they worried about how seriously to take this threat, Scott was talking about Derek as if he were any other person.

"If you want to leave, Jamie, then we'll leave," Scott said seriously.

"He hasn't done anything, indicated anything," Jamie said. "He's been polite. He even gave us information about the kittens. If he does act, I think we'll have warning of some kind."

In reality Jamie didn't want to run because the only places they could go were farther from Marisol and he didn't like being this far from her, especially when she was caring for eggs. She needed him nearby, and she needed him safe. If he could find safety here, no matter how temporary, he was going to stay. Jamie sighed.

"I think I've found a safe place for the kittens," he said. It was partially true. He hadn't found an exact location but with Zuri and the unicorn's help he would find one soon. "They'll be protected nearby and I'll visit them and care for them."

"Where is it? Do you want to check it out now?"

"No," Jamie said, and paused. "It might be safest if you don't know where it is. I'll go there again tonight to make sure it's safe, and bring the kittens there soon. Janna and Tiger will have to go, too," he added sadly.

Scott squeezed his hand. "But they'll be safe?"

"Yes."

"I won't ask," Scott said. "If you think they're safe, I'll trust you. I know there are some secrets only for Queens."

Scott thought he was taking the cats to the nesting grounds, Jamie realized. Since Jamie had never explained that the reason they were in Spokane and not with Marisol was because of the kittens, he had never mentioned that the kittens couldn't go in nesting grounds. He hated lying to Scott but this wasn't a lie, not really. Scott hadn't stated that he thought the cats would go there. He had only said that some secrets were for Queens, and that was absolutely true. This was a secret that Jamie held, as a Queen, and could never reveal to anyone. He just hoped Zuri and Rayne found a safe enough place for his feline family. He would be devastated if anything happened to them and still shuddered at the nightmare flight that had brought them here when Janna and Tiger had clung to him for dear life so they weren't dropped from dragonback. And the kittens, though a little more protected in a pillow cover, could have easily been hurt in the rough flight. They had all survived and he was eternally grateful, and he would make sure the unicorns knew exactly how much they needed to take care of his cats.

"If the Elder holds a grudge against anyone, it ought to be Margot," Scott said with a hint of anger. "She's the one who made you kill him."

Jamie shivered. That day was still burned into his memory. It didn't haunt him anymore, but as he drifted into sleep the sight of blood sometimes flashed through his mind. More than the sight, though, was the feel. The pressure he had been forced to place on the blade to break the skin, then the quick slide once the blade had severed the skin. The feel of blood spraying across his body, his face. And the hot scent of blood and pain that had swamped him.

With the enhanced senses he had gained from bonding with Marisol, he had experienced the death far more vividly than he suspected most people would. He had learned to handle himself without experiencing the kind of sensory overload that had nearly killed him when he first bonded and struggled to enter Marisol's world. For the most part, everything was second nature to him now. Certain colors tended to trigger strong emotions from him, and when Ashton had died, the colors had been what seared into his mind. The hot red of the blood, the subdued red of the flesh, the ashy white of the skin, the black of his robes, all of it had combined into an overwhelming agony. He had recovered quickly from it, but the feel of those colors still swamped him when the nights grew long and sleep wouldn't come.

He had come to understand why Margot had ordered the killing, but he hadn't forgiven her. The person in charge of executions was either the Queen or the head of council. Since there was no head of council at the time, since Ashton had been removed but no replacement named yet, it had fallen to Jamie. But technically, Margot could have done it herself. She was the acting council head when it happened and she was just as qualified to kill Ashton as Jamie was, but she hadn't done it.

Now that Jamie knew about the Elder's feelings and how the Elder had loved Ashton, according to Derek, and he knew that it was Ashton's death that had caused to Elder to leave, he wondered if the reason Margot hadn't killed Ashton was because she didn't want to call the Elder's wrath on her. If she had killed Ashton then the Elder would be after her, not Jamie. He and Jamie would still be at odds because he was a murderer and had manipulated his way into being Derek's mate, but the Elder wouldn't be plotting revenge against Jamie. He would be focused on Margot. And she had to know it.

Jamie wondered if the Elder understood why Jamie had killed Ashton, that Margot had been the one to order it. Did he give any of the blame to Margot? If so, then perhaps he would be more willing to side with Jamie over Margot. Jamie was still Queen, after all, so if he followed protocol then the Elder would support

Jamie in this conflict. All signs indicated that this was the case. But whether the Elder protected him passively or he actively helped Jamie against Margot remained to be seen. He had told them about the kittens; would that kind of help continue? Could Jamie trust him if he did keep helping? At least now Jamie knew to be wary and knew what exactly to look out for.

"I'm sorry, Jamie," Scott said.

Jamie realized he had curled into Scott's body and his boyfriend was cradling him. Scott kissed the top of his head and wiped tears from his cheeks, tears Jamie wasn't even aware of. They were stray tears, as Jamie wasn't exactly crying, but he was upset and a few tears had slipped out. The memories of killing Ashton were just so strong.

"It's fine, Scott," Jamie said, nestling against Scott's chest and kissing his neck. "It just hits sometimes, you know?"

"Yeah," Scott said, rubbing his back. "Do you want to talk? Is there anything I can do?"

"Just hold me," Jamie murmured, finding strength in his boyfriend. The clean dandelion and honey scent of Scott was washing away the painful memories and he inhaled deeply. There was a hint of clover; Scott had been near Narné recently. He let his mind fill with the love he felt for Scott and tried to push away everything else. At least for the moment. He needed to reestablish balance within himself. Finding out about his father had destabilized him and having that followed up by the danger with the Elder had thrown him off considerably. He hoped no one had noticed how off he was feeling today. Seeing Derek's mom and having her mention his mating flight had been the final straw in his composure, though he doubted anyone noticed. He had learned how to control his expressions and look calm when he wasn't. He had learned to fake a lot in the years since his father had died. With Scott, though, he didn't have to fake. He also didn't have to worry. Scott would protect him.

He tilted his head back and gazed into Scott's beautiful eyes.

He pushed his lips against Scott's, wondering what kind of mood Scott was in. He just wanted to lose himself in Scott's body but Scott was still delicate. He wouldn't push. When Scott grabbed the back of his head and dove into his mouth, however, he grinned. Scott was more than ready to give him what he wanted, and he felt his body start to respond. He was cuddled so tightly against Scott that he knew his boyfriend could feel his instant response and he felt a growing hardness against his thigh as well.

They kissed and kissed, then Scott picked him up and tipped him onto the bed. Jamie laughed and stripped off his shirt. Scott straddled him and began kissing his chest, his tongue lingering on the thin horizontal scars that were the legacy of his desperate youth. Sometimes when Scott did this it depressed him, as it reminded him of things better left unsaid, but usually Scott's complete acceptance and need for him despite his flaws was a turn on. Today, it was a definite turn on and he moaned and grabbed Scott's back, feeling along Scott's scar which – unlike the thin streaks along Jamie's arms and legs – was from a dragon.

Scott kissed down Jamie's chest, his hands busy at Jamie's pants as he pulled them off. His tongue flicked against the dragon scars across Jamie's belly and then, as Scott yanked off his pants, his tongue licked Jamie's cock. Jamie moaned softly and clung to Scott's head as Scott slid his cock into his mouth. He loved being inside Scott like this, feeling Scott's tongue and throat around him. His hips hitched forward, bringing him deep into Scott's throat and Scott's hands gripped his hips tightly so he was in control of the pace as Jamie tossed his head and started to lose control.

Scott caressed and adored his cock for a long time as Jamie gasped and moaned and tried to hang on, and then Scott withdrew and pulled his own pants off. He was hard and dripping as he pushed Jamie's legs up and leaned against him. Jamie felt the tip of his cock against his entrance and tried to relax. Then Scott plunged inside him and he bit back a cry. In Portland they could be as loud as they wanted since no one was nearby, but here they needed to keep quiet. As Scott began thrusting into him, their minds linked and he gasped as he felt Scott fully, their bodies moving in perfect unison.

Often when they had sex one of them kept their minds partially closed. There were a lot of reasons for that, often quite innocuous, but today their minds were wide open and Jamie felt everything that Scott felt, the doubled sensations of fucking and getting fucked blasting through his mind and body with a wall of heat. Jamie gasped and arched his back, driving himself further onto Scott as the dual sensations grew stronger and stronger. He could feel Scott's pleasure and his increasing loss of control that matched Jamie's own.

Another solid thrust and Jamie stifled a cry as his body exploded into an orgasm. He felt Scott's orgasm again double his sensations and long minutes passed before they lay panting and exhausted on the bed together. As Scott withdrew, the link between them faded and Jamie pulled Scott close and kissed him.

"I love you, Scott," he whispered. "Stay with me here, okay?"

"I won't leave your side," Scott promised.

CHAPTER THIRTEEN

Nameless

C hris stroked the brunette nestled beside him, mentally comparing him to Derek. This student didn't match up at all, but he was pleasant enough. Derek was tall, dark-haired, with flashing dark eyes and an arrogance that faded into surprising sweetness when he submitted. The student next to him was like most students: handsome, but not striking, and a little too eager to please an older, more experienced man.

The student had just ended his sophomore year, making him the same age as Jamie, though he didn't compare to Jamie either. It was a little hard for anyone to compare to Jamie, even Derek to some degree, because of how Jamie had appeared in that mating flight. He wasn't interested in Jamie, but the sight of Jamie's face twisted in pleasure and the need to join the flight was seared into his brain. The summons to Derek's flight hadn't been like that, and maybe that was why he had lost. Derek hadn't wanted him enough. Next time, he would.

At first Chris had worried that getting someone new in his bed would be a challenge but he needn't have been so concerned. He had met with indifference in the first two students he approached but when the third seemed uninterested as well, he had pushed. Normally the students started out desperate for him and he didn't need to do much to get them into bed but with just a little persuasion, this student had turned from dis-interested to entranced in a matter of minutes. A little flattery, a few exaggerations, a few meaningful glances as he pressed against the student and made his intentions known, and the student had asked him if he had any plans for the evening with an endearing blush.

The student had been sweet in bed, willing to do anything he asked, and he missed Derek's forcefulness and the unexpectedness of Derek's surrender. Derek liked to dominate as well as submit and it was always a game to see what Derek's mood was and what he would want. Chris had been indulgent with him, giving him whatever he wanted, and he regretted that now. He had been too easy and Derek hadn't valued him enough. Margot was right. He needed to sharpen his skills. It shouldn't have been Derek's choice what they did. It should have been his, and Derek would have enjoyed that just as much. Perhaps more. He would have been willing to fight for it more, Chris was certain.

Chris got up and considered the student, who was still sound asleep. It was a little rude to just leave, but he had no desire in waking the student up and talking to him. He couldn't even remember the student's name. He was just one more in a long line of men that Chris used but didn't care about. Only two men had ever stood out in that long line: Ashton and Derek.

He left a note with thanks and a false desire to see him again after dressing, then slipped out of the room and through the dorms. He didn't especially care if anyone saw him here but it was a little unusual for an adult who wasn't on the council to be here. Members of the council were often in the dorms, not just for illicit purposes but also because most of them were teachers or advisors. They often had very legitimate reasons for being here and in fact he passed a member of the council on his way out.

The councilmember seemed surprised to see him, but the disgust he usually associated with the council now wasn't there. The man seemed to consider him, pausing in his path to watch him walk by. And as he left the dorm and headed to the dragon canyon, another man appeared from the shadows and began walking with him. Chris nearly stopped in his tracks when the man joined him. It was Gerald, and he gestured for them to continue even as Chris wondered what his presence meant. Surely he couldn't get in trouble for sleeping with a student. That would be beyond hypocritical.

"You're doing well," Gerald said blandly, and Chris eyed him.

"I'm better," he said.

"Who was the student?"

"A sophomore."

"No name?"

"Does there need to be?"

Gerald's lips curled to a smile. "No, but is there?"

Chris wracked him mind, not knowing why this was important. The student had introduced himself, of course, but Chris hadn't been paying attention. He had been focused on his own wants and desires, not caring about anything the student had to say.

"Do I need to go back and get his name?" Chris asked. "I'd rather not."

Gerald's smile widened. "I'm surprised. Margot indicated that you just needed some inspiration to return to usual. I hadn't expected how quickly you would act."

"She was right," Chris said. "Derek chose the Elder because I failed."

"And you don't plan on failing again?"

"I was careless with him," Chris said, looking down. They were almost at the canyon. "I forgot what Ashton taught me and I lost him because of it."

"Ashton was wrong on one tradition," Gerald said. "But remember that he was right on all the others. You lost sight of your duty and you've paid for it dearly. But you've paid enough. It's time to put you back on the council."

Chris paused, staring at Gerald in surprise. "What?"

"Margot did tell you, didn't she?" Gerald asked.

"I didn't expect it this soon."

"Your student was a good choice," Gerald said with a shrug. "You picked at random, he looks nothing like Derek but he's also not the opposite of Derek, and you can't even remember his name. You were using him as prey, as you should. That's enough for me, and for the others."

"Students are prey," Chris pointed out.

"Nothing was prey to you after Derek," Gerald said. "You lost sight of everything."

Chris was silent as they wound through the paths of the canyon. It was true. He hadn't noticed anyone after losing Derek. Even before then, he hadn't seen anyone else. There was only Derek, and no one else mattered. He had assumed Derek felt the same despite Derek's feelings for Scott, feelings that Chris himself had fanned. He should have known that if Derek were capable of loving Scott, he was capable of drifting away from Chris. Chris hadn't made a mistake letting Derek and Scott be together, he didn't think, but he had made a mistake letting Derek's attentions wander when Scott wasn't there in person. They were headed towards the council chamber, he realized in surprise. He stopped.

"You mean right now?"

"Do you object?"

"No," Chris said, a little stunned. "None of you have problems with this?"

"Some do," Gerald said. "But everyone who ranks above you is fine with it, and I trust you understand how to put the others in their place once your own place has been restored."

Chris nodded, thinking of Carys. Carys ranked below him even though Carys had been one of Ashton's pets, and Chris had used that rank difference to his advantage. And when Chris's rank had been stripped, Carys had used that to devastating effect. If someone challenged him after this, he needed to be able to handle it. Rape among council members was not uncommon and was a generally accepted way of dealing with rank disputes. Chris's encounter with the student had been consensual but he suspected he would have no problems forcing someone to do his will if necessary. Even a few days ago the thought of that would have been unbearable, but now he was ready. He needed to be on the council so that he could practice seducing students in order to win Derek back. He would discipline anyone who got between him and that goal.

"Mike is on the council now," Gerald added.

"I'm not surprised."

"His rank is similar to yours," he warned. "When you return to Spokane, you two will have to sort it out."

"He's still a child," Chris said, offended that Mike already had so much power. Chris had dedicated his life to Ashton and the council and had earned his place as one of Ashton's closest servants. He was the highest ranking councilmember who had never been a pet, and Ashton had assured him that he would have been a pet if the timing had been better. "Is he even inner circle?"

"As I said, you'll have to sort it out," Gerard said. "The Spokane council doesn't have an inner circle per se, but Mike has already met those requirements as well."

"I thought we were leaving him alone," Chris said.

That had been the policy when Chris was still on the council. Mike had been shattered by Ashton's death. It was always hard for pets to adapt to the loss of Ashton's attention but Ashton never ignored them completely and assisted them when necessary. With Mike, though, there had been some debate as to how to handle him. Some of the council wanted to offer him comfort, since Mike would still be addicted to Ashton's touch, but most wanted to leave him alone until he stabilized on his own. Mike had been closer to Ashton than any other pet in anyone's memory, but because of that closeness, Ashton had abused Mike in a way he had never abused anyone else. And Mike had betrayed him, and indirectly caused his death. No one really knew how to handle Mike but the final decision was to keep an eye on him, treat him gently, and only offer to comfort him if he asked.

"Derek pushed him on the council before he had fully recovered," Gerard said. "He needed a little assistance to get back on track. Like you, in many ways."

Chris looked up sharply. "I do not need help from any of you."

"But you did need someone to talk to you," Gerard pointed out. "You weren't recovering on your own. Something had to be done."

That was true, Chris realized. If Margot hadn't talked to him and inspired hope, he would have continued as he was, sinking lower and lower until he would have lost everything. He shivered. He loved Derek. But losing Derek shouldn't mean losing his life, and it almost had. He remembered how at first he had wanted to beg Margot to erase everything, and how when he realized she couldn't help, he had wanted to end everything. Love should be positive. It should add to life. It shouldn't end life.

"Gerard," Chris said, pulling the man to a stop just outside the entrance. "Margot said I would know what happened to Jamie if I returned to the council. Is that true, or will it fall outside of what I'm allowed to know since I wasn't council when it happened?"

Gerald hesitated. "Margot told you that?"

"She just gave a vague answer when I asked. Is he safe?"

"We have every reason to believe Jamie and Scott are safe," Gerard said. "You won't be allowed to know the exact details, unfortunately. You know our policy. But they are as safe as they could be."

"Where are they?"

"Who would you tell if I told you that?"

Chris frowned. "What do you mean? Is it a secret from part of the council? I can keep silent if you want."

"Chris, we've always known your closeness with Margot and the female council," Gerard said, to Chris's surprise. There wasn't anything wrong with acting as a spy for the women, but it also wasn't something to acknowledge out loud. "We know Margot has a reason for wanting you back on the council or she wouldn't have instigated this. Why does she want you?"

"You clearly know that I talk to her sometimes," Chris said uncomfortably. These things were better left unsaid. "Apparently none of you are as talkative."

"Then you want back on to be her spy," Gerard said, and Chris's eyes widened. None of this ought to be said out loud, not this directly. "The two councils have split since you left, Chris. Things you learn from us cannot be passed to her, or anyone on her council. Do you understand?"

Chris was silent, wondering how to answer. Margot could easily pressure him into sharing secrets because she was the one getting him back on the council. She had a lot of leverage over him. But his loyalty to his peers came first.

"It would help if I knew some things that were acceptable for her to know," Chris said slowly. "Things you expressly told me I could pass on."

"You're willing to limit what you tell her?"

"You are my council head," Chris said. "Not her. I hadn't realized we had divided, but there's no question where I stand. I'll obey you."

He paused and considered. "Is there some reason you don't want Margot and the women knowing where Jamie is?"

"No one knows where he is, but if you learn something, you should tell me and me alone," Gerard said.

Chris nodded, but inwardly he was frustrated. Something had happened while he wasn't on the council and because of that, he would never learn about it. The council didn't share anything they didn't have to and council matters remained private even after one joined. He hadn't realized he had lost out on such a potentially important piece of information as what had happened to Jamie. But why hide anything from Margot? Had something happened between Margot and Jamie? They had always gotten along, as far as he could tell. They had never been friends, but she had quietly supported him against Ashton and had helped smooth the transition after Ashton's death. It was unlikely that Jamie would turn against her, or she against Jamie. But there was no way to know unless he figured it out eavesdropping on the other councilmembers. A long shot, but the only one he had.

Gerard pulled him into the council room and he saw the entire inner circle and many of the rest. The inner circle seemed almost happy to see him, though they had shown their disgust for his actions the most. There were several lower circle members and they didn't look as pleased. They were probably the ones who would try to challenge him in some way but if the upper circle supported him, they didn't matter. He examined them and decided they weren't a threat. Some he had dealt with before; they should have known better. The others didn't have enough rank to matter.

Gerard brought him to the center of the room as everyone circled him. When he joined the council this had been an intimidating experience but he had been dedicated to Ashton and would do anything for the man, so he survived. But now that he knew his place and he knew it was higher than most of the other people's, he felt no fear as they circled him. Nothing would be required that he couldn't give. His fears were gone. He was ready to rejoin his council.

CHAPTER FOURTEEN

Understanding Motives

D erek's summer class was much the same as his classes
during the semester had been: an attempt to teach him
to handle being Queen with the Elder as his mate. He
was constantly reminded not to drop his guard around the Elder
even while he learned how queens and their mates normally
worked, because he had to know those rules even if they weren't
following them exactly. The Elder followed protocol and Derek
needed to know everything about that protocol so the Elder
couldn't lie to him or manipulate him and it was an enormous
amount to learn. He did his best and his classes were ungraded,
but he knew he wasn't picking up as much as they would have
liked. He wondered what Jamie's classes were like and if Jamie
were bombarded by all this information all the time. Jamie's life
didn't depend on him understanding protocol, though, so the
other queen probably learned at a reasonable pace.

He still felt guilty about causing panic for Jamie and Scott.
The Elder seemed perfectly normal even though Jamie was here.
He hadn't indicated an ill intent in any way and Derek shouldn't
have assumed the worst about him. Of course, his teachers
wanted him to assume the worst at all times. But he ignored
them quite a bit when it came to handling the Elder. They didn't
have to live with the man. He did.

He had thanked Ethan for dealing with his mom and he was
amazed that the council had been uniformly behind him when

she was here. Apparently she had encountered several other council members while touring with Ethan and every single one of them had backed Derek without hesitation. After the tour, Ethan had insisted that his mom leave without another good-bye and Derek was extremely grateful. He owed Ethan for that but he didn't think Ethan would take advantage of the situation. He would almost certainly ask for something at some point, but Derek didn't think it would be unreasonable.

Jamie and Scott were keeping as low a profile as possible and while Derek saw them every day, usually in the apartments as they came and went, he hadn't spent any significant time with them. They were almost always together, though he had noticed Jamie slipping away at night and heading to the forest. He wondered what exactly had happened in the woods that made Jamie realize his heritage and suspected there was more to the story than Jamie had let on, but he didn't push.

The day was almost done as Derek stretched and entered his apartment. As usual, it smelled delicious. The Elder was an extraordinary cook and had quickly learned what Derek liked to eat. Tonight was enchiladas, a dish that the Elder hadn't been familiar with but had learned to cook quickly. They probably weren't very authentic but Derek loved them, and he smiled as the Elder took his bag and gestured for him to sit. The Elder placed a dish in front of him and sat across, and they began eating. As always, it was delicious and Derek complimented him as he dove in. There was no dessert, since it was a weekday. The Elder often made desserts on the weekends or for other occasions but they had both agreed that too many sweets might be fattening. Derek worked out, but avoiding sweets was a good strategy in general.

"Did your class go well?" the Elder asked, as he usually did after dinner. They had moved to the living area and were sitting together on the couch, Derek lying against the older man.

"Fine," Derek said noncommittally. Sometimes he had more to say, either because he learned something cool or because the teachers had irritated him, but often he left it with fine. He liked that the Elder asked, though, despite his often brief replies.

"Did you see the other Queen and her mate today? I couldn't find them anywhere."

"Were you looking for them?" Derek asked a little nervously. Was the Elder keeping tabs on them? If so, was it to protect them or so he could target them more easily?

"No, but I often see them. The campus is small."

"I'm not sure where they went," Derek said. "I saw them this morning but that was it."

He paused, thinking of his fears about the Elder's intentions. The Elder had been extremely honest when he told Derek about hating Jamie right after the mating flight. At that time, Derek had been trying to win Scott and didn't have any positive feelings for Jamie so there was no threat that Derek would share that information. Did the Elder even remember telling Derek?

"Are they safe here?" Derek asked.

"Margot's unlikely to find them," the Elder said. "She wouldn't think they'd come here."

"Why not?"

"Because I'm here," the Elder said. "She thinks I would kill Jamie if he came here."

"But you won't?"

The Elder stared at him and Derek realized he had put too much emphasis on that question, asked it a little too desperately. He gulped.

"I mean, it's just that I know you don't especially like Jamie, because of Ashton," he said slowly. "Is Jamie safe here?"

"It depends on his actions," the Elder said, equally slow as if he were considering each word. "It's very unlikely that he's in danger from me. He is not what I expected."

"What did you expect?"

"I expected him to be strong, intelligent, and he is," the Elder said. "But he's also very, very young. I had forgotten how naïve young people can be sometimes. He's strong enough that he should have refused to kill Ashton, but I don't think he knew he had a choice."

"I didn't know he did," Derek said, puzzled. "I thought it was his responsibility, since he was Queen."

"There were other options," the Elder said. "Queens are not intended to kill."

Derek let out a silent sigh at that, since it meant he wouldn't be asked to kill anyone again. Killing Alan was a highly traumatic event in his life and he never wanted to repeat it. He had been given a choice, he considered. He could have refused. And the council had seemed to accept his revulsion at killing people and it hadn't turned them against him. Killing one person was enough for them. He was glad there weren't any rules that would require another murder. The Elder stroked his hair and kissed his forehead.

"You will never need to kill again," he said softly, probably knowing exactly what Derek had been thinking about. "If it ever comes up, I'll do it for you. But it should be Ethan's responsibility."

"I'm glad," Derek whispered. "So you don't blame Jamie anymore?"

"He still did it," the Elder said. "I won't forgive him. But perhaps I'm a little more understanding of his reasons. He isn't in danger from me because of that."

"But he is in danger?"

"He'll always be in danger," the Elder said. "As are you. You're Queens. There will always be those trying to take advantage of you and manipulate you. That's why your mate is so important. The Queen's mate is supposed to be the strongest, most experienced man on campus. Usually it's the council head. That consolidates power and gives the queen someone to lean on when others turn against them. But neither Jamie's mate nor yours are traditional."

"Scott would do anything for Jamie," Derek said.

"Not if he doesn't know what he needs to do," the Elder pointed out. "His dragon is powerful, but Scott is nearly as young as Jamie. They haven't lived in Tarragon society long enough to understand how it operates and Scott can't properly shield Jamie because he doesn't know what to look for."

Derek shivered. "You protect me, right?"

"Yes," the Elder said with a kiss. "And I know exactly how. But my role on this campus is limited. Much of the protection offered by a queen's mate comes from their influence on the council and I have almost no contact with them."

"I'm not changing my mind on that," Derek warned, and the Elder huffed in laughter.

"So strong," he murmured. "I wouldn't try to change your mind. I'm just telling you why I can't offer as much protection as a traditional mate."

"You offer enough," Derek said, snuggling into the Elder. He wondered if they would have sex tonight. Probably. He was in the right mood and the Elder always seemed to be in the mood. Occasionally Derek wasn't interested and the Elder never insisted, though as Derek's mate he could demand it of him. His teachers gave him so many warnings about what the Elder could do to him, what he might do, but so far the Elder hadn't hurt him at all. He was extremely considerate of Derek's mood and feelings and while he seemed to think he wasn't fully protecting Derek, he was keeping him safe and content. With Jettie gone, that was more important than ever. He reached out to Jettie and felt her asleep with her eggs. He smiled.

"Jettie's asleep," he said. "Where's yours?"

"He's sleeping, too," the Elder said fondly. "When we were alone he slept for weeks on end, as did I. Time didn't seem to matter. We slept to escape. Now he's so busy he sleeps to restore his body."

The Elder was smiling and Derek smiled with him. It was obvious how much the Elder loved his dragon. He rarely spoke about the centuries he had been in Mount Tarragon. Derek had never really thought about what that must have been like. He was trapped, though it was by choice. Tarragon society had turned against him and he had left things to Ashton. Derek didn't know what would have happened if Ashton hadn't died, if the Elder would have remained in stasis for centuries more. Ashton's death had revived him and inspired him to return to Tarragon society seeking revenge, but he didn't seem to be interested in that revenge anymore. At least not as strongly, if he were willing to leave Jamie alone.

Perhaps the Elder had found other reasons to live besides vengeance and that was why his drive had lessened. He was the Queen's mate now, after all, and seemed to enjoy Derek. Maybe because he had power and a good Queen he was as content as Derek was. He hoped so. He would be pleased if the Elder stopped actively working against Tarragon society and stopped being a threat, even though he knew it was unlikely to happen. The Elder needed to kill dragons to survive and sooner or later, he would kill again. As Derek's teachers warned him, it would happen eventually and he needed to be prepared for when it did.

"It's late," the Elder said, raising the last pitch to make it a question. Derek grinned.

"I'm not tired," he said. "But we could go to bed."

The Elder laughed and kissed him, then helped him to his feet.

"I'm sure we'll find some way to help you fall asleep," he murmured, and Derek pressed against him and kissed him. This was the best part of having him as a mate, he decided. Being dominated by the Elder was unlike anything else and he loved it even while he tried to fight it. The fight made it more fun and sometimes he even won. The Elder's arms wrapped around him and unexpectedly tickled him.

Derek burst into laughter and batted him away playfully. The

Elder had only recently discovered that Derek was ticklish but had been merciless since then. As they headed into the bedroom, Derek decided that whatever hesitations he had about his mate, his teachers had to be exaggerating. He wouldn't return to killing dragons. Would he?

CHAPTER FIFTEEN

Gentle Farewell

J amie examined the kittens and wondered how he was going to carry all of them. Janna and Tiger could walk; how would the kittens get to safety? He had met with Zuri several times, though he hadn't seen the unicorn since that first meeting. He longed to see her again, but it was likely that unicorns didn't like to reveal themselves often. Even though Jamie wasn't exactly a stranger, he wasn't in their tribe. But they had agreed to take in the kittens until they were old enough to return, and it was finally time to say goodbye.

Scott had already said goodbye to them earlier in the evening, a tearful event that wasn't helped by the fact that he didn't know where the kittens were going. He didn't know they would be safe. He just had to trust Jamie. But he did trust, and so he had reluctantly said farewell to his beloved Tiger and the rest of the family. Jamie would have to say goodbye soon, too, and he wasn't looking forward to it. He had so many fears about parting from them and even though he knew they were going somewhere safe, that only helped so much.

Even if the cats were happy and safe, they would still be far away. He couldn't cuddle with Janna at night. Sure, he would have Scott to cuddle with, but he would miss how Janna frequently climbed onto his chest in the middle of the night and curl up right on top of him, her whiskers tickling his chin. He wouldn't wake up to Tiger's purring as Tiger kneaded Scott's legs. The cats were such a big part of their lives and they would be gone. Safe, but gone. It was going to be a hard adjustment.

When he had flown to Spokane, Jamie had carried the kittens in a pillowcase. They were bigger, but maybe it would work. He couldn't imagine any other way to get them into the woods where Zuri could pick them up. Maybe a tray of some sort, he considered. He needed something. He searched the apartment for a better way to carry the kittens and couldn't think of anything better than a pillowcase or sheet to wrap them up. They weren't big enough to follow him the way Janna and Tiger could. They were too small, barely stumbling around in the nest Janna had built them, and far too fragile.

There was a knock at the door and he left the kittens with Janna in the closet. He cracked the door and nearly slammed it again. It was the Elder. What was he doing here? There was no one else. Jamie didn't open the door any further, but he didn't slam it.

"Do you need something?" he asked as politely as possible, wondering if he needed to get Scott. He reached out to Marisol and she was carefully monitoring the situation.

"I assume you're moving the kittens soon," the Elder said, and set something on the ground. "Perhaps this could help."

Without another word, the Elder left down the hall and Jamie opened the door to examine what he had left. It was a cat carrier. A fairly large one, too, that could easily hold all of the kittens. He looked down the hall, but the Elder had already entered his own room. An odd gift. What was the purpose of it? Was it really just a thoughtful gesture, or did he have his own reasons for doing it? He had to have his own reasons. He probably did want the kittens gone so he could use his ability, whatever it was. Perhaps he just wanted to help. Perhaps he wanted to trick Jamie into lowering his defenses. Well, it didn't matter. He would take the help, because this was exactly what he needed.

He brought the carrier into the bedroom and Janna stood up

and sniffed it. Tiger nuzzled it. Neither seemed to have any problems with it so he coaxed the little babies into the carrier. They were so incredibly fluffy as he scooted them in. The featherlike texture of their fur was so different than Janna's, even though Janna was incredibly soft. The kittens were fluffy, too, with that feather fur puffing into a ball of fluff around them. They were so incredibly cute and as he moved them, Janna sat and licked one of them. Then he gently picked up that final kitten and set her in the carrier. The kittens mewed and cuddled with each other. Janna tried to get in with her but he knew that would be too heavy to carry all the way to the woods so he gently diverted her every time she tried to climb in. She meowed once, but finally stopped trying. He zipped the carrier and slung it over his shoulder. It was pretty heavy; he was grateful Janna wasn't inside.

"Come with me, Janna, Tiger," he said, and headed out.

It was dark outside, as it always was when he left to visit the woods. He didn't want anyone following him and revealing the other tribe in the woods. Janna and Tiger trotted along with him as he slunk across campus. He glanced up and noticed a figure in the window of the apartment building, in what he thought was Derek and the Elder's room. Was it Derek or the Elder? He had noticed Derek in the window before when he went out at night, but it could easily be the Elder tonight, since the Elder obviously knew he was about to leave. Would either of them try to follow him? He hoped not. He rather suspected that the mist wouldn't lead him to Zuri if he were followed.

Soon, he was enveloped in the mist. It was mostly silent, with the occasional mew from the carrier. When that happened, Janna would wind around his legs as if asking to see her kittens, but he kept walking. They would reach their new home soon and nothing would separate them. His breath caught. A new home. Away from him. Because being near him was too dangerous.

There was a crack of a branch and he stopped. It was Zuri and she smiled at him as she left the woods to enter the path. She knelt and Janna approached her cautiously. Zuri stretched

110

out her hand palm-up and Janna sniffed her, then retreated to Jamie's side. Tiger, on the other hand, sniffed her and then head-butted her hand.

"What gorgeous cats," she said. "This must be Tiger, right? He's a sweetie."

Tiger rolled over and she rubbed his tummy, and Jamie let out an indulgent laugh. Tiger was such a show-stealer. He wanted all the attention, all the time. Janna nuzzled his leg and put her front paws on his left foot. She held her head up, trying to see into the carrier. He set the carrier down and Janna meowed softly at the kittens inside.

"Yeah, and this is Janna. We haven't really named the kittens yet, but they're in here."

"Good thinking on the carrier," she said. "I'll carry them back to our community. You said they were outside cats, right?"

"They like being inside but they do like to go out," he said. "I'd prefer the kittens stay inside. They've been staying in my closet with Janna. She doesn't leave them much."

"Perfect," Zuri said. "I've got a huge closet that they'll love. The unicorns will keep an eye on them when they leave my house. I've got the food you requested, and we're all set up to take care of them. Food, water, kitty litter, pillows and blankets, and we'll give them as much attention as they let us give."

"Thank you, Zuri," Jamie said, and knelt. Janna cuddled him, her front paws reaching to his shoulders as she seemed to embrace him. He hugged her and scooped her up, kissing her nose, then her forehead, then nuzzling her. He didn't want to be apart from her. She had been at his side ever since he had adopted her and she had saved his memory. She was precious to him, far more than any other pet he'd ever had. Tiger was dear, the kittens were dear, but Janna was everything to him and tears filled his eyes as she licked his cheek and purred.

"Bye, sweetie," he whispered, then set Janna down. "Go with Zuri, now."

He hadn't even thought that Janna might try to follow him home, that she might not want to go with a stranger when he was right here. But she meowed, licked him again, and went to sit by Zuri and Tiger. Jamie rubbed Tiger's tummy and then gestured to the kittens.

"Take good care of them," he said, his voice nearly breaking with tears.

"I swear, they'll be safe and happy and I'll do everything in my power to protect them," Zuri said solemnly.

There was a whisper of air and then Rayne stepped into the path. Jamie's breath caught. The unicorn was impossibly beautiful and he was filled with awe, and peace. His tears dried.

"I will protect them," Rayne said in that golden voice in his head. Janna approached her and sniffed her hoof, then intertwined around her legs. Rayne snorted softly, with clear pleasure. He was glad that the unicorn liked his cat, and very reassured. Tiger trotted over, eager to meet the unicorn as well, and Rayne lowered her head to meet his nose in a nuzzle. Tiger sneezed and Jamie laughed. Tiger laid down between her front hooves. Jamie still had tears in his eyes, but they were of relief, now. Janna and Tiger would be safe. The kittens would be safe. He would miss them dearly, but they would be safe and Zuri would make sure they were happy as well.

"Janna, Tiger," Zuri said, picking up the cat carrier. "Let's go, cuties."

The two cats looked back at Jamie as if to say goodbye, then followed Zuri into the mist. Rayne didn't leave, and dipped her horn.

"You will not be able to visit them at our community, but we will bring them back to you when you need them, or when they are ready. Have your dragon contact me. They will be happy with us, though they will not forget you."

"Thank you," Jamie whispered, one of his fears lightening. He was terrified that because they were feral cats, they might forget him if they were away for too long. He would be devastated if Janna, who he adored like family, didn't recognize and love him. But if Rayne said they would remember, then they would. He trusted her completely.

Rayne turned and vanished into the mist and Jamie slowly returned, letting his tears run as he walked but taking a moment to dry them before entering campus. Scott would probably be in their apartment already, he considered. Scott had left for a while to give Jamie the privacy to take the kittens to safety, but he would be back now. He wished they were still in Portland, still somewhere safe. He wished Margot hadn't acted against them. But they were here, and it would be months before he could see the kittens again. He would get through it, with Scott's help.

CHAPTER SIXTEEN

An Unexpected Death

Scott couldn't hide his sorrow when he and Jamie woke up and there were no cats on top of them, and no mewing coming from the closet. Jamie seemed to brace himself and Scott knew he was mourning them as well, though he had assured Scott over and over again that they were safe. He kept assuring himself that they were feral cats and quite capable of taking care of themselves wherever Jamie had stowed them. If Jamie trusted them to be safe, then he would too. But both of them were subdued as they dressed and he knew it was because the kittens were gone.

They ate cereal in quiet, and Scott wondered how they were supposed to spend their days now. Several of the councilmembers had mentioned that Jamie ought to be in summer school, since that was what he would be doing in Portland, but Scott had graduated. Or at least he had finished his senior year. He hadn't technically graduated and he wondered about that. Should he ask about it? He did want to graduate and get a degree, after all. He had worked hard for three years to earn a degree. It wasn't his fault the last year or so had been so punctuated by drama. Mike would know, he decided. And maybe Mike would offer to teach Jamie, since they already felt comfortable with him.

"I'm going to talk to Mike today," Scott said hesitantly, wondering if Jamie would want to go with him.

"That sounds good."

"Do you want to come?"

Jamie stared silently in his cereal for a moment, then sighed. "No. I'll probably stay here and then get lunch. Do you want to meet up at the cafeteria later today?"

Scott agreed and hoped Jamie didn't get too depressed staying in this room without the cats. It was one reason he was anxious to leave; every time he looked around, he was reminded of Tiger. They didn't say anything else until Scott gave him a kiss goodbye, and then it was only a simple farewell. He hoped things didn't stay like this long. They were alone in a dangerous place and losing the cats was further isolating them, but they would recover. Tiger and Janna were safe with the kittens, and he and Jamie were as safe as they could be given the situation.

Scott headed out to the campus with very little idea where to go. Mike managed to find him and Jamie on most days but he had no idea what the man actually did during the day. He wasn't teaching, Scott didn't think. There were some summer classes in session, including Derek's, but Mike was only involved in first-year students and there weren't any yet. Last spring, Mike had been Jamie's representative on campus and that kept him busy, but now that he had rejoined the council, Ethan had been given those responsibilities.

Unlike many of the councilmembers here, Ethan's loyalty to Ashton had evaporated early and he had joined Jamie and Scott in the hatching grounds when they were preparing to go to war. The men's council had a very rigid hierarchy but luckily Gerald and Ethan, the two highest ranking men, valued the rule of law above Ashton and had sided with Jamie when given a choice. He wasn't sure the other councilmembers would have accepted a lower-ranking member being given control over the Spokane council. But maybe they would have. There were a lot of layers to the hierarchy and Scott didn't understand most of it. As long as they obeyed Jamie, he would let them keep their secrets and hierarchies and whatever else they didn't want other people to know. And it did seem that they obeyed Jamie, and, perhaps more importantly here in Spokane, Derek.

As he searched the campus for Mike, he kept an eye out for Derek as well. He frequently saw Derek on the way to and from his classes, or going on a walk around campus. When he was walking around campus, however, the Elder was often with him and Scott had no desire to encounter that man. Derek might have overreacted that night, but he was still a threat. Finally, he caught a glimpse of a blonde striding across the knoll and he hurried forward.

"Mike," he called, and the man turned.

Mike smiled at him, but looked around as if expecting someone else.

"Where's Jamie?"

"He wanted some time alone," Scott said. He wouldn't have been that honest with anyone else, but he trusted Mike. In spite of everything Mike had once done to him, he trusted the man. After all, Mike was his first love. That love had been trampled and dragged through the mud in the years since Mike had forced him into sex and then broke up with him, but their relationship was recovering. He had forgiven Mike for what he had done and could push past the negatives to focus on the positive.

"Mike, I wondered about-"

He froze as a wave of panic swept over him, coming from Narné. Mike stiffened as well and both turned in the direction of the queens. Without a word, both of them started running towards Jamie and Derek. The panic from their dragons lessened and Scott demanded to know what had happened from his dragon.

A dragon has died, Narné said, and Scott drew in a sharp breath. The Elder had killed, and Jamie was right next to him. He broke into a sprint and Mike was right with him, a grim look on his face. Did he understand the danger? He had to. But surely the Elder wouldn't kill Jamie like this. Marisol didn't feel threatened. When she was frightened, she tended to tell all the dragons about it and none were reacting to her fear. So what was happening?

They dashed into the apartment and ran into Ethan, who was coming from the other direction. They all came to the hallway and Scott froze, his heart thudding loudly. Jamie stood on one side of the hall and the Elder on the other. Derek was between them, his hands outstretched as if to stop a confrontation. Jamie looked furious. Scott had seen him kill Ashton and knew he was capable of killing, but for the first time, he actually looked like he wanted to do it. The Elder, for his part, looked worried. Had he not expected to get caught? How did he possibly think he could get away with this?

After a moment of hesitation, Scott rushed past Derek to plant himself firmly at Jamie's side. Mike and Ethan looked between Jamie and the Elder as if unsure what to do. Whatever happened, they would side with Jamie. Scott was sure of it. If the Elder had broken his promise and started killing dragons again, then they wouldn't tolerate it. They were on Jamie's side, on Derek's side, and the Elder had to know it. So why had he done it?

"I know what you think, but I didn't do this," the Elder said calmly.

"He didn't, Jamie," Derek said, still standing between them. "He's been with me this entire time."

"His dragon is the one who kills, not him," Jamie hissed.

"Elder," Ethan said, stepping forward cautiously. "If you believe you are innocent, then you should submit to the council's justice. If we investigate and find you blameless, we'll let you go."

The Elder glared at him, then at Jamie. After a long moment, he sighed.

"If that's what it takes," he said. "I surrender to the council until my innocence has been proven."

Scott blinked in surprise. He was giving up? But if he had broken one rule, then what was to stop him from killing all of them, including the council? He no longer had to abide by Tarragon law, after all. Was this a trap? Was he trying to trick them, lull them, and then he would attack all of them while their backs were turned?

"Your dragon must also surrender," Ethan said.

"Very well," the Elder said. "You can check him for any signs of blood when he returns."

"Where is he?"

"Flying," the Elder said in a tight voice. "Dragons fly."

Scott narrowed his eyes. It was true that dragons often enjoyed soaring around in the sky and they were frequently flying during the day when their humans were busy with human affairs. But it was highly suspicious that his dragon just happened to be gone when a dragon was killed.

"Was the human killed?" the Elder asked.

"Don't you know?" Jamie asked in a harsh voice. "Or didn't you have time?"

"I assume they're alive," the Elder said, ignoring the anger in Jamie's voice. "You should deal with them before worrying about me. I won't fight, nor will my dragon."

Ethan instructed him to have his dragon land on the campus and Scott knew the dragon would be surrounded, but he was such a large dragon it wasn't a very good way of keeping him. Ethan ordered Mike to get restraints for the Elder and Mike left quickly. The Elder glared.

"Is that really necessary? You have my word that I won't resist."

"Until we know for sure you're keeping your word, we're not taking chances," Ethan said. Then he came to Derek's side and pushed him towards Jamie. "Stay with the Queen, Derek. I'll handle things here. Scott, keep them safe."

Ethan gestured towards the outside and Scott led Jamie and Derek out, wondering how he was supposed to be keeping them safe.

"We need to check on the boy whose dragon died," Derek said softly. "He might try to kill himself."

Jamie nodded and the two of them set off into the campus with Scott quick at their feet, hoping he could protect them wherever they went. Derek was probably safe, he figured. Even if the Elder broke his word, he would still want to be a Queen's mate and that meant keeping his Queen. But Jamie was in grave danger and he didn't like Jamie wandering around where the Elder's dragon could snatch him away like this. They needed to get inside.

"Do you know what happened?" Scott asked as he hurried them towards one of the dorms where the boy must be.

"A dragon was killed suddenly," Derek said. "It's exactly what happened when the dragons were going missing. But it wasn't the Elder this time."

"You don't know that," Jamie said darkly.

"I do," Derek said. "I've been with him. I was with him when it happened. Isn't something supposed to happen when a dragon kills another dragon like that? Some physical change? Isn't that why Ashton killed those dragons?"

Jamie seemed startled. "He did change when his dragon fed," Jamie said. "Mike told me he suddenly looked younger and Arion grew, too."

"Well, nothing happened to the Elder. He didn't do it."

"Derek," Scott began, but Derek turned to him in anger.

"He didn't do it. I'm telling you."

Scott swallowed his words. It looked like their worst fears were confirmed and the Elder had sway over Derek. He had worried when he saw how well Derek was getting along with the Elder, but he hadn't wanted to believe it. But why had the Elder done it? It still didn't make sense. And if he really hadn't done it, then who else would dare?

CHAPTER SEVENTEEN

Warm Comfort

I t wasn't hard to find handcuffs for the Elder. The nearest councilmember had some, though Mike didn't ask why. Ethan probably had some as well, he considered, but might have forgotten in the heat of the moment. No councilmember used the handcuffs to bind enemies, after all. They were used for more pleasurable experiences. But Mike was grateful and the other councilmember followed him back a ways, asking for more information. Everyone knew a dragon had died. The boy whose dragon died was in custody, he was glad to hear, and wouldn't be allowed to kill himself.

But he had to tell the councilmember not to enter the building. The councilmember, who ranked higher than Mike, had at first scoffed, but hearing that Ethan had ordered privacy finally got him to back off. He would ignore Mike, but not Ethan, and Mike was just glad the council respected the law and the hierarchy so well. Ethan hadn't technically said not to enter, but Mike knew he wanted it, so he was only partially lying.

When he returned, it was just the Elder and Ethan. The Elder was sitting on the couch outside the Queen's room appearing calm, but there was a hint of rage in his eyes that frightened him. Ethan gestured for the Elder to stand and he did, turning around and putting his hands behind his back without a fight. Mike was the one to close the handcuffs around his wrists and he hoped the Elder didn't remember that if he broke loose and started killing. Then the Elder smiled at them, a pained smile.

"Are you satisfied now?"

"You'll stay under council watch until this has been decided," Ethan said. He sounded a little nervous and Mike didn't blame him. The Elder's eyes narrowed.

"You realize if I had killed a dragon and broken my vow, I wouldn't be cooperating now, don't you? Derek was telling the truth. I didn't do this."

"The Queen thinks you did, and we obey him," Ethan said.

"Derek is the first Queen on this campus," the Elder pointed out. It was true, but Derek wasn't thinking clearly right now.

"If both Queens agreed, we would let you go," Ethan said firmly. "But as long as one Queen feels threatened, you stay under watch."

"Fine," the Elder said tightly. "I'll obey you as long as you act within Tarragon law, which I still follow. But step outside of those bounds, and I'll consider you to have broken the promise between me and this council."

Ethan went a little pale at that and Mike shivered. The Elder was still following the law right now in submitting to them. Was it actually possible he didn't do it? Ethan led the Elder outside with Mike behind them. When they reached the door to the outside, Mike noticed several councilmembers, including the one he had brushed aside. He glanced at Ethan, who didn't seem surprised. As they left, the councilmembers surrounded the Elder without a word. Even the one Mike had pushed away didn't say a word to him to indicate that he knew Mike had been lying, and normally that type of subversion by a lower-ranking member of the council would be punished. Maybe he would be punished later, he considered. Keeping the Elder under control was far more important.

"Mike, we'll take care of this," Ethan said. "Can you see to the students?"

"Of course," Mike said, remembering the days when dragons

121

were regularly disappearing and that was one of his primary duties. He hadn't ever thought they would return to those days.

Mike headed to the dorms and his mind suddenly went to TK. He must be terrified. He hadn't been here when the dragons were disappearing; this was his first experience with a dragon death. As he walked, he had Eraxes ask the most frightened students to head to his location. He also instructed his dragon to keep the other dragons near the campus under close watch. And, of course, he mentioned that Eraxes should ask Devon, TK's dragon, to stay especially close and to make sure TK came to him as well. He didn't know if TK would be one of the most frightened students but didn't want to take the chance he wasn't. He needed to see TK and make sure he was safe.

Students were already gathering when he arrived in the open space between the three dorms. They were the upperclassmen dorms; the freshmen, when they arrived, would be on the other side of campus where they was no chance of them finding out about dragons. He smiled at the students and patted the shoulders of a few as he entered, and soon they converged on him with tears on their faces. Several pushed forward for a hug and he embraced them, and tried to give them whatever comfort they needed. After he thought everyone had gathered, he pulled away from a particularly distraught girl and went to the bench built into the open space. It was solid concrete, so he didn't have to worry about falling off or the bench lurching unexpectedly, and it would give him the height to see all of them and be seen.

When he stepped up, he caught a glimpse of TK's dark face at the back and his heart clenched briefly, then he felt something inside him relax. TK was safe. Even though he had known it wasn't TK's dragon who had been killed, he had still harbored that fear. But Marisol would have told him instantly if anything happened to Devon. She knew Mike and TK were together.

"Listen, everyone, we're going back to the buddy system for a while," he said. "You need a partner at all times, and your dragons do, too."

"Are more dragons going to be killed?" asked one boy, terrified. "What happened?"

"We don't think anymore will be killed," he said, wishing he could be more certain of that. "This is different than last time."

"But a dragon was killed!"

A chorus of voices chimed in, all frightened, and he didn't blame them. The Elder had targeted young dragons who wouldn't be able to fight him, so the youngest students were particularly terrorized by the attacks. All of the students here right now were sophomores, he realized. Apparently none of the upperclassmen were frightened enough that Eraxes had summoned them for a personal consolation.

He started talking to them, soothing them, reminding them of their options and their responsibilities and the fact that they were safe as long as they stuck together. Then he encouraged all of them to talk to him personally and seek out other councilmembers as well if they needed help. They would all go to him, he knew. They trusted him because he had been in charge of their first year and they didn't know the other councilmembers yet. He wondered if any councilmember would try to take advantage of a student's fear to get them into bed. Probably. But most wouldn't, and they would help reassure the students. As he stepped back down, the students swarmed him again. He had them form an informal line so he could speak to all of them individually and he noticed that TK was at the back of the line. Good, because when he got to TK, he might not be able to turn to anyone else. He wanted to snatch TK out of here and bring him to his apartment, where he would be completely safe. But he helped all of the students first, soothing them in whatever way they needed, hugging them and reassuring them and letting them describe their fears in tight, high-pitched voices while he listened and patted their shoulders. When they left his side, they were quieted. They were still afraid, but it was reasonable fear. Everyone dispersed after talking to him and soon it was just him with a couple of students and TK. He went to the other students first one by one, then, when they were alone, he went to TK and hugged him tightly. He breathed in TK's scent of summer sunshine with the hint of rain, a scent he had grown more attracted to in the weeks they had been sleeping together.

"I was so worried about you," Mike confessed as he held TK.

"Aren't you supposed to be reassuring me?" TK asked, but he didn't sound nearly as frightened as the others.

"I will reassure you in any way you need, but first let me hold you."

TK obediently put his arms around Mike, then shivered. It seemed as though he was holding his fears back but being held like this was bringing them to the fore.

"Can we go inside?" he asked in a shaky voice. He probably didn't want to burst into tears in the open like this. Without a word, Mike took his hand. TK pulled in the direction of his dorm, since that was where they always went, but Mike headed to his own apartment. TK had never been there and when he realized where they were going, his pace quickened. No doubt he was curious. Mike wondered idly why he had never taken TK here, but he had never brought his conquests into his personal space. Not even Scott had been to his room when they were dating. This would be a first, but the circumstances required it.

Mike flipped the lights and TK looked around as if surprised. Mike kept his space perfectly clean except his large desk, which was covered in papers even though the semester was over. He would weed through them and toss the unimportant ones later. He always seemed to put off doing that and every semester, the pile grew deeper. He had purged everything when he came to Spokane but in Portland, the piles had been overwhelming.

It was a clean, stark room. He preferred clean lines in his furniture and had modern tastes, so everything was fairly neutral other than a few accent pieces here and there. TK entered and walked around, running his hand across the kitchen counter as Mike led him past the galley kitchen into the living area. It wasn't a big apartment, though it was considerably larger than the dorms. He hadn't wanted a big apartment. Too much to keep clean. Most of the council had rooms twice as large as this, but they also tended to use their rooms to seduce. Mike kept his affairs elsewhere and as such, needed less space.

"This is really nice," TK said, but there was an edge of fear still in his voice.

"Come with me," Mike said, taking his hand and pulling him to the comfortable couch. As he sat beside TK, who immediately leaned into him, his mind flashed back to him leaning into Ashton on this very couch. He had brought all of his belongings from Portland and sometimes sat in this couch, remembering his former lover. He remembered how sweet Ashton had been at times. He only wanted to remember the good, because the rest was too painful.

At the thought of Ashton, his body stirred and he held TK closer. Would sex right now be too much, or would it be exactly what TK needed? He pulled TK against his chest and kissed the top of his head. TK leaned into him further and let out a sigh.

"This has happened before, right? And it stopped eventually? Is Devon safe?"

"Devon is safe," he confirmed. "As long as he stays with other dragons at all times."

"If dragons are safe together, then how did so many die last time?"

"Dragons aren't always obedient," Mike said slowly. "And humans aren't, either. They made mistakes, and paid dearly."

"But he'll be safe with the others."

"Yes."

TK was silent for a moment, then turned to look at Mike.

"Wasn't the Elder the one doing it last time? Is Jamie in trouble?"

"We have the Elder in custody, and his dragon under watch,"

Mike reassured him. "It shouldn't happen again."

"But Jamie?"

"Jamie is protected," Mike affirmed. "And Marisol isn't even here."

"Jamie's the vulnerable one," TK said. "Marisol's too big, isn't she? But Jamie could easily be killed."

"The Elder is in custody," Mike repeated. "He won't hurt Jamie."

Another silence. "What if it wasn't the Elder? What if it's someone else that we don't know, and he's targeting Jamie but no one knows to expect it?"

Mike considered. It was possible. The Elder wasn't acting guilty, so it was possible it was someone else. But wouldn't Jamie know if another dragon did it? He could sense all of the dragons. Marisol at least could sense all of them, and no dragon would protect a dragon who had killed other dragons. Ashton had learned that the hard way.

"Scott is with him," he said without thinking, and TK's eyes narrowed. "Jamie can take care of himself," he quickly added, not wanting to drive TK into trying to protect Jamie. If TK did something foolish again like he had when going out to find a dragon egg out of season, then he would be in danger and Mike wouldn't allow that. He had to distract TK out of those thoughts and without thinking it through, he kissed TK.

TK pulled back as if surprised. Mike put his hand against the back of TK's neck to hold him in place and kissed him again. This time, TK kissed back. Mike ran his hands over TK's strong body and slid his hand under his shirt, feeling his muscles and the bump of his nipples. He fingered them playfully and TK's breathing quickened, his heart racing under Mike's hand.

"Come to my bedroom," Mike said, half-requesting and half-commanding. TK disentangled himself and stood, then held his hand out to Mike.

"Okay."

CHAPTER EIGHTEEN

Alternative Theory

J amie was fuming and grieving all at once. Mike had taken care of the students and Ethan would be taking care of the student whose dragon had died and he couldn't even imagine the pain he was going through. He wondered if Mike was reliving when Ashton had killed Kale and nearly killed Eraxes. But Mike had experience with this, unfortunately, from when the Elder had been terrorizing the campus, and so did Ethan. He had to trust them to take care of this situation. He took a deep breath. In some ways, his anger was a way to distract from his own pain and he knew it. But he was furious at the Elder.

He should have known something was wrong when the Elder gave him that cat carrier, because the instant the cats were gone – the instant the Elder could use his powers again – he had struck. Whatever power it was, the cats had clearly been preventing it and now it was unleashed with deadly consequences. Should he go to Rayne and ask for the kittens back? Should he at least get one of them to protect the campus? But it didn't seem like one or two were a threat; it was all of them together that impacted a dragon's ability. How had he not seen this coming?

But the Elder wasn't acting guilty. He was acting surprisingly innocent, no doubt because he hadn't expected to get caught like that. Maybe his dragon had acted without his direction. That had to be it. The Elder was planning on killing again but his dragon grew impatient and with the kittens gone, he acted on his own.

Poor planning on the dragon's part, since now they had the Elder in custody. Ethan was fairly certain they could keep him contained, but warned there was almost nothing they could do to contain the dragon.

Jamie took another deep breath. He needed to pull himself together because others were counting on him. Derek had clearly been compromised. He was blindly siding with the Elder just as they all feared would happen. Even if he had been with the Elder the entire time, the Elder's dragon could easily have killed and the Elder could have kept it from him. He wished it were otherwise, but the sacrifices he had made to keep Derek on their side had been in vain. Derek was the Elder's, and there was little he could do about it now. He shut his eyes against that pain, because keeping Derek on their side had cost him dearly. His relationship with Scott, though on firm ground now, had nearly been shattered because of what Scott had been forced to do to get Derek back. Not just once, either. Multiple times, Jamie had sacrificed. And all of it was wasted. Derek belonged to the Elder.

The council felt the same; until Derek saw the error of his misguided belief, the council was unlikely to follow him and that meant Jamie needed to step up and take command. It would be difficult, as Derek might fight him for control, but it needed to be done. He wouldn't allow Ethan to take over, no matter how much Ethan's loyalties seemed to be with him right now. He would not let the head of council gain too much power from this.

With yet another deep breath, he left his room and found Ethan waiting. He had needed a few minutes to think and figure things out, but now he was ready to face the world.

"I don't think his dragon did it," Ethan began without preamble. "We found no trace of blood on him. And we searched. The other dragons couldn't smell blood, either."

"I'm sure he knows how to get rid of the scent," Jamie said bitterly, thinking of all the other dragons he had likely killed. "And he didn't return for several minutes. That's enough time to get rid of the evidence."

"He was coming from the wrong direction," Ethan said. "We found the dragon's body."

Jamie flinched. "Had it been eaten?"

There was a chance, just the slightest chance, that the dragon had died on its own. Dragons did die sometimes. For a moment, he grasped the thin hope that perhaps this wasn't the Elder's doing. Because if the Elder truly turned against them, it would be another war and this time, a great number of dragons would die.

"Yes," Ethan said grimly, destroying that slim ray of hope.

"Then it has to be him. I want to talk to him. Maybe if confesses..."

Jamie wasn't sure how to finish that thought. If he confessed, what would Jamie do? Forgive him as long as he went back to obeying Tarragon law? That was certainly safer than letting him run riot and kill at will. But if he allowed the Elder back after the Elder had deliberately broken his word and killed a dragon, then what was to stop him from doing it again? Nothing. He couldn't forgive the Elder. He also couldn't leave the Elder alive. Wherever he went, the Elder would be a threat. He was strong enough to overpower any community he found. He would always be a threat, no matter what they did to him. Only killing him would prevent that fate. He wondered if he would have to be the one to do it. Probably. Ethan would make him, just as Margot had made him. And maybe he wanted to do it this time. He sighed. No, he didn't want to kill. No amount of anger would justify that. He would insist on Ethan doing it, since it really was Ethan's job. But the Elder would have to die, and die before his dragon managed to free him or kill again.

"What if he confesses?" Ethan asked, glancing over at him as they began walking to where the Elder was being kept.

"Nothing," Jamie said. "He gets nothing even if he does confess."

"You think we should kill him?"

"That's the law."

"He's going to fight."

"Can you handle that?"

Ethan was silent. "There has to be a trial," he said slowly. "No one will accept his death without a trial. He's still the Queen's mate, after all. But if he's found guilty of murder, then we can hold him long enough to kill him."

Jamie fumed. He remembered how angry he had been when Ashton had killed Kale's dragon, nearly killed Mike's, and then fought Jamie and Scott. But when the council had arrived, when Jamie thought they would be saved, Margot insisted on a trial. It was only because Marisol and the other dragons were in agreement on the punishment that they were able to kill Ashton. But he could sense that the dragons weren't in agreement on the Elder. Jamie knew what had happened, but Marisol wasn't so sure. She couldn't sense the Elder dragon, after all, so there was no proof of what had happened. The dragons had known what Ashton was doing, for the most part; they had no clue what the Elder was up to. And without Marisol's support, it was likely that a trial would end in a stalemate and the Elder would have enough time to escape.

The Elder was being kept underneath the apartments where most of the councilmembers lived. It was essentially a dungeon, though there was really no need for it. It resembled the dark, forbidding council chamber in Portland and he wondered if that were why they built it, if they felt more comfortable in the darkness of this room than the normal room they met in formally here in Spokane. He wondered if Derek had ever been to this room. Was this were Alan had been killed, or had he been killed above, in the official council chamber? He shivered at the thought of Alan. It was probably best to put him out of mind right now. He didn't want to get distracted facing the Elder.

The Elder was in what was essentially a cell. His hands were behind his back and he was locked in by bars. There were two councilmembers standing on either side of the opening to his cell, and several others in the room. He seemed secure and Jamie relaxed slightly. They had him under control. Maybe they could hold the trial here to prevent the Elder from escaping. And since it was underground, it was unlikely that the Elder dragon could break through the building to rescue him. That was at least something.

Jamie came close enough to the bars to talk, but not too close. The Elder stood an equal distance on the other side, his face impassive.

"Why did you do it?" Jamie asked.

"I didn't," the Elder said. "I told you. You have another killer on the loose. You should be looking for him, not accusing me without cause."

"Who else would possibly kill a dragon?" Jamie hissed.

There was a sound from the entrance and Jamie looked back to see Scott enter. Scott looked less than pleased to find Jamie here. Maybe Jamie should have let Scott know he was coming to confront the Elder. But as Scott came to his side, he glanced at Jamie.

"He might not have done it," Scott said in a low voice.

Jamie started in surprise, then whirled to face Scott.

"What?"

Scott flushed and glared at the Elder before answering. "His dragon doesn't have a trace of blood, and wasn't anywhere nearby."

"If it were a different dragon, I would know," Jamie said angrily. "I can sense every dragon, and I know that none of them did it."

"Not every dragon," Scott said, and Jamie narrowed his eyes. What was Scott getting at? "Remember the guard Ashton put on you once, who you didn't even know was there? He got past you."

"But Marisol knew about him," Jamie pointed out, then paused to consider. Was it possible? There were dragons that confused him. Alan's dragon, for example. He couldn't read its loyalties and that was why he had never quite trusted the man. Were there dragons he wouldn't be able to read? He turned to Ethan.

"Are there dragons who can hide from other dragons? You would know, wouldn't you?"

His mind was whirling. Because it was true that the Elder was not acting the way he would if he had just killed. And he wouldn't have killed that recklessly. And if his dragon showed no signs, then was it possible someone else had done it?

"Yes," Ethan said, sounding surprised. He must not have realized it. "The man Ashton had guard you. He can prevent people from noticing him, but his dragon can also escape detection if she wants. It's difficult, but possible."

"Where is he?"

"He ran after Ashton was killed," Ethan said. "You know we've never really tracked them down."

That was true, Jamie knew. There was still a group of Ashton loyalists out there and he knew they had come to Spokane in the hopes that Derek would become another Ashton. He looked at the Elder, who appeared to be barely holding back his anger. Why would he be angry if he were guilty and they were finding someone else to blame? He ought to look relieved.

"If someone has framed me, then I demand the right to kill him," the Elder said angrily.

"We have to catch him first, and confirm this," Ethan said. "He'll be put on trial."

"And me?" the Elder demanded. "I suppose you'll still put me on trial?"

"If he confesses, then there's no need," Ethan said. "But until we catch him, you must stay in custody."

"There's no need for strict custody like this," the Elder said. "Even if I were accused of killing a dragon, you wouldn't treat me like this unless you knew it was me. Now you know it wasn't. I demand to be kept under house arrest, if you insist on keeping me."

Ethan looked at Jamie. "That is the policy. Unless we're certain of guilt, we don't hold people like this."

Jamie bit his lip. If the Elder were the killer, then releasing him now would give him the chance to escape and start killing again. But if they held him unlawfully, then he might view it as them breaking their agreement, escape, and start killing again. He would have to follow Tarragon law and hope the Elder were sincere in this. He couldn't imagine anyone else doing this, but it was possible.

"We'll follow the law," Jamie said, and Ethan looked a little relieved. "But you'll remain under guard until we're certain."

The Elder nodded in agreement. Ethan opened the door to the cell and Jamie tensed as he went behind the Elder and unhooked his hands. The Elder rubbed his wrists, then strode out of the cell.

"I'll still have privacy with my mate," he said. "Where is Derek?"

"Somewhere safe," Jamie said, his eyes narrowed. Derek was actually at class. It wasn't scheduled, but he had insisted on sticking with Jamie to try to prove the Elder's innocence and one of his teachers had forced him into a special session to try to distract him.

"You'll be able to speak to him in private," Ethan added. "That is the law."

The last was directed at Jamie and he felt his anger returning. So they would let the Elder get his claws into Derek again? But if it was the law, then they had to obey it. He tried to release the tension in his body, knowing the others could easily see how upset he was by this situation. He needed to be calm. He was a Queen. He needed to be calm and rational and above the emotions that were swirling through him.

"I'll make sure he's updated on the situation," Jamie said. "He's in class right now."

The Elder's eyes narrowed. He knew Derek didn't have a class and probably suspected they were using the class to try to convince Derek he was guilty. It was a fair assessment, since he suspected that was exactly what the teacher was trying to do. But what if the Elder weren't guilty? What if this really were just someone else framing the Elder? He tried to quell his anger at the Elder. After all, the Elder was still following law and protocol perfectly. It was even within his rights to demand to kill the man. If he were really guilty, he would be acting right now to escape, not just standing there. But why would anyone else kill a dragon like that? He took a deep breath and met the Elder's eyes, trying to push aside his anger at this man.

"Why would someone else kill a dragon?"

"Was the dragon eaten?"

Jamie nodded.

"Surely you know why dragons eat each other."

Jamie shivered. "But why would he act now, when he hasn't before?"

"You're here now," the Elder said. "Perhaps he knew you would jump to the conclusion that it was me. If Derek were in charge, I would not have been treated this way. Derek knows I'm innocent."

Jamie considered. It was very true. The only reason they were able to take the Elder into custody so quickly was because Jamie had ordered it. Derek would have insisted on him being free until a trial, no matter what Ethan wanted. The Queen outranked the council, after all. But why hadn't the killer acted as soon as Jamie got here, if that were the case?

The kittens, he realized suddenly. The man's dragon could only hide itself by using its ability, and that had been blocked until the kittens were taken away. It couldn't be coincidence that the day after the kittens left, this happened. He had thought it was because the Elder was ready to strike, but what if someone else had suddenly realized that their dragon was able to use its ability again? The Elder had already thought of this, he realized as he met the Elder's gaze again. But he wouldn't say anything in front of the other councilmembers like this. He was keeping the kittens a secret and for some reason, that deeply reassured Jamie.

"If you are innocent, then I apologize for how we've treated you," he said stiffly, knowing that if the Elder really were innocent, he would need to work hard to mend this rift between them. After all, he and Scott were stuck here for the near future and he needed to stay on good terms with this man. Because as he thought about it, it seemed more and more likely that the Elder was innocent.

"Anyone would reach the conclusion you reached," the Elder said. "And as long as you continue to follow the law and find the one who did this, then no apologies are necessary."

A threat, but also an offer of conciliation. Interesting. Well, he would follow the law, and if someone else did it, then they would find him. He thought back to the guard. At the time, Ashton had been trying to keep Jamie and Scott from making up after their first real fight. Jamie had wondered why Scott wasn't coming to him, what was keeping him away, and had thought Scott just didn't care anymore. Instead, there had been a guard who threatened and beat Scott up when he wouldn't leave Jamie alone. And Jamie hadn't known anything, because the man was completely blocked from his sensory perception.

He reached out to Marisol. She agreed. It was possible for a dragon like that to escape detection. The dragon was still escaping detection, she added. She knew which dragon it was now and if it showed up in her senses, she would let him know and order the other dragons to surround it instantly.

"Marisol is helping to look," Jamie said, and the Elder's eyes narrowed.

"You shouldn't stress her too much while she's so far away and nesting."

"It requires almost no effort on her part," he said. "Other dragons will act if the guilty dragon is found."

The Elder nodded and Jamie wondered at that odd show of concern for Marisol. Maybe he was relying on Marisol too much, he considered. She was incredibly far away and it took effort to communicate with her at more than a surface level, and he had been sharing a lot of deep information with her to try to figure out Margot and now this. And she had her eggs to look out for. He wondered if the Elder had known other queens and this was a genuine warning. Probably. He had been alive long enough. So the Elder probably knew what he was talking about and maybe he should go a little easier on Marisol. He wouldn't be doing it because the Elder recommended it, though, he decided. He would do it because he didn't want to stress out his dragon. Maybe the Elder had pointed it out, but he didn't want to be taking the man's advice even if he was innocent in this one instance. Because even if he hadn't killed this dragon, he had killed others and would do so again at some point in the future. It was almost inevitable. All they could do was hope they were safe for now, and it seemed they would be for a little while longer.

CHAPTER NINETEEN

House Arrest

"The Elder has been moved to house arrest," the teacher said unexpectedly. He had been grilling Derek on the strategies they had taught him to avoid manipulation by the Elder and Derek was growing increasingly frustrated. He knew the Elder was innocent. Not only had they been together all day, they had actually been talking about their dragons. They had spent a luxurious morning in the most pleasant way possible, then, as they lay in bed exhausted, Derek had asked about his dragon. The Elder dragon, he had been informed, was currently trying to match paces with the crows in the area. Dragons occasionally tried to pace themselves with the birds and it was always entertaining watching them try to slow down enough. He wouldn't have expected the Elder dragon to be engaging in such youthful games. Jettie was keeping her eggs warm, he had reported, which was less interesting but far more important. And then Jettie had blasted him with the message: a dragon was dead.

The Elder hadn't gotten that message and been confused by Derek's sudden tension. He had asked if the other Queen needed him, and Derek had stared at him in surprise. But the Elder's dragon wasn't in communication with the other dragons and wouldn't immediately know what had happened to them. It was that question more than anything else that had confirmed the Elder's innocence in his mind. He genuinely didn't know what had happened. Derek's immediate, instinctive distrust was quelled even as it began, but he had known that Jamie wouldn't understand and would jump to the wrong conclusion. He started dressing and hastily explaining the situation to the Elder, who had, for one brief moment, seemed afraid. That confirmed his innocence as well, because he knew he would be blamed and probably thought he would be killed, or at least be driven out.

And then Scott and Jamie had dragged him away from protecting his mate and shut him in a classroom with this teacher that Derek had always despised. This man had never taught him anything valuable. It was all about opposing the Elder, resisting him, trying to convince Derek that dragons shouldn't be killed, but he already knew all of that already. He would never allow a dragon to be harmed and that was what was so infuriating now. They were acting like he had forgotten, like he was letting the Elder get away with this. But he wasn't. The Elder was innocent.

"What does it mean that he was moved?" Derek asked, trying to hide his resentment.

"He's no longer the primary suspect, I would guess," the teacher said, sounding puzzled. "But there is no one else."

"There has to be," Derek said. "That's what I've been telling you. It wasn't him."

"You can't just blindly believe him, Derek," the teacher warned, but Derek slashed his hand through the air.

"I don't," he said angrily. "You think I didn't assume he did it when I first heard? But I was with him. I know he didn't do it, and I know his dragon didn't do it. I know perfectly well that he's going to kill again. You think I'm not listening? But he didn't do this. And it looks like the council finally figured that out as well."

"You have permission to leave," the teacher said, clearly not liking have to say that. "I disagree with the council, but they have authority here."

Derek stood up and practically bolted from the room. He rushed back to his apartment. Ethan and four councilmembers were in the hall outside and for a moment, he remembered how they used to station guards outside to make sure the Elder wasn't hurting him. He slowed down and walked to the door calmly. Ethan put a hand on the door to stop him.

"Derek," he started, but Derek cut him off.

"I am still your Queen," he said coldly. "You have no right to keep me out."

"How did you know he was innocent?" Ethan asked. "Then I'll let you in."

Derek glared. His conversations with the Elder ought to be private, but he suspected that unless he cleared himself of suspicion right now, they would think his judgement was permanently warped and he would lose all his power over the council.

"We were together when it happened," he said. "Jettie told me immediately. He didn't know what had happened. I had to tell him."

"He could have been pretending not to know."

"When I told him, he looked scared," Derek said, not really wanting to share that personal bit of information but suspecting it was one of the only things that might sway them. "I've never seen him look like that. He knew you were going to accuse him. He probably thought you would kill him. He didn't do it."

Ethan nodded and lowered his hand from the door. "We have reason to believe it was one of Ashton's people. Jamie has already apologized to the Elder, but he remains under watch until we've caught the man."

"If he did it, don't you think he would have acted against you?" Derek asked. "You should have trusted me when I told you he was innocent. You should have known I would have good reasons for thinking that. I would never protect him if I thought he had actually killed a dragon."

Ethan stared at him for a long moment, studying him. Then he bowed his head.

"I apologize, Queen. We acted without thought. It will not happen again."

"See that it doesn't," Derek said, still angry that they had mistrusted him. But at least he had regained their respect. He didn't think they would turn against him again. He opened the door and entered, then shut the door firmly. Then he turned to see the Elder on the sofa looking disgruntled.

"Did they stop you from entering?" he asked in a dangerous voice.

"No," Derek said. "They just wanted to talk first."

He stared at the Elder. "Do you know what you almost cost me?"

A slight smile appeared on the Elder's lips.

"Then they're back on your side? Good. I would hate to think I was responsible for you losing all authority here."

"You're responsible for a lot," Derek said, stepping closer aggressively. "None of this would have happened if-"

He paused. It wasn't really fair to blame the Elder for this. It wasn't like the Elder had planned this in any way, or known about it.

"If you didn't have a history of killing dragons," he finished, though he didn't say it as strongly as he would have liked. But the Elder couldn't change his past, either. In all the time Derek had known him, he had always followed the law and protocol and never killed. But he remembered the very first time he had seen the Elder, when the mist had taken him with the Elder's dragon into the cave where he was hiding. The Elder had kissed him then, and Derek had tasted blood on his lips. He wasn't innocent. But in this one case, he was.

"Do you expect me to apologize for staying alive?" the Elder asked, and Derek sighed.

"Will you ever kill a dragon again?"

Silence, and Derek's heart sank. Of course he would. Not now, it didn't seem. Probably not in the near future. But eventually, the Elder would grow old and need to kill dragons to stay young. Why couldn't he just accept fate and let himself die? Why did he feel driven to kill rather than accept what would inevitably happen?

"Do you want an answer to that, sweetheart?" the Elder asked, standing and coming to his side. The Elder cradled his cheek in his hand.

"Not really," Derek said softly. He knew the answer and didn't want to hear it confirmed. He wanted to think of the Elder as innocent, not as someone who was just biding his time before killing again.

"They're looking for the killer now," the Elder said. "They would find him faster if I helped. My dragon is quite good at scenting blood."

"Then why don't you ask to help?"

"They're keeping my dragon contained right now," he said. "As long as there's any suspicion of me at all, neither me nor my dragon will be free."

"What do you want me to do, then? You know I can't ask them for favors involving you," he pointed out. "Not after I just won them back to my side."

"Jamie might listen to you," the Elder said. "If he ordered it, then it would be done. His impartiality isn't in question. And if you ask him, not the council, then no one would have to know you spoke on my behalf. Any more than you already have," he added, then stroked Derek's cheek. "Thank you for trusting me."

"It was obvious you didn't do it," Derek said uncomfortably. His impartiality was definitely in question, he knew. Even though he had insisted to the council that he was capable of making independent decisions without relying on the Elder, he wondered. Could the Elder have manipulated him? It didn't seem like he had this time, but what if he did it in the future? If anything like this ever happened again, would he be able to catch any manipulation? Or would he assume that any future times were like this one, when the Elder actually was innocent?

"Will you consider talking to Jamie?"

"I'll talk to him," Derek said gruffly. He didn't want to admit that the council would follow Jamie's orders more than his, but it was the truth. He couldn't risk the trust he had just won back from them. And if the Elder really could help, they might need it. "You won't try to run?"

"I want the killer brought to justice," the Elder said with clear anger in his voice. "He nearly ruined everything for me here. He nearly cost me everything I've built. I won't let him go free."

Derek nodded. The Elder seemed sincere enough, and his desire to kill the man was obvious and probably justified. After all, he had built a lot of power here. He wasn't allowed to hold a traditional role in the council, but he was given quite a bit of power as the Queen's mate. It was certainly better than a lot of his options, and he had nearly lost it because of whoever had killed the dragon. Derek couldn't help but shiver. Someone else was killing dragons. And they didn't know who.

CHAPTER TWENTY

First Priority

Scott watched the Elder dragon warily as it bolted into the air. He hated letting it leave like this, but Jamie had commanded it. The Elder dragon had the best chance of tracking down the killer, so they would rely on its strengths. Even though Scott was fairly confident that the Elder hadn't done this, it was still dangerous. What if the Elder hadn't done this, but it gave him the excuse to start? They couldn't control his dragon and now the creature had free reign to go where it pleased. Dangerous.

"If the Elder were lying, that dragon would have killed all of us by now," Ethan said, also looking at the dragon spiraling into the air and immediately heading towards the location where the dragon's body had been found. It wasn't far from campus, which was worrying. They had found the body of a small green dragon about two miles outside of the campus in the forest with its throat ripped out. Scott and Ethan had just returned from the site, but there wasn't much to be learned there. It was highly unlikely that the Elder dragon had done it. Ethan had noticed that the bite size was far too small for a dragon like that. But the Elder did kill. Just not in this one instance. They couldn't relax too much, and he didn't like letting the dragon fly wherever it wanted.

Other dragons were going with it, of course. The Elder's dragon couldn't communicate with the other dragons so it had

143

to be with others who could communicate on its behalf. But what if the Elder dragon killed the dragons sent with it? Narné wasn't allowed to join the hunt, nor was Ethan's dragon. They didn't want to take the risk. Mike's dragon Eraxes was with them, and was representing the council's dragons. Scott suspected that since he was the newest member of the council, his dragon was stuck with the task. Then again, Eraxes was one of the largest dragons on campus and that might also be the reason. He couldn't quite tell what Mike's rank in the council was. He was new, but seemed to command a lot of respect. Part of it had to do with the responsibilities Jamie had given him before he was on the council. Because Mike was one of the few people Jamie trusted, he had been Jamie's representative on campus and essentially held the same power as Ethan. Somehow, that had never caused problems and Scott suspected that they had met privately to sort out how to deal with their ranks so that Ethan could retain complete control over campus but Mike could have the access he needed. Now that Mike was on the council, though, he obeyed Ethan and Ethan had ordered Eraxes to go with the Elder dragon.

They returned to campus to wait for news and caught up with Mike, since he was the one keeping an eye on the Elder dragon. He seemed a little tense as they sat in the center of campus near the construction where they could have some privacy. They were in the shade and it was comfortable out. The sky was bright blue but there were clouds on the horizon. In Portland, that would have meant rain, but here it didn't necessarily mean anything. He hoped it didn't mean rain because it would be harder to track the killer dragon if the rain washed the scent away.

"The Elder dragon has the scent," Mike offered after a long time. "He's searching."

"I don't trust him," Scott muttered.

"We don't have a choice," Ethan pointed out. "Our Queen wants him helping, and I really don't think he'll try anything."

"He's innocent this time, but what about next time?" Scott

asked.

Silence. There was nothing they could say to that because it was true. The next time a dragon died on campus, it would almost certainly be the Elder's fault. They could delay it, but it was inevitable. Another dragon would die at some point, and they would be stuck with the task of bringing the Elder to justice.

"We'll worry about that when it happens," Ethan finally said. "He's content for now, and has no reason to kill. I think as long as he has Derek, he'll stay contained."

Scott scowled at the thought that the Elder controlled Derek but it was true. He didn't like to think that Derek had automatically assumed the Elder was innocent, even though Derek had his reasons. He didn't want Derek in that situation. His feelings for Derek weren't exactly the same as they had once been, but he still loved the man. He didn't want to see him hurt.

Mike sat up suddenly, drawing in a sharp breath.

"He's found the dragon," he said, his eyes shut, then winced. "He's attacking."

"He's killing the other dragon?" Ethan asked, leaping to his feet. "I have to get the Elder back in custody."

"No," Mike said. "Not killing. Just hurting."

He winced again. "He's bringing the dragon back here. The dragons have the area surrounded. We need to get people there to track down his partner."

"I'll authorize twenty people to get there as soon as possible," Ethan said. "Let's get back."

It wasn't far; one of the reasons they had chosen that spot to sit was the closeness to where the dragons had been keeping the Elder dragon under watch. It was nearly twenty minutes before the Elder dragon's shape appeared in the sky. It was weighed down by a limp dragon in its arms and Scott flinched. He hadn't expected the dragon to be strong enough to carry an entire dragon on its own, but it was. The dragon dropped the unconscious dragon to the ground and settled nearby, hissing at the still form.

Blood dripped from several deep gashes on the unconscious dragon's hide but he was alive. Scott let out a sigh of relief. It hadn't even occurred to him that the Elder dragon might kill the offending dragon. He had been worried the Elder dragon would turn on Eraxes and the others, but the Elder wanted to kill the man who had framed him. Of course his dragon would want to kill the dragon who had helped.

The Elder dragon licked its lips and Scott shivered at the sight of blood on its tongue.

"Eraxes says they've spotted the man," Mike said. "Others are on the way to get him."

"Good," Ethan said, then turned to the others on call. "Keep the Elder dragon here, and get this dragon some care."

He gestured to Scott. "As soon as the man is brought back, we'll have a trial. First, though, we need to officially tell the Elder that the culprit has been caught."

Scott agreed and as they were walking, a student sprinted towards them and stumbled to a halt in front of them.

"Derek requests your presence," he said, a little out of breath.

Ethan and Scott looked at each other. Telling the Elder was important, but the Queen took precedence.

"Where is he?" Scott asked.

"He's at Lampasas," the boy said, and Scott blinked. It was time for Derek's class to start. He must have heard that the dragon was caught and wanted to be informed first. Smart thinking. Whoever was told first would have the most authority on the issue and of course that needed to be Derek, the Queen on campus. Scott had assumed Derek would be with the Elder but if he wasn't, they needed to go to Lampasas first. Ethan wore a faint smile and they switched direction without a word. He probably understood Derek's reasoning as well and appreciated the move. Scott wondered if he had known Derek was at class and had been trying to undermine his authority or if he, like Scott, had forgotten. Derek had lost quite a lot of power by standing up for the Elder but Ethan's willingness to go to him first indicated that he still held sway over campus matters.

They arrived at Lampasas and quickly found Derek and the council member in charge of teaching him. The council member smiled at them and gestured for Derek to be excused. He looked relieved and went into the hall with them.

"Well?" he asked tersely.

"The Elder dragon has brought the killer dragon into our custody," Ethan said. "We should have the killer in custody soon as well. What would you like us to do with them?"

Derek nodded and seemed a little pleased, probably that Ethan was giving him the chance to choose what happened to the killer and his dragon.

"Is the dragon under watch?"

"He's unconscious," Ethan said. "We'll bind him down in case he wakes up."

"Why is he unconscious?" Derek asked, puzzled, and Ethan sighed.

"The Elder dragon attacked him."

Derek's eyes narrowed. "But he's alive?"

"Alive, just with a few scars," Ethan confirmed.

"And the Elder dragon?"

"Nearby, under watch as before."

Derek nodded. "When the killer is found, I want him brought to the council chambers immediately."

"With all due respect, Queen, you should not be the one ruling over the trial," Ethan said politely, and Derek glared.

"Why not?"

Scott tensed as well. Another power play to challenge Derek? But Ethan didn't look like he was trying to steal any power for himself or challenge Derek in any way. He looked almost apologetic.

"You have absolute authority on our campus," Ethan said, and Derek relaxed. Slightly. Scott could almost hear the "but" coming in Ethan's words. "But a case like this should be overseen by the Queen from Portland."

"Why?" Derek asked warily.

"This is a Spokane matter," Scott added. He did not want Jamie in charge of this trial because it was almost certain to end in the man's execution. Jamie was still haunted by memories of killing Ashton. Scott would never let that happen to him again.

"Any case that involves death should be overseen by the first Queen," Ethan said.

Derek scoffed. "I've overseen a trial that led to an execution, and I carried out that execution."

Although his words were strong, Scott noticed his hands tremble slightly. He was probably as affected by killing Alan as Jamie was by killing Ashton. Their society should not insist on executions being carried out by the Queens, he thought angrily.

"I don't mean the sentence," Ethan said. "I mean the crime. And I don't mean human deaths. Any case involving the death of a dragon must be overseen by the Queen from Portland."

He glanced at Scott sympathetically. "And Jamie won't be the one to carry out the sentence," he said. "The Elder has already claimed that right. No one will challenge it."

Scott shut his eyes briefly. Good. Jamie wouldn't be weighed down by another murder. Derek didn't look satisfied but he didn't protest. Instead, he sighed and gestured towards the hall.

"I still want you to bring him to the council chamber. I assume I can at least be present," he added sharply.

"Of course, Queen," Ethan said. "This is your campus. You will cede control to Jamie for the duration of the trial only, then reclaim your position as our first Queen."

"Very well," he said. "Jettie informs me that he's just been caught and is on his way here. Will the two of you accompany me?"

"Of course," Ethan said, and Scott smiled and patted Derek's shoulder. He clearly wasn't pleased by this situation but he wouldn't question it and Scott was just glad his position as head of the campus seemed unchallenged for now. He would have a lot of work to do recovering from this, but Scott would do his best to help.

CHAPTER TWENTY-ONE

The Trial

J amie sat alone in his room with his head cradled in his hands. The killer had been caught, and he and his dragon were in custody. Jettie had informed him that Derek had ordered the man brought to the council chambers. Since he didn't want to stress Marisol, he had been asking other dragons for information on the issue directly. Eraxes had shown him the Elder dragon's attack and while he was angry that the dragon had attacked like that, at least the other dragon was still alive. He stood up and went to the mirror. He looked stressed, but otherwise suitable to lead a trial. Ethan's dragon had politely informed him that he would need to be the one to lead the trial. He had never really done that, he realized. When Ashton was on trial, Margot had led it. He had no idea what he was supposed to do. Was there anyone he could ask for help before it started?

He stood up and thought of Mike. He sent a thought to Eraxes for Mike to meet him and discovered that Mike was nearby. Ethan and Scott were across campus with Derek, according to Narné, and he would have a chance to talk to Mike first. Good, because he wanted to know what he was getting himself into.

As he left his apartment building, Mike approached and bowed to him formally.

"Queen," he said. "My dragon says you wish to speak."

"You don't need to be formal," Jamie said with a smile.

"You spoke directly to Eraxes," Mike pointed out. "He was sure you wanted something important."

"I just don't want to exhaust Marisol making her go between everyone like this," Jamie explained. "Since I can talk to everyone directly, there's no reason not to."

"You might have to tell that to the other dragons you're talking to," Mike said. "They might assume you're talking to them for formal reasons. But you did want to talk to me, right?"

"Yeah," Jamie said, looking around. They were alone. He didn't want anyone else to know how ignorant he was of his responsibilities. "Ethan's dragon told me I would need to lead the trial. I've never done that before. I haven't learned about it, either. What am I supposed to do?"

"Oh," Mike said, startled. "I hadn't realized you wouldn't know what to do. Ethan must not know, either. But I guess there's no real reason to teach you that yet so it wouldn't be in your classes. It's not a common occurence."

"So what do I do?"

Mike began filling him in on his responsibilities and he relaxed slightly. This didn't seem too hard. He mostly had to call other people up to speak and wouldn't have to say much himself. Once the verdict was reached – and it would almost certainly be a death sentence – he would have to call on the Elder to carry out the sentence. He was a little nervous about that but if the Elder hadn't acted against them yet, this was not the time he would start.

"Ethan will have a sword for you," Mike said. "He'll give it to you when you enter. You'll need to wear it at your waist until the verdict, then draw it and hand it to the Elder."

"He could easily kill me with it," Jamie said nervously.

"I don't think he will," Mike said, but didn't sound positive. "And it's Tarragon law. The Queen carries out executions, so if you want to give that right to someone else, which you have to do now that the Elder claimed the right to kill him, you have to hand him the sword yourself."

Jamie nodded. He didn't have any options, but surely nothing would happen. There was no way the Elder would go through all of this just to kill Jamie right when he was freed of suspicion. Feeling a little more reassured, he and Mike headed to the council chamber. Narné let him know that the others had gathered and were ready for him. He took a deep breath as they reached the building, and then Mike opened the door for him. No one seemed surprised that Mike was at his side even though Mike quickly took his place among the rest of the council. Everyone knew he and Mike were close and it wasn't unexpected that they should be together when arriving. As Mike had indicated, Ethan handed him a sword in a sheath attached to a belt. He wound it around his waist and it hung heavily at his side, a reminder of his responsibility. Ethan was at his side as he approached the other side of the room where Derek, Scott, and the Elder waited.

The Elder was only barely holding back his rage and Jamie just hoped it was directed at the accused man, not against him for automatically assuming he was guilty. It was dangerous being so close to him but he was Derek's mate and had a place here in front of everyone else. Jamie stood between Derek and Scott and looked around. It looked like everyone was here and as if his presence were the signal, two council members entered with the accused man.

Jamie had never seen him before, though he had apparently beaten Scott up multiple times. Scott's eyes narrowed; clearly he did remember him. He was dragged to the center of the room and glared around the room before fixing his gaze on Derek.

"I'm innocent," he said before anyone else spoke. "It's your mate that killed that dragon. I would never kill a dragon."

Ethan stepped forward. He was also at the front, on the Elder's other side.

"We'll have time to present evidence, and you'll have your chance to speak," he said coldly. "But you don't have that right yet."

The man scowled and Ethan looked at Derek.

"Queen Derek, this man stands accused of killing and eating another dragon," he said. "Will you preside?"

"Though I am the first Queen here in Spokane," Derek said, looking around as if challenging anyone to defy him, "I will lay aside my claim and allow the Queen of Portland to preside, as this matter impacts all dragons."

"Thank you, Queen," Jamie said as formally as he could. He looked out at the council and remembered what Mike had told him. Despite the council's rigorous reliance on protocol and rules, there wasn't actually a set way of holding trials. It tended to rely heavily on the crime in question. When Ashton was in charge, sometimes he didn't even bother with the trial part and skipped straight to the punishment. But Mike had encouraged Jamie to hold a fair trial and he knew it was good advice. He didn't want to give the council here the impression that they could ignore due process just because the end result was certain. Jamie looked at Ethan, since Mike had recommended calling him first.

"Council head Ethan, will you please lay out the evidence against this man as best you know?"

Ethan bowed to him and went to the center of the room near the accused. No one had even said his name yet, Jamie realized. It probably didn't matter who he was, or maybe the council here assumed everyone knew him. Well, whatever the reason, he was nameless for now and Jamie wasn't going to expose his ignorance by asking for it. Ethan laid out everything that he knew clearly and succinctly, pointing out the various reasons why they knew the Elder hadn't done it, since one of the main goals here was to prove that this man, not the Elder, had committed the crime. Jamie was reassured as he listened. The Elder was innocent. He had believed the others and had reached that conclusion on his own, but hearing it laid out like this was reassuring.

He called on Scott next, who seemed a little unnerved to be called on in front of everyone. Technically he should have gone first as his status was higher, but Mike had recommended calling Ethan first so Scott would know what he was supposed to do. He didn't have much to add but it was important that there were multiple witnesses to everything. Jamie called Mike next, who added what he knew of when the Elder had searched for and found the killer dragon. Then Jamie glanced at the Elder and hesitated. Mike had been firm on the fact that the Elder himself needed to testify, since so much of it relied on him being innocent. Assuming this man was found guilty, there would no trial for the Elder but Mike said he needed a chance to speak on his own behalf. Cautiously, Jamie called him forward.

The Elder went to the center of the room slowly, locking his gaze with the accused man, who went white with fear. Jamie could practically taste the Elder's desire to kill this man and he tensed, wondering if the Elder would just kill him without waiting for the decision to be reached. He drew close to the man, who flinched. Then the Elder turned to face Jamie and bowed.

Considering how angry the Elder was, he sounded completely composed as he explained his side of things, focusing mainly on his dragon's efforts to catch the killer. He apologized for his dragon's actions in attacking the killer dragon with not a hint of apology in his voice. Clearly his dragon would have killed the other dragon if he had his way, but he was obeying Tarragon law and Jamie was grateful. When he finished, he glared at the man again and then returned to Derek's side. Jamie took another deep breath. Those were the only people he needed to call, but he asked if anyone else had evidence to add. There was silence, and then he looked at the accused.

"You may speak for yourself against the accusations made against you," he said.

The man looked at the Elder nervously and licked his lips. He had probably hoped to still pin the blame on the Elder but with all the evidence laid out like that, it was obvious that not only was the Elder innocent, there wasn't a single person in this room who thought the Elder might possibly be guilty.

He started blustering excuses, claiming innocence, accusing the Elder, but it quickly turned to pleading for his life. He knew he had no case and no chance.

"You can't convict me," he pleaded. "You can't know for sure my dragon did it. You have no evidence."

"We have plenty of evidence," Jamie said, since the others looked at him as if waiting for his answer. He reached out to the man's dragon and was surprised to find that she was just waking up. He reached into her mind, far deeper than he had ever reached into a dragon before, and pulled out her memories. He scowled.

"Your dragon remembers killing," he said. "Even if all of this wasn't evidence enough, I have seen your dragon's memories. She is guilty, and so are you."

"You can't see her memories," the man said, sounding shocked. "No one can see a dragon's mind like that."

"Well, I can, and your dragon is guilty without question," Jamie said. "But I won't rush to judgement. Would the council care to discuss the matter and offer me their verdict?"

It was a little late to ask for their opinion since he had clearly just reached his own, but he couldn't ignore them. He needed to show that he respected them. He wondered idly what he would do if they opposed him and requested leniency, or found the man innocent. He didn't think they would since the evidence was so overwhelming, but they might just to see his reaction. No, he thought, glancing at the Elder. Reaching the wrong conclusion would alienate the Elder as well. If they found this man innocent, there was a very good chance the Elder would see that as breaking Tarragon law and attack all of them. They wouldn't risk it.

The council members looked at each other, but no one spoke. Then Ethan stepped forward.

"I believe our decision is unanimous," he said, and no one objected. They all understood the dangers in even appearing to consider this man innocent. No one wanted to cross Jamie and the Elder, though they probably feared the Elder a lot more. They probably had reason to, though Jamie's title should have made him the larger threat.

"The man is guilty," Ethan announced. "Does the Queen agree?"

"Yes," Jamie said, and turned to Derek, wanting to make sure that the council here continued to respect his position. "Does the second Queen agree?"

"I do," Derek said solemnly, though he looked grateful to be included. Mike had said Derek didn't need to be part of the trial at all but Jamie wanted him to start reclaiming his power. He didn't want the council here growing too powerful and while he had his doubts about Derek, the man was a necessary counterbalance to both Ethan and the Elder. He needed Derek to maintain his role as a strong Queen on campus.

Jamie nodded. "The only sentence that can be given in a case of killing and eating another dragon is death. Elder, you have requested the right to execute this man. You have permission."

The Elder grinned and Jamie shivered. This was the part he worried about most. The Elder was getting permission to kill, and might not be satisfied after killing one person. Would the blood of the killing spark something in him and drive him to kill more? But there were no options. The Elder had claimed the right and there was no reason to deny it. Mike had been firm on this. Refusing to let the Elder kill him would violate Tarragon policy and then he really would start killing. So Jamie drew the sword from his waist and the Elder went in front of him. He hesitated. He could kill the Elder right now and be rid of him. Or the Elder could kill him. He would have to obey Tarragon law and trust the Elder to do the same. He handed the sword to the Elder and met his eyes. They were dominated by rage, but there was some amusement as well. He probably knew what had gone through Jamie's mind before handing over the sword.

The Elder went to the man as the council backed away from him. Jamie realized he had no idea how the Elder would kill him. When he had killed Ashton, Margot had instructed him to slit his throat. But the council members had let go of the man completely. Wouldn't they have stayed to hold him in place if he was going to slit his throat? He glanced at Derek, wondering if he should ask the other Queen to leave. Derek looked nervous. He had killed someone in this very room, Jamie realized. And this was his mate that was going to do the killing. He really shouldn't be here, but there was no way Jamie could ask for him to leave that wouldn't diminish his power. He turned back to the Elder and braced himself. The man fell to his knees, pleading for mercy. The Elder raised the weapon to one side and swung.

Jamie gasped as the Elder sliced off the man's head. It fell to the ground and Jamie's stomach leapt. He struggled not to vomit as the body collapsed and blood spilled across the floor. The rest of the council looked shocked as well. Blood was splattered across the robes of the nearest members and quite a few of them looked as disturbed as Jamie felt. He looked to make sure Derek was okay. He looked incredibly pale and was trembling slightly, but other than that he looked fine. Jamie took a deep breath. He was deeply shaken, but the trial wasn't technically over yet. The Elder turned to him. He was covered in blood, as was the sword he extended to Jamie. Jamie's hand shook as he took the sword back, shivering as his hand made contact with the wet substance as their hands brushed. It was all he could do to sheathe the sword again.

"Elder, you have been cleared in this crime," he said, though it was hard to call the man innocent when he was drenched in someone's blood and had just taken a life.

Now the trial was officially over.

Ethan went to Derek first, touching his cheek briefly and asking him something too soft to hear. Derek nodded, and then he came to Jamie. Jamie unbuckled the sword from his waist and practically shoved it at him, not wanting to be near the blood any more than necessary. The Elder bowed to him but didn't go to Derek, to his surprise. Instead, he went to the council members around the body. Maybe he knew there was no way Derek would tolerate him covered in blood like that. Ethan went to Derek again and spoke softly, and then they headed out of the room, probably to get Derek back to his apartment where he could recover from the shock.

"Jamie," Scott said, probably just as softly. "Let's go. They don't need us here anymore."

Jamie nodded and allowed Scott to lead him away. The scene played through his mind over and over again. He hadn't even imagined someone could be strong enough to do that. He had struggled to pierce Ashton's skin with his blade, but the Elder had chopped the man's entire head off. His stomach churned and he knew that as soon as he was in private and didn't need to appear strong, he was going to throw up. Looking over at Scott, he realized his mate felt the same way. They were both deeply shaken, but at least the killer was dead. No other dragons would be killed. Until the Elder really did turn on them, he thought grimly. He didn't want to be on the other side of the Elder's sword but it would happen eventually. It was inevitable. He just hoped they could handle him when that day finally came.

CHAPTER TWENTY-TWO

Handling Questions

Chris opened his eyes and stared at the blonde head on the pillow beside him. The student was still sound asleep as he got up and dressed. He would shower when he got back to his room. He didn't want to spend any more time here than necessary and it was always annoying when the students woke up and tried to extend the relationship. Sometimes he allowed it, if they really performed well the night before, but usually he just left a note and that was that. Most councilmembers operated that way, he knew. They also tended to target the same group of students, he had found. Some students were extremely impressed by the council and frequently invited them into their bed, so they were used to being abandoned the next morning. It was fairly rare to get a student who had never slept with another council member but it did happen. Chris looked for those students specifically and often scouted the first-year students for his partners. That was how he had connected with Derek, after all.

The thought of Derek didn't hurt as much as it usually did. Margot and Gerard had both recommended working on his seduction skills and he agreed. There was no reason Derek should have slipped away from him so easily. He had been poised to win, but the Elder had seduced Derek away and he wouldn't let it happen again. Inwardly he wondered how he was even going to get into Derek's next mating flight. The Elder would likely ban him and since it was up to the council who participated and the council was unlikely to go against the Elder's wishes, the ban would probably stay. He would also have to be in Spokane for the mating flight, equally unlikely. But Gerard and Margot both seemed to have a plan and he wouldn't question it. Yet.

He stretched as soon as he got home and went to the shower. Summer had passed in a blur for him. He was part of the council again and relished having access to everything going on, but he was disturbed by the lack of news about Jamie and Scott. He had tried to coax information out of the others but they had seemed uneasy about what had happened and refused to talk about it. The refusal he expected, but it was clear they didn't like whatever had happened. Had Jamie and Scott been attacked and that was why they had fled? Did the council know who had attacked them? He didn't know, and it bothered him.

Over three months had passed since Jamie and Scott had unexpectedly left and school would be starting in a matter of weeks. They needed to be here to take their classes, or at least Jamie did. Scott had graduated, but he was still in training as Queen's mate. He might not be taking formal classes the way Jamie still was, but he was still needed. What were they thinking staying away this long? Jamie had always seemed almost paranoid about keeping the council in check and without him here, Gerard and Margot were gaining an enormous amount of power. It was like Jamie didn't even exist anymore, like the Queen didn't matter. They acted as if Jamie would never return, but of course he would. This was his campus.

Marisol would be ready to leave her eggs soon, he knew. Jamie had convinced her to leave her eggs before the first year exam and it was almost time for her to leave, if they were still keeping to their original schedule. Or maybe Jamie and Scott were at the nesting grounds with Narné. It was possible. No one else seemed to know where they were and it didn't seem like they were lying about that. They seemed to know why he had left, but not where he was. Margot was especially keen to hear news of their location and Gerard didn't mind him sharing his lack of knowledge, but he suspected if Chris ever did find out, he would be forbidden from telling her. He would respect his council head over Margot, he knew, even if she had been the primary reason he was allowed back on the council.

After he showered and dressed for the day, he headed out to find another council member and see if he could learn anything else. He had other responsibilities now since his position on the council had been restored, but he could safely ignore them for a few hours. He was in charge of coordinating with the German community, making sure their needs were met and they stayed subservient to Portland and the Queen. It was increasingly difficult with Jamie's absence and both Gerard and Margot had encouraged him to recommend loyalty to the council again, not to Jamie. Germany was resistant to that idea, though. Chris knew they were the first nation to join Jamie when he turned against Ashton and their dragons had already been halfway to

Portland by the time Ashton was killed. They were Jamie's most loyal allies and they were demanding information on Jamie's whereabouts that Chris just couldn't give. All he could say was that Jamie was completely safe and away from Portland of his own accord. With the school year about to start, though, he knew he was going to get more pointed questions about Jamie's absence, questions that he himself shared. Maybe he could get more information from Gerard that would help with his job as well.

Gerard was speaking to two other council members when he found him near one of the academic buildings in upper campus. There were a few students milling around as it was between classes for summer school, but it was mostly empty. Even though he outranked both of the other council members, he waited for them to finish without interrupting. They couldn't do anything to him but he was still a little wary alienating other members of the council after his expulsion. He'd already had to put three challengers in their place since he was reinstated and while it wasn't difficult, it was a hassle that he'd prefer to avoid. So he let them finish and go on their way before he approached Gerard, who wore a resigned smile.

"I'm sure I can guess why you're here, Chris," he said. "I don't have any news."

"The school year's starting in a couple of weeks," Chris said. "Why aren't they back yet?"

"They might not come back for fall semester," Gerard said, and Chris blinked. That was the first time anyone had indicated that they might remain wherever they were.

"Are they in Spokane?"

"I doubt it, since the Elder is there," he said. "And I'm pretty sure we would have heard something by now."

He pushed aside his usual anger at the mention of the Elder. At the start of the summer there had been an incident in Spokane. Another dragon had been killed, and Chris had been desperate to go to Derek's side and comfort him the way he had comforted him when the other dragons were killed by the Elder. Somehow, the Elder wasn't responsible and they had caught the man, an Ashton loyalist, and he had been put on trial and executed by the Elder. Chris's heart went out to his love for not only having to preside over that kind of thing, but also to have to watch his mate kill someone. Derek knew the Elder was a killer, of course, but there was something different about seeing someone kill in person. The first time Chris had seen Ashton kill someone, he had been shaken to his core. His love for Ashton hadn't changed after that, but he was far warier around the man than he had been before. Ashton seemed to encourage it, as fear was a necessary driving force in keeping the council in check. He didn't like to think of the Elder using that fear against Derek, who was already almost helpless to him. But Gerard had a good point about Jamie being there. Even if he were willing to risk the Elder, they would have heard something. Communication between the campus's was sparse, but he knew Gerard was in frequent contact with Ethan, the head of council there.

"If they're not on a campus, they can't take classes," Chris said. "Do you have any way of getting in touch with them?"

"You have just as good a chance," he pointed out, and Chris sighed. It was true. Marisol was capable of speaking to all dragons and their partners and he had approached her on the subject a few times, though it was strange to be able to do so. He suspected his dragon knew exactly where Jamie and Scott were and just refused to say, and Marisol had refused as well except to say that they were safe. He had tried to ask her when they were returning but he only ever got the same answer, that they were safe, and had given up. He got the feeling that she was asked that a lot, by a large number of people, and he didn't want to add any stress when she was taking care of her eggs.

"Marisol was due to leave soon," he said. "Can't we just track her and see where she goes? She'll almost certainly go straight to Jamie. And if she stays where she is, isn't that a good sign that he's with her right now?"

"We're not tracking the Queen," Gerard said firmly. "If she wanted us to know more, she would tell us. If and when she leaves, we will let her leave freely."

"Our dragons will know where she is," Chris pointed out.

"If they're not telling us anything now, I doubt they'll start just because Marisol leaves."

"I need something to tell the Germans," he warned. "They're starting to demand to see Jamie. You know how they feel about him."

"Just keep telling them he's safe, and will be back," Gerard said. "I'm sure you know how to be convincing, Chris. Bothering me about this won't help, and you do have a job to do."

Chris bowed. That was a pretty clear dismissal. Gerard wasn't as ruthless as Ashton but he was still head of the council and Chris didn't want to cross him in any way. He headed back across upper campus when he noticed a limo nearby. He tensed, and sure enough, Margot got out. Her eyes went straight to him and she smiled. She rarely visited campus and it was dangerous talking to him openly, since people might guess that he was her spy, but she gestured him over and he had to obey.

"How are things on the men's campus?" she asked, and he looked around nervously. She laughed. "No need to hide it," she said. "Gerard has already scolded me about you, and I've heard from other council-members that everyone knows who you work for."

"That's still no reason to approach me in the open like this," he said.

"Watch yourself," she said, and he flinched. Like Gerard, she was head of council, but she was far more like Ashton than he. He wouldn't contradict or challenge her again.

"So what news is there?"

"Germany continues to demand to see Jamie," he said. Most of the news he could give her was about their international affairs, since the countries were split between the men and women's councils and she often had little idea what was happening with their half of the inter-national community. Before, Margot reported her campus's news to Ashton and he coordinated everything, but while Margot was trying to take on that role, many of the men's council were hesitant to fully trust her.

"Any news of when that will happen?" she asked. "You were just talking to Gerard. What did he say?"

Chris hesitated. Was this something he could share? Well, Gerard hadn't specifically warned him against sharing it and he usually did if it was something he didn't want Margot to know.

"He said he didn't know if Jamie and Scott were coming back for the semester," he said slowly. "He said they might stay wherever they are longer. I told him they needed to be in classes, or Jamie at least does. I think he agrees, but he still doesn't know if they'll be back."

"Jamie does need to return," Margot said. "Tarragon society will lose all need for him if he stays away too long."

"Marisol is still keeping the dragons in order," Chris pointed out. "They'll respect her as first queen no matter what. It's just Jamie that's losing influence. Are you sure you don't know where he is? I tried tell-ing Marisol he needed to return and she refuses to talk to me."

"I'm sure Marisol is having trouble handling everyone, and she has her eggs to care for as well," Margot said. "It would be a shame if this year's first year exam didn't go smoothly. Then Marisol might lose her influence as well."

For some reason, she sounded almost pleased by that prospect. Chris must be misjudging her tone of voice, because no one would want the first year exam to go poorly. He would have liked to call Mike back here, since he had handled the first year students so well the last two years, but Mike was needed to keep an eye on the Elder. He and Mike would need to sort things out eventually, he knew. He would need to put Mike in his place, since they apparently had similar roles in the council and he would not let anyone rank higher than him who didn't fully earn that place. Mike was a child; there was no way he should rank higher than Chris. Eventually, they would deal with it, but for now, Mike was needed in Spokane and Chris was just glad someone was there to look after Derek.

"Spokane is quiet," he said, and Margot looked at him sharply.

"You think Jamie is in Spokane?"

"What?" Chris asked, startled. "No, I was thinking of Derek. Jamie wouldn't go to Spokane with the Elder there, would he? Especially since he doesn't have Marisol with him. I just meant that we haven't heard anything from Derek since that dragon's death."

"Spokane seems to be running well," Margot said. "Their Queen at least is responsible."

She sighed and patted his shoulder. "I know you're still thinking about Derek, but you need to be focused on winning him back, not worrying about what's happening to him right now. There's nothing you can do about the present. You have to prepare for the future."

"I know," he said. "I am. When it's time for his next mating flight, I'll be ready."

"Good," she said, then looked around. "I need to talk to Gerard. I'm sure you have other things to do."

Just as clear a dismissal as Gerard's, but far softer. Good, because she was more vindictive than him and he didn't want to push her. He nodded and began retreating to his home in dragon canyon. He would spend some time dealing with Germany, then find another student to practice his seduction skills on. As he walked, he wondered where Jamie and Scott had spent their summer, but his mind drifted to Derek, trapped somewhere with a killer. It had been so long since he had seen Derek that his mental image of the boy was starting to fade. The immediacy of his presence was dimmed, and he knew Derek would be feeling the same about him. If he did get into Derek's second mating flight, would he still have the advantage? Or would Derek have been seduced by the Elder just as his dragon had been? He shivered. It wasn't worth thinking about. He would keep up his skills here and when he entered Derek's flight, he wouldn't lose.

CHAPTER TWENTY-THREE

Unpleasant Arrival

D erek opened his eyes lazily to the sight of the Elder's handsome profile relaxed in sleep. He watched the Elder's slow breathing for a long time. It had been months since the trial where the Elder had killed, but he couldn't get it out of his head. He had been shaken for days afterwards and refused to have any contact with his mate. The Elder slept in a separate room and avoided him for the most part and Derek was grateful, because he had the right to order Derek into his bed if he wanted. But he had given Derek the space he needed and when the shock and horror wore off, he slowly integrated himself back into his life. Now it was almost like it had been before, except that now Derek knew what he was capable of.

The Elder's breathing changed and his eyes opened. His lips curled in a smile as he turned to look at Derek. Ever since the trial, the Elder had been unusually gentle. Derek had grown to enjoy it. He felt treasured when the Elder held him close and cradled him and said sweet things to him. He wasn't always gentle in bed; Derek would have disappointed if the Elder's strategies in the bedroom changed completely. He enjoyed the Elder just the way he was and when he had finally invited the Elder back into his bed after nearly two weeks, the Elder had blasted past any reservations he had until he was begging for more.

"You're awake," the Elder said, stroking his cheek. "Did you sleep well?"

"No nightmares," he said. His dreams were haunted by death now, both by the man who had been killed by the Elder and by Alan, the man he himself had killed. The Elder had once reassured him that he would never have to kill again because as Queen, that wasn't his responsibility. He hadn't realized that watching an execution would be just as bad.

The Elder tilted his head forward and kissed Derek gently. Then his hand tightened around the back of Derek's head and he rolled so he was on top with Derek pinned under him. Derek's breath hitched and his heart jumped.

"You don't have any classes today," the Elder said, tracing his hand down Derek's neck to his bare collarbone. The air conditioner wasn't the best and it was so hot he usually just slept in boxers. The Elder frequently slept nude, which Derek never minded. He was so handsome it was hard to argue when he was naked.

The Elder kissed him again, his hands sliding down Derek's body to the waistband of his boxers. He flinched. They sometimes had sex in the morning, but never immediately after waking up. Still, the thought turned him on and he helped peel off his boxers until their naked bodies were pressed against each other. The Elder ground against him and he let out a hiss of pleasure. He wrapped his arms around the Elder's shoulders but wasn't surprised when the Elder pushed his arms above his head. He obediently wound his hands together and gave the Elder free reign over his body, and soon he was moaning and panting as the Elder's tongue snaked across his chest and teased his nipples. The Elder's hand began stroking him slowly, tantalizing him as he shifted to try to get more traction. His arms lifted for a moment, longing to pull the Elder down on him, and abruptly the Elder withdrew. Derek bit his lip and flattened his arms again. He was not in control here. The Elder was. With a nip along his neck, the Elder returned to teasing his body and in moments, he was desperate for more.

"Please," he begged. "Inside me."

The Elder grinned and stroked lower, to his ass, and shifted so that he was positioned at his opening. Derek crooked on leg around the Elder's waist, giving him permission to do whatever he wanted, and he moaned softly as the Elder entered him in one smooth, swift motion. The Elder didn't give him any time to adjust as he started thrusting and Derek moaned again, needed every pounding pulse against him. He arched his back in time with the rhythm and started to grab the Elder when his hands were once again pinned down over his head. His heart beat rapidly and his lungs felt as though they were suffocating it felt so good, and the Elder had barely started. The Elder kissed him as he thrust, and as the pleasure sifted through his senses, he felt something else in his mind. A flickering of something familiar, a familiar voice trying to get through to him.

"Not now, Jettie," he murmured, though saying it aloud wouldn't have any impact. Still, she didn't seem to be listening to his mental pleas not to disturb him. She never bothered him when he was having sex. She enjoyed it with him or ignored it, depending on what else she was doing, but she had never interrupted him before.

As soon as he spoke, the Elder's pace slowed, then stopped. Derek shifted, desperate for the motion to continue, for the enormous cock lodged in his body to shift in time with him. But the Elder pinned him in place and didn't thrust.

"What does Jettie need?"

"Nothing," he said. "She's fine. Don't stop."

The Elder sighed and pulled out of him completely, and he cried out at the loss.

"Communicate with Jettie and tell me what she wants," he ordered.

Obediently, knowing he wouldn't get any more sex until he

did what he was told, he reached out to Jettie. And winced.

"What is it?" the Elder asked, sounding worried.

"It's- it doesn't matter. She's fine. It doesn't involve her. Let's just keep going."

"Not until you tell me what it is," the Elder said. Derek sighed.

"It's my mother," he said. "She just showed up on campus. Ethan is taking care of her. See? We have plenty of time to be together before I have to go deal with that."

The Elder ran a finger down the center of Derek's chest, stopping just short of his belly button and nowhere hear his erect cock. He shifted, trying to get closer to that touch.

"If Jettie is worried, you should deal with this now," he said, sitting up.

Derek's eyes flew wide open and he gasped. "You can't leave me like this," he protested. He was practically at the brink of orgasm. Just a few more minutes and he would be there. This interruption would be forgotten as soon as the Elder was back inside him and surely the man wanted more as well. Didn't he? But the Elder rolled off him and to his surprise, he saw that the Elder's penis was losing its rigidity.

"No, you can't do this to me," he said. "This isn't important. We don't have to stop."

"Get up, and get dressed," the Elder said, leaning to kiss his forehead. "After you handle this situation, we can continue."

He protested again, to no avail. The Elder stood up and went into their bathroom, leaving Derek in shock. He grabbed his cock and stroked. If he couldn't have the Elder's help, then he would do it himself. He desperately needed release, after all. He let his hand explore his shaft but it wasn't the same and as he climaxed, it lacked the intensity he could have had if Jettie hadn't interrupted them. No. Jettie wasn't the problem. His mother was the problem. What was she doing here?

Now that he had come and his mind felt a little clearer, he joined the Elder in the bathroom to clean himself up. The Elder grinned at him, no doubt having guessed that Derek would finish himself. He was tempted to stick his tongue out at the man for refusing to help but didn't want to resort to the childish gesture with his mom on campus. He settled for a pout and as he cleaned himself, the Elder came over and kissed his shoulder.

"I'd like to meet her," he said.

"I don't really want you to," Derek said. "I don't want anyone to meet her."

"You really think I'll think of you differently if I meet her?"

He blushed. That was why he didn't want anyone meeting his mom. He now knew that Ethan at least wouldn't turn against him because of her, and it seemed like the rest of the council was on his side against her as well, but he still didn't want to risk it. And he did not want to risk her meeting the Elder. He would have to talk to her and then get her to leave. He wished there were some way out of talking to her, but there was no way she would leave until she saw him. Would she listen? Or would she try to stay a few days again? Everyone would back his decision if he wanted her to go, but what if she just kept showing up unexpectedly like this? He supposed he should be thankful she hadn't dropped by sooner. She had waited over three months before coming back. That was a long time, for her. But it didn't seem like any time had passed at all to him. A lot had happened since then, of course, but it felt like yesterday that he was trying to convince her to leave. And now he had to do it all over again.

He finished getting ready but before he could leave, the Elder took his shoulders and stared into his eyes.

"Why don't you want me to meet her?" he asked. "I know she'll be nothing like you. The women Ashton was drawn to tended to be women who flattered him, who weren't really worthy of him. I'm sure your mother is the same. You're not like that. You took after your father. I won't think poorly of you no matter what she's like."

"Then why do you want to meet her?" he asked, frustrated.

"She's someone you care about," he said. "Even if you don't take after her, I want to know the important people in your life. Or is it that you don't want her to meet me?"

"Well, there's that, too," Derek said slowly. The Elder smiled faintly.

"I doubt she knows anything about me, or why it's so unusual that I'm your mate," he said.

"You don't have a real name," Derek pointed out. "If I just call you the Elder, she'll think it's weird."

"That is my name, now," he said. "I don't think she'll find it as unusual as you fear. So introduce me to her."

"You don't control me outside of the bedroom," Derek said angrily, backing away from the Elder's grip. "You can't make me do this."

"I'm not making you," the Elder said soothingly. "I'm asking you. Can I please meet your mother?"

Derek eyed him warily. Was there some secret reason the Elder wanted this? Or was it as simple as he said and he just wanted to meet her because she was his mother? He didn't really have any reasons not to introduce her if it didn't change the Elder's view, and it probably wouldn't. He was uncomfortable explaining the Elder to his mom, but it wouldn't be too difficult. And Ethan would likely be there as well, which would smooth things over. He nodded.

"Fine," he said. "She's not staying long, though."

"You're the Queen," the Elder said. "She'll stay as long as you allow, and not a moment longer. Everyone on campus will back you up on that."

Derek nodded again, slower. It was true. He had the campus behind him. He had lost their support for a week or two after the Elder was accused of murder, but he had reclaimed everything since then. Not even Jamie's presence on campus was taking away from his authority, mostly because Jamie and Scott were being extremely good about keeping a low profile. He knew Jamie and Ethan talked nearly every day about what was happening in Portland, since Ethan regularly exchanged news with the other campus and it was Jamie's only real way of keeping in touch with things there, but Jamie had never challenged Derek in any way. They might not ever be friends, but they were friendly now, and he even went out of his way to spend time with Jamie sometimes.

They headed out of the apartments together towards the main campus where Jettie indicated Ethan and his mom would be. As soon as they entered the grassy area between the buildings, he heard his mom call his name. He sighed as he saw her approaching rapidly with Ethan following behind her at a much slower pace. She embraced him tightly, then stepped back and smiled flirtatiously at the Elder.

"I don't think I've ever seen you before," she said. "Are you on the council?"

A fair question, since the robes the Elder wore were similar to the council's robes minus the dragon on the breast.

"I'm the Queen's mate," he said, and her eyes widened. She looked at Derek, then back at the Elder, then at Derek again.

"What a lucky son I have," she said. "What's your name?"

"You can call me the Elder," he said, and she reached out to shake his head without the slightest hesitation.

"An odd name," she said, but didn't follow up with any other comments. On that, at least. She grinned at Derek. "I thought you said you didn't get the mate that you wanted. How could you possibly not want someone like him?"

Heat flooded his cheeks and he noticed that the Elder looked amused. Well, everyone knew that Derek had wanted Chris for his mate, not the Elder. It wasn't like his mom was sharing any secrets. But he still didn't like her just throwing that into the open like that.

"And where is the Queen? I was hoping to see him again today," his mom said, looking around.

"Derek is our Queen," Ethan said.

"The real Queen," she said, rolling her eyes as if to indicate how little she thought of Derek's rank. He felt his hackles rising and tried to stay calm. She was always like this. She always did this. He couldn't let it get to him. But it was still hard.

"I am the real Queen, mom," he said icily. "I don't know why you choose today to come, but I think you should leave."

"I'll just be here for a day or two," she said with a smile. "I'm sure the head of council here or your mate can arrange for my stay."

"I've told you, the Queen has the final say on everything," Ethan said in an annoyed voice. "His word is final."

"Hmm, the Queen's mate does outrank the council, doesn't he?" she asked in a scheming voice, then smiled sweetly at the Elder. "I'm sure there's a place for me, just for a day or two."

"I serve my Queen," the Elder said. Derek noticed a hint of amusement in his voice and wondered if he possibly found this situation funny. But at least he was backing up Derek. That was the important thing.

His mom looked around as if seeking anyone else with authority, then her eyes lit up.

"Well, I'll just ask the other Queen."

Derek followed her gaze and noticed Jamie sitting with someone in the shade on a bench along the building. Jamie was facing them and he couldn't see who was with him, but it wasn't Scott. Derek would recognize Scott anywhere. And then, to his shock, Jamie leaned forward and kissed whoever he was with.

Derek gasped. Jamie was kissing someone besides Scott? Jamie, who was allowed to be mates with the man of his choosing, who had fought tooth and nail to be able to be at Scott's side, who had hated Derek because he thought Derek was stealing him, *that* Jamie was kissing someone else? Without a thought, Derek stormed over to them, vaguely aware of Ethan trying to intercept him. Jamie noticed him about ten feet away and leapt to his feet, looking shocked and guilty. The other man rose to his feet as well. It was TK, the student from Africa. Derek had heard rumors of something between Jamie and TK but he hadn't believed it. Why would Jamie possibly want anyone else when he had Scott?

Derek squared off in front of Jamie and was only barely aware of the others around them. This was between him and Jamie, and Scott was on the line.

CHAPTER TWENTY-FOUR

Misplaced Kiss

"Hey, Jamie, want to talk?"

Jamie turned to see TK approaching. They were in a fairly isolated spot on campus and he looked around. There were a few people walking nearby, as the weather was perfect, but no one was paying attention to him. He was glad; he had come here to walk for a while without attracting notice and TK was the first one to approach him. He considered, then nodded. He really shouldn't be talking to TK without getting permission from Scott, but it wasn't like they were going to do anything.

"Let's sit down in the shade," TK suggested, and they went to one of the benches along the nearby building that was shaded by the large maple trees nearby. The campus had been constructed carefully to preserve as many of the existing trees as possible, as they provided excellent shade. Apparently it would be a hassle in the fall and they would have to employ a large staff to keep the grounds raked, but there was money for it. Tarragon Academy turned quite a profit and everyone on the council was extremely rich. After some discussion, Ashton's wealth had been divided between Jamie, the heir to his power, and Derek, his son. Derek had tried to insist that they track down all of Ashton's children and split the money evenly between them, not giving any to Jamie, and Jamie would have agreed to that – he didn't really want the money – but the council had insisted. The two queens would receive the money. Jamie had promptly reinvested some of his money in the campus itself, but had also discovered that bribery smoothed things over with the council quite well. Thanks to Ashton's greed over the past century or so, there was more than enough to provide for Jamie the rest of his life, and he made more each year as the first queen.

Jamie was hardly thinking about TK as he sat down next to him but when TK took his hand, his attention snapped back instantly. He drew in a sharp breath and realized TK was smiling shyly at him, his dark eyes glittering. He was so handsome, Jamie thought wistfully.

"Are you staying here fall semester?" TK asked. "I didn't think you'd stay this long."

"I don't know," Jamie said. It was starting to become a problem. He needed to figure out a way to deal with Margot. He had been trying to persuade Gerard in Portland to assist him as soon as Marisol left her eggs. The council would need to unite around Jamie immediately and there would likely be casualties since Margot would strike when cornered. But Gerard warned that not all of the council would obey if there was a risk to them. Her dragon could only erase one person's memory at a time and there seemed to be a limit on how frequently she could do it, but no one knew the exact limitations of her ability because she hid it so well. Gerard had a few guesses, as did Ethan. The three of them were in constant communication trying to figure out the problem. Gerard had warned that the situation was starting to become dire not just because of the pressing matter of classes but because of the other countries. Jamie was needed to represent Tarragon Academy to the world. The other nations were keeping in line but without a Queen, the strong worldwide network of nations was starting to fracture. Ashton had kept them together through force and all had been willing to follow Jamie and maintain the same tight alliance and obedience, but without Jamie there, there was friction. He needed to return.

Well, Marisol had left Portland earlier today and was headed here, so at least that would be taken care of. She would arrive soon and then he could start seriously planning his return. He needed to return. He couldn't hide from Margot forever. Another week, maybe two, but he needed to return before the start of the semester. There were no other options.

"I don't think I'll be here for the semester," he added. "All of my teachers are in Portland."

"Why are you spending the summer with us, anyway?" TK asked. "I'm not complaining, I love that you're here, but why?"

"I just wanted to leave for a while," Jamie said with an uncomfortable shrug. TK smiled and stroked his hand.

"Well, I'm glad I get to spend the time with you. You always seem so busy here. I haven't had a chance to talk to you alone this whole summer."

It was true. Normally Jamie was with Scott or Ethan, so it was rare that he was alone. He saw TK regularly, but never when he was by himself and Scott always made sure to steer them away whenever TK showed up. It was a little unfair; Scott got to see Derek almost every day but Jamie had to keep away from his crush? There was nothing left between TK and Jamie anymore, after all. Scott was back in his heart.

They chatted a little, TK keeping Jamie's hand in his and stroking it softly. It felt good. Scott was rarely this gentle in his shows of affection, he reflected. He tended to be passionate, but this subtle gesture of love was touching in its simplicity. Jamie found himself scooting slightly closer to TK until their thighs were pressed against each other. They continued talking as he observed TK, remembering why he had liked the man. TK was so intelligent, with a wit that frequently had Jamie dissolving into laughter. It felt good to laugh. He was so stressed most of the time but with TK, the stress melted away. That had always been true of TK, he thought. He had met TK when Scott was here in

176

Spokane having sex with Derek, and then Scott was kidnapped by the Elder, and TK had been his relief from that trauma. TK was his comfort. The one person he felt safe and relaxed around, the one person who would never betray him. He knew TK was seeing Mike now but he didn't mind, because he and TK weren't a couple anymore. TK could be with whoever he wanted and he was glad it was Mike, because he would treat TK as well as he deserved. And he did deserve someone wonderful, Jamie decided as he laughed at TK's turn of phrase. He squeezed TK's hand and then, without a second thought, leaned forward and kissed him.

TK's eyes went wide as Jamie's lips briefly pressed against his.

"What was that?" he asked softly.

"I just missed you," Jamie said. There was movement to his right and he tensed. Had someone seen that? Then he saw the figure angrily approaching and paled, leaping to his feet and backing up a little. It was Derek. Ethan, the Elder, and a woman who he recognized as Derek's mom were here too. What were they doing here? And why did Derek look like he wanted to kill him? TK stood at his side rather protectively as Derek confronted Jamie.

"What the hell do you think you're doing?" Derek said in a low, angry voice.

"What does it matter to you?" Jamie asked.

"You belong to Scott," Derek hissed, and Jamie's eyes narrowed.

"I don't *belong* to anyone," he said. "I'm a Queen."

"And Scott is your mate," Derek snapped. "How dare you kiss someone else when he's your mate."

"I can kiss anyone I want," Jamie said, drawing himself up and not liking the utter resentment in Derek's gaze. Why did he care so much?

"You don't deserve him," Derek said, and Jamie stiffened. "He should have someone who loves him."

"I do love him," Jamie said.

"He should have better."

"And I suppose you're better?" Jamie said, taking an aggressive step forward. "You think you know Scott just because he fucked you a couple of times, against his will? He doesn't love you. You were just a boy he had to seduce."

Derek gasped as though struck, and started forward- Ethan grabbed him and yanked him back a step.

"Stop, you two," he said. "TK, you should leave."

TK looked between Jamie and Derek nervously, then nodded and quickly made his way towards the main campus. Jamie glared at Ethan, then turned his rage back on Derek. He opened his mouth to challenge Derek.

"Stop," Ethan said, cutting him off before he even began. Ethan was still holding Derek, though Derek wasn't struggling, just tense and looking like he wanted to attack. Jamie wanted to attack, too. "Jamie, go cool off. I think it's best if you two stay away from each other for a while."

"You can't tell me what to do," Jamie snapped.

"Please, Queen," Ethan said. "I think it would be best."

Jamie looked at Derek. If they fought, Jamie would probably lose. Derek was a lot bigger and stronger and Jamie didn't know how to fight. Maybe it would be better if he left right now. But he wouldn't go without getting the last word.

"You mean nothing to him," Jamie said with a glare.

Derek hissed. "At least I love him."

The Elder came to Jamie's side and gently pushed him away from Derek. He flinched away from the man's touch, though it was perfectly polite and respectful. Whirling on his toe, he set off towards the woods. He needed to be alone. To think. It was a lie to say that Scott didn't love Derek. He did love him. Derek wasn't just some assignment; he had genuine feelings towards the other Queen. And Jamie's love of Scott ought to be unquestioned. But if he loved Scott, why had he kissed TK?

He rubbed his lips as he entered the thick trees that marked the edge of campus. There was hardly any mist since it was daytime, but he vaguely remembered the path he had taken to bring Jana, Tiger, and the kittens to Zuri for protection. He had come here many times over the past few months, but always at night with the mist guiding him. Why had he kissed TK? It had seemed so natural. TK was such a comfort to him. Did he love TK? He wasn't sure. Not in the same way he loved Scott. He would die for Scott. But he did have feelings for TK. He enjoyed spending time with him, loved talking to him, and loved his body, too. They had never had sex or anything, since Scott controlled his bed, but they had been intimate together and had held each other and kissed with nothing between them. He missed that comfort. There was so much between him and Scott and while it had gotten better after Scott had nearly lost his memories, it wasn't perfect the way it had once been.

He reached the clearing where he usually met Zuri and sat down in the dry undergrowth, leaning against a tree. No, he considered. It had never been perfect. From their very first days there had been conflict. But they had persisted and worked through obstacle after obstacle because they loved each other. Scott was more important than anything else and he had sacrificed for Scott, even killed for him. So why was he drawn to TK now that things were going well between him and Scott?

"Jamie?" a voice asked, and he looked up to see Zuri. "Is everything all right?"

She was alone and his heart clenched. He had been hoping to see Jana, he realized. But the cats would be wherever Zuri's community was. She often gave him news and updates, and the occasional picture, but they never came to visit him and he hadn't seen them a single time since giving them up. The unicorn tribe must have noticed him approaching and sent her out to stop him from getting too close. It wasn't a danger at night when the mist would stop him, but without that protection he might stumble upon their community and he knew they didn't want that. He wondered how long he had been sitting here, trapped in his worries. Quite a while, probably.

"I just needed to be alone," he said. "Is Jana nearby?"

"She was with the kittens when I left," Zuri said. "Should I get her?"

"No," Jamie said with a sigh. "I don't want to upset her."

"What's wrong?"

Jamie stared at the dried grass and leaves on the ground around him. What was wrong? Everything. Nothing was going well in his life. He had been given one brief moment of comfort with TK and now everything was even worse. Then he felt something reaching out to him and drew in a breath, looking up. Zuri looked up as well and flinched as something enormous flew overhead. It was Marisol, and her crimson scales glittered in the sunlight as she twirled above him.

"Is that your dragon?" Zuri asked in awe. "I've never seen a red one before."

"I'll have her come down nearby," Jamie offered. "You can meet her."

Zuri looked delighted and Marisol indicated that there was a clearing nearby when she could safely land. In a few minutes they were in the clearing and Jamie bolted to her, wrapping his arms around her snout and squeezing his eyes tight against the tears. This was what he needed. His dragon. She was his everything. She would always be his comfort. No one could get mad at him for loving her. He took several long, long minutes feeling

180

the need and ache in his heart begin to fill up, then backed away, though he kept one hand in contact with her scales. He turned to Zuri, who looked almost frightened.

"This is Marisol," he said. "You can touch her. She likes having her scales rubbed."

"Will she hurt me? She's looking at me like she wants to eat me.

"Of course not," Jamie said with a laugh. "She's curious about you. That's why she's looking at you. She knows you're taking care of Jana and the others right now, and that you're connected to unicorns. She'd like to meet you."

Zuri took a few steps into the clearing and, with Jamie's encouragement, reached out to lay a hand on Marisol's shoulder. She gasped.

"You're so warm," she said. "And soft. I thought you would be hard."

"She's beautiful, isn't she?" Jamie said proudly, and Zuri smiled.

"And you can talk to her with your mind? She's yours, and no one else's?"

"She's mine, and I'm hers," Jamie said, scratching Marisol's eye ridges. The dragon practically purred in delight and let Jamie know exactly how long it had been since she was close enough to a human to get this kind of treatment. She was going to need to be spoiled for days, he could tell.

"I'm so jealous," she said. "The unicorns have people they prefer, but they don't belong to anyone, and we don't necessarily belong to them. I don't really want to change that, but still... I'm jealous."

Jamie smiled. "I'm glad you get to meet her."

"You need to get back to your campus, don't you?" she asked.

"It's dangerous to have both of you so close."

He nodded. Having him close to their community wasn't a major problem but having a dragon nearby might be a threat. The other dragons might see Marisol and wonder why she was here, and might come to investigate. They said goodbye and he climbed on Marisol's back, delighted to have her strong form under him again. She nuzzled him and took to the air. He sighed. He was going to need to deal with a lot of issues now that Marisol was here, but Scott and Derek would probably need to be first. And TK.

CHAPTER TWENTY-FIVE

Careless Mistakes

Mike was heading towards the center of campus at Eraxes' request when he saw TK storming towards him. The boy didn't even see him until they were right in front of each other and instead of his face warming into a smile, he continued to look furious.

"TK, what's wrong?" Mike asked, reaching out to comfort him as he was clearly upset.

"Nothing," TK snapped, shoving off Mike's hand and shouldering past. "I don't want to talk to you right now."

He stormed off and Mike watched him go, puzzled. Then he continued into the center of campus until he saw Derek facing off with Ethan with the Elder and his mother nearby. Mike hurried up, since this was likely why Eraxes had summoned him here, and they looked over at him as he approached. Derek's gaze was utterly dismissive and he shivered.

"Elder," Ethan said. "Why don't you show Angela around campus until she leaves? I'm sure she'll be ready to leave soon."

"Ethan," she started, but the look Ethan shot her was nearly as potent as Derek's glare. She seemed to realize she was outnumbered, swallowed hard, and meekly allowed the Elder to escort her away. Mike wondered if it were really a good idea, but wasn't going to argue since he had no idea what was going on.

"Derek, I think you need to go somewhere and cool down as well," Ethan said. "Should I send someone to go with you?"

"You think I'm a child?" Derek asked angrily. "And I don't need to calm down. He's at fault, he should apologize and he shouldn't be allowed to have Scott as his mate."

Mike's eyes narrowed. Derek and Jamie must have fought about Scott. He had wondered when that was going to happen. It was a miracle it hadn't already happened, to be honest. The council had quietly talked about how to handle the situation if the two Queens turned against each other. Jamie was in danger and needed to be here, but Derek was their Queen. They hadn't come to any good plans and when the two Queens seemed to be getting along unexpectedly well, they had stopped talking about it. Jamie and Derek had been downright friendly with each other, in fact. But maybe it was inevitable this would happen.

"Scott and Jamie's relationship is their own," Ethan said. "Let them handle things between them. You have your own relationships that you should be focusing on. Why don't you go back to your room until the Elder returns, and then the two of you can talk."

"You want me turning to him?" Derek asked in a low voice. "What about not trusting him? About not becoming reliant on him?"

"He's still your mate," Ethan said, though Derek raised a good point. "Maybe talking to your mate will help you understand that the relationship between a Queen and his mate is often a lot more complex than it appears on the surface. You shouldn't question Jamie and Scott."

Derek scowled, but didn't say another word as he stormed off in loosely the same direction TK had gone, towards his apartment. As soon as he was out of sight, Ethan whirled to Mike with murder in his eyes and Mike flinched.

"Why weren't you with TK?" Ethan asked.

"What?"

"TK," Ethan said. "He was unattended. He found Jamie and they just kissed in front of Derek. What were you thinking? Why is he even still interested in Jamie?"

Mike's jaw dropped. They had kissed? That was impossible. Wasn't it? He knew TK still had feelings for Jamie. It was obvious. But most of his feelings now were dedicated to Mike. That was why TK had been so angry just now, he realized.

"Did he kiss Jamie or did Jamie kiss him?"

"Does it matter?"

"He might still be in love with Jamie, but not to that extent anymore," Mike said, because he knew why Ethan was angry and it was dangerous. It was Mike's job to keep TK's attention away from Jamie so that this exact type of situation could be avoided. Ethan checked in with him every once in a while, emphasizing that Mike needed to stay on top of TK to prevent this from happening. And it had happened despite all of that. As head of the council, Ethan could do anything to him for disobeying him and allowing this to happen. Mike was the newest member of the council and while his rank within the council was fairly high, he was still new and he hadn't faced any punishment yet. He had heard some of the stories about what Ashton did to people who disobeyed him. He didn't know how similar Ethan would be but he didn't want to find out.

"I've done everything I can," Mike said nervously, because Ethan was still angry. "I can't be with him every moment of the day, and Jamie was his first love. That's not easily replaced."

"You're still in love with Scott, aren't you?" Ethan said in a dark voice. "But most people lose interest far faster than that."

Mike blushed. Then Ethan sighed and shook his head.

"Jamie initiated the kiss. I'm sure you've done your best. Your failure will need to be addressed, but not right now. Right now, you need to go to TK and make sure he doesn't get any ideas. I don't want him anywhere near Jamie again, and he needs to stay away from Derek now as well. Understand?"

"I understand," Mike said meekly. He would have to make sure TK was nowhere near either of them ever again, because he didn't want to know what Ethan would do if he really disobeyed. He bowed to Ethan nervously, then hastened towards TK. The boy had been heading back to the dorms; hopefully that was where he had ended up. He sent a thought to Eraxes to see if Devon, TK's dragon, knew anything, but all Eraxes could tell was that Devon was angry. Everyone was angry, it seemed, and Mike was the one to pay the price. Why had Jamie kissed him? What was he thinking? TK wouldn't have invited it. Mike was sure. Almost sure. Fairly certain, at least. TK loved him now, not Jamie. Didn't he?

He knocked on TK's door and to his relief, he heard someone on the other side.

"Who is it?"

"It's me," Mike said. There was a long pause, then the door opened. TK didn't let him in, however.

"I don't want to talk to you right now."

"I think we need to talk," he said. "I heard what just happened. I heard Jamie kissed you."

"Which is why I don't want to be around you right now," TK snapped.

"My boyfriend just kissed someone else," Mike said. Now he was getting angry. "Don't I deserve to know why?"

"We're not boyfriends," TK said rather bitterly. "We just sleep together."

"I didn't think the title mattered that much to you," Mike said. Had he erred in not calling himself TK's boyfriend sooner? They were boyfriends except in name. Did the name matter? "I consider you my boyfriend. I guess I thought you did to."

"Then why didn't you ever ask me to go out?"

"I ask you to go out on dates all the time," Mike pointed out.

"Dates," TK said scornfully. "But not to be with me."

"TK, will you go out with me?" Mike asked. "Will you be exclusive with me? I'm already exclusive with you."

TK scowled, but let him in the room. They sat next to each other on the coach and Mike wrapped his arm around TK's tense shoulders.

"I don't know if I want to be exclusive with you," TK said, and ran a finger over his lips. "I thought Jamie didn't want me. I thought he wanted Scott. I thought I wanted you, not Jamie, because I couldn't have Jamie. But he does want me. He's just trapped by damn Tarragon tradition into having Scott. It isn't fair. He should be able to have whoever he wants, not just the person whose dragon caught his in some mating flight."

"Jamie did choose Scott," Mike said. "He's always chosen Scott. Over and over again. No matter what odds were stacked against them. Their love is truer than any I've ever seen."

"But he also loves me," TK said, meeting Mike's eyes as if daring him to challenge that assertion.

"Maybe," Mike admitted. "But not the same way he loves Scott. If he had to choose between the two of you, there wouldn't be any competition."

"That's not true," TK said. "I saw it in his eyes today. He's worried. He's desperate. He needs someone who understands him and I understand him."

Mike was silent for a moment. It was probably true that Jamie was worried and desperate, but not because of his relationship with Scott. It was because of his situation and whatever had driven him here to Spokane where it was so dangerous for him to be. TK was sensitive enough to Jamie that he was accurately picking up his emotions, which were generally quite hidden, but he was completely misinterpreting things and it was dangerous. Should Mike tell him about Jamie's situation? About the danger Jamie was in, the danger he was running from? Or would TK just be more determined to protect him?

"He may be worried about something else entirely," Mike pointed out.

"It doesn't matter what's causing his worry," TK said. "He wants someone to comfort him. Clearly Scott isn't doing it, so I will. Scott has never been there for him. Scott betrays him, not comforts him. He needs me."

"He doesn't need you-"

"He kissed me," TK said, lifting his head and meeting Mike's gaze again. "If he didn't need me, why would he kiss me?"

Mike struggled for an answer to that. Why had Jamie kissed TK? It didn't seem to make sense. Jamie and Scott had always had an unusual relationship. There were so many things between them that ought to drive them apart, but they still fought to be together. He knew Derek was a big sticking point between them. Scott had seduced Derek on multiple occasions and Mike knew Derek held an important place in Scott's heart, and Jamie had been forced to sit back and let that happen because Tarragon society would have fallen apart if he hadn't. Mike had been there the first time Scott was assigned to seduce Derek. Ashton was behind that, because he probably knew Jamie wouldn't be able to handle it and such a thing would drive the two of them apart. But Mike had helped Jamie get through it and Jamie had forgiven Scott, to some extent at least. Scott had needed to sleep with Derek again to prevent him from falling into the Elder's trap, and later again, again to keep him from the Elder. Jamie hadn't been able to argue with any of it; he just had to sit back and watch his mate cheat. If Scott didn't care about Derek it probably wouldn't have hurt Jamie as much, but it was clear Scott genuinely cared for Derek.

Everyone had expected Jamie and Derek to fight over Scott at some point. The two Queens had always borderline hated each other because of their relationships with Scott. Both were in love with him, both wanted him, and even though Scott had clearly chosen Jamie, he had been forced into bed with Derek enough that both sides could claim victory. Mike had known this fight would eventually break out, but not with TK as the catalyst. He could see it, though: Derek wanted Scott and couldn't have him because Scott wasn't his mate, and if he thought that Jamie didn't appreciate being Scott's mate, he would lash out. He knew without question that Derek had started the fight. Jamie wouldn't risk a fight, for one, and also had no reason to attack Derek since nothing had happened between him and Scott. But if Derek had seen Jamie kissing TK, his jealousy would almost certainly flare to the surface and Jamie would have responded in kind, since the relationship between the two was so incredibly fragile. He wasn't sure what to do now, though. He couldn't have TK trying to form a new relationship with Jamie. It was dangerous not just to himself because of Ethan's warning, but also to Tarragon society. The Queens needed to be working together. They might not ever be friends, maybe, but they needed to cooperate.

"TK, I know you don't approve of a lot of the way Tarragon society is run," Mike said slowly. "I know you think Jamie is trapped. But he's not. He's our Queen. If he wanted to change something, he could. If he didn't want to be with Scott, he could change the rules so he wouldn't have to be. He's choosing to be with Scott because he loves him."

"Scott just hurts him," TK said, his eyes filling with tears. "Maybe he just can't imagine being with someone who doesn't hurt him. He just needs to be with me and he'll see what a real relationship could be like."

"And what about me?" Mike asked, stroking his cheek. He was

running out of ideas and needed to get this contained. "What about our relationship? You'll hurt me just to stop Jamie from being hurt? How is that fair?"

"You wouldn't be hurt if I left," TK said, again with a bitterness in his voice. "I don't mean anything to you."

"Yes, you do," Mike said firmly, tightening his grip on TK's shoulders. He should have been clearer about their relationship, he realized. He should have called TK his boyfriend, and been more expressive. He hadn't even realized TK wanted that. "You're my boyfriend, and I love you."

TK's eyes widened.

"You... love me?"

"Yes," Mike said, pulling him close for a kiss. TK allowed it for a moment, then pushed away, looking confused.

"You can't love me. You're on the council. You've probably slept with dozens of boys like me."

"No," Mike said. "I just joined the council. You're my first, and I don't want any others."

"I know I'm not your first," TK said with narrowed eyes, and Mike laughed.

"I don't mean my first boyfriend, or my first lover," he said. "I just mean my first real relationship since I joined the council that I wanted to continue long term. You're right, most council-members have flings with as many students as they can get into their beds. But I have you. I'm not interested in anyone else."

That was true, he realized. He wasn't interested in anything else and under the worry of disappointing Ethan was a gnawing sense of jealousy that TK still wanted Jamie and didn't want him. He had failed in seducing TK properly and it stung. TK should have been thinking of him and loving him, and he wasn't.

"I guess... I didn't think of that," TK said slowly. "You don't have anyone else. You really think of me as your boyfriend?"

"Yes, but I didn't want to pressure you with titles and you never seemed to care," Mike said. "If I had known, I would have asked you a long time ago."

"But you'll be my boyfriend now?"

"Yes."

TK seemed deep in thought, then nodded slowly. "All right. I'll be your boyfriend."

"That means you can't go chasing after Jamie," Mike warned. "You're loyal to me now."

"If you're right and Jamie's choosing to be with Scott, then I can let it go. But if he comes to me again, if he wants me again, I can't guarantee anything. I still love him."

Mike inwardly winced, but he could tell this was the best he was going to get.

"All right," he said, then slid his hand down TK's body suggestively. "Now that we're boyfriends…"

TK laughed and snuggled closer, leaning in to kiss him. If Mike could fully ensnare him, body and mind, then he wouldn't have to worry about TK running to Jamie again. He wasn't as good at seduction as the other council members. He had never needed to learn the skills the way they had. But he would keep TK hooked because if he didn't, he would face Ethan's punishment and he would do anything to avoid that.

CHAPTER TWENTY-SIX

Hidden Betrayal

Scott looked up at the knock on his door. Jamie had gone out earlier, wanting some time alone, and he had decided to stay here and lounge. He stretched and opened the door to see Derek looking upset. Derek pushed past him into the apartment without a word and Scott let him in, puzzled. He shut the door and turned to ask Derek what was wrong when the man hugged him tightly, suddenly. Scott hugged him back gently, wondering what was driving Derek.

"What's wrong?" he asked, stroking Derek's back as they embraced. He thought of the Elder and his eyes narrowed. "Has anyone hurt you?"

Derek and the Elder seemed to get along well but maybe it was just an act. They had always seemed to get along well, after all, and Derek had never complained to anyone, but it was obvious the Elder was trying to manipulate him. Maybe the Elder really was hurting him and had just persuaded him not to say anything. After the Elder had executed the killer at the trial months ago, Derek had pushed the Elder away and he had allowed it, but what if he had punished Derek for that public display of disobedience as soon as they were back together? Was Derek safe with that man?

"It's Jamie," Derek whispered, his voice hot against Scott's neck.

"Is Jamie safe?" Scott asked sharply, though really he should sense it if Jamie were in trouble. Marisol would say something, wouldn't she? But she was on her way here, he knew. Maybe she wouldn't notice something wrong with Jamie because she was flying.

"He did something," Derek said. "To you. Against you. He cheated on you."

"What do you mean?" Scott asked, puzzled.

Derek drew back far enough to meet his eyes. They were bright with tears.

"If you were my mate, I would love you with all of my heart," Derek said in a shaky voice. "I would never betray you."

"What happened?" Scott asked, worried now.

"Jamie kissed that other student, the one from Africa," Derek said, and Scott's heart clenched. TK. Scott had been so careful to keep Jamie away from him and in all fairness, Jamie didn't show any real interest in talking to the man. TK was with Mike now, at Ethan's request, he knew, so that was preventing TK from starting anything. Jamie had gone out to be alone, but what if he had gone out to meet up with TK? Jamie often went out alone, he realized. At least two or three times a week. What if he always went to meet up with TK? What if he and TK had been having an affair under his very nose?

"I would never do that to you," Derek said, and hugged Scott tight again. Scott's breathing was ragged as he absently patted Derek's back. Would Jamie do something like that? Trick Scott? Lie to him? Go behind his back to be with the person he had flirted with when Scott was trapped by the Elder? He remembered how betrayed he had felt when the Elder had released him and he finally came back to Jamie – only to discover that Jamie had been with someone else the entire time he had been a prisoner. It was a level of betrayal he had never expected. While their relationship had been far more stable ever since he had nearly lost his memories and that had seemed to reshape his priorities, they had never fully put everything behind them. He had forgiven Jamie, but was still on edge with TK here. The man was a threat to his relationship and the thought that Jamie had betrayed him again left him feeling sick to his stomach.

Scott clutched Derek to him as his mind whirled with the possibilities. He reached out to Narné and the dragon reassured him, but he could tell he was uncertain as well. Jamie was in the woods, Narné informed him. Alone. Marisol would be here soon and would go straight to him, then bring him back to campus. Derek shivered in his arms and Scott stroked his cheek.

"Derek, are you all right?" he asked, because he was the one who ought to be upset, not Derek, but Derek seemed deeply shaken by this.

"Why does he get everything?" Derek asked in a helpless voice. "He always gets whatever he wants, everything he wants, and he never has to do anything to earn it. He doesn't deserve any of this."

"He has never gotten anything without paying a high price," Scott said sharply. "Just because you don't see him suffering doesn't mean he doesn't."

"He gets you as his mate," Derek said, shutting his eyes as another tear escaped. "He gets to have the person he wants as his mate, and he spurns you. He wants someone else instead. Why should he deserve to keep you?"

"I love him," Scott said, and Derek shook his head.

"I know," he whispered. "That's what makes it worse. I've seen how important he is to you. When I rescued your memories, I saw you, Scott. I saw your soul. I know how large a role Jamie plays in everything you do. And he betrayed you. How could he? How is that fair?"

Scott sighed. He wanted to defend Jamie. After all, Jamie had paid a higher price for what he had than Derek could possibly imagine. But he couldn't defend Jamie, because Derek was right. Jamie had betrayed him. He let go of Derek and went to sit on the couch. Derek joined him and stroked his back.

"You don't have to pretend, Scott," he said softly. "I know you love him. I do. But he keeps hurting you. He doesn't deserve you."

"I'm not going to turn to you, no matter what you hope," Scott said, taking Derek's hand. "You have your own mate to worry about."

Derek hissed and looked away. "It isn't fair that Jamie gets you and I get him."

"No, it isn't fair," Scott said, bringing Derek's hand to his lips and kissing it. "He hasn't been hurting you, has he?"

"No, he's always treated me well," Derek said. "Are you worried?"

"I'm always worried. I don't trust him."

"I don't trust him in some things, but I do trust that he won't hurt me," Derek said. "He would get nothing out of that. But I don't want to think about him."

"There's nothing you can do to help me and Jamie," Scott said. "We have to work this out on our own. Again. We've never had a smooth relationship, Derek. Ever. But I love him, and he loves me. Even if he did kiss TK, even if he did more, I know he loves me."

"How can you say he loves you when he hurts you like this?"

"I hurt him first," Scott said, thinking of all the ways he had betrayed Jamie. The first blow to their relationship had come from Scott; no matter what Jamie did, it would always be in retaliation because Scott had sent the first fracture into their love. He still remembered finding out that the council was planning on assigning someone to Jamie because he was still a virgin and resisting attempts to seduce him. He had watched Jamie and fallen in love, and had sworn away his freedom for the right to be with Jamie. But because he was assigned to have sex with Jamie and not pursuing a relationship naturally, Jamie had been deeply betrayed. And later, when Derek showed up... Yes, it was always Scott who hurt Jamie first. Never the other way around. Scott had betrayed him time after time, and really, Jamie had only betrayed him once. Now twice. He could survive. As long as Jamie still wanted him, he could survive. He felt something slide down his cheek and realized in shock that it was a tear. What would he do if Jamie didn't want him? What if Jamie had finally decided that he couldn't forgive Scott, that he wanted someone else? There was no way he could recover from that.

Derek pulled him into an embrace and he relaxed into the other man's arms, clinging to the support he offered. He was usually the one comforting Derek, he realized as his grief and fear started to overcome him. Derek had never held him like this before. He shut his eyes and wondered if he would lose Jamie. If after everything they had been through, Jamie would choose someone else and abandon him. What would he do? He was still Jamie's mate and they were stuck together until the next mating flight. Would Jamie let someone else win the flight? TK's dragon might be big enough to participate. Probably not big enough to win but Narné had won against worse odds. Would Scott try? Would Narné chase Marisol and attempt to claim her again, or would he accept defeat and let someone else have his Queen? Why would Jamie abandon him like this?

There was another knock at the door and Scott pulled back from Derek abruptly, realizing how intimately he was holding the Queen and how open he was being with his emotions. Derek was in tears as well and they both wiped their eyes before standing and going to the door. Derek had obviously been crying and he wondered if people could tell he had been as well. Probably, but there was another knock at the door so he didn't want to wait. He opened it to see Ethan, to his surprise, and when Ethan noticed Derek next to him, his eyes turned hard.

"What is the Queen doing here?" he asked coldly. "You two shouldn't be alone together. Especially not right now."

"We weren't doing anything," Scott said, and Derek bristled.

"I told him what happened," Derek said. "He deserved to know."

"And I was about to tell him," Ethan said. "You shouldn't have come here, Derek."

"We didn't do anything, Ethan," Scott said, though he realized why the man was upset. If Jamie had just cheated on Scott, then he probably wanted to avoid Scott cheating on Jamie with his past lover. Even if he knew Scott and Derek wouldn't have sex because of Tarragon law which gave the Elder control over Derek's bed, they still might have done enough to anger both Jamie and the Elder. But they hadn't. They had just held each other and cried.

"I was comforting him," Derek said defensively. "Someone has to take care of him."

"It's not your place, Derek," Ethan said, but he said it gently. "Jamie and Scott need to work things out on their own, and you have your own relationships to consider. Why don't you go to your room. The Elder will be here in a minute or two and I don't want him catching you two together."

Derek and Scott exchanged a look. Derek clearly didn't want to go but Scott didn't want the Elder jumping to any conclusions, so he pushed Derek slightly. With a sigh, Derek headed down the hall to his room. Ethan studied Scott.

"So he told you what happened?"

"Jamie really kissed TK?"

Ethan nodded.

"Do you know anything else? Have they meeting up at other times, too? Have you seen them together?"

"This is the first time they've seen each other alone," Ethan said.

"You're sure about that?"

"Yes," Ethan said. "You know TK and Mike are seeing each other. Mike's been keeping an eye on the matter and this is the first time they've gotten near each other when no one else is around."

Something loosened in Scott's chest. Jamie hadn't been sneaking out and seeing TK behind his back. He hadn't realized Mike had been helping keep an eye on TK and wondered if the relationship between the two was genuine or if Ethan had ordered Mike to do it to prevent Jamie and TK from doing anything. Either seemed possible. Or maybe it was a blend. Mike had no problems seducing on command for the council, but they had been together for months now and it was unlikely Mike hadn't developed feelings for him. Mike wasn't heartless like the other councilmembers. He cared about the people he slept with. So he must care for TK, and that meant he must be feeling the same betrayal Scott was feeling right now. But this was the first time they had seen each other, he reminded himself. This was a one time betrayal. It wasn't much better.

"TK will not be an issue in the future," Ethan added. "I've spoken to Mike about it."

"Thank you," Scott said. He had never thought he would be grateful for the council's interference like this. He reached to Marisol and felt that she had arrived. "Marisol and Jamie just returned. I should greet them."

"If you need any help, Scott, the council would be happy to assist," Ethan said seriously. "We cannot have you and Jamie at odds, and we cannot have the Queens fighting. Not right now."

"I know," Scott said. Now that Marisol was here, after all, they needed to start planning how to get back to Portland. They couldn't afford to lose focus because of relationship problems.

"I'll talk to Jamie. I can handle this. As long as it was just this one time, it's fine. Keep TK away and it won't be an issue again. But I don't know how to get Derek and Jamie back on good terms."

"They were doing so well," Ethan said, shaking his head. "I thought we could avoid this. I know you've been helping keep them civil. Thank you for that."

"If I could talk to Derek, I might be able to help him, but it's probably best if I don't have contact with him right now, isn't it?"

"I don't want to alienate the Elder," Ethan said, agreeing with him. "The Queens will have to settle this on their own. I just hope it happens quickly."

He felt a pulse from Narné and Marisol and sighed, running a hand through his hair and leaving the room.

"Marisol just landed. We should greet her properly."

CHAPTER TWENTY-SEVEN

Fear or Desire

J amie stayed low to the ground as the sun started to lower on the horizon, circling the campus once before another dragon joined them in the air. It was the Elder dragon and Jamie eyed it warily. Marisol was larger than him, but just barely. He could sense her uneasiness to be near such an enormous dragon but he didn't threaten them in the air. He was escorting them to the field nearest the apartments where Jamie was staying. Marisol flew beside him as they finished circling campus and then landed. The Elder dragon landed at a safe distance. Narné was waiting and Jamie could tell he was displeased by the Elder dragon's move, but couldn't argue. Jamie looked around for Scott but didn't see him. Instead, the Elder was nearby and as Marisol settled lower, the Elder approached and offered to help him off just as he had when Jamie had come on Narné with a barely responsive Scott and all of the kittens. Like then, Jamie allowed the Elder to help him slide down because it was protocol.

"Welcome, Queen," the Elder said.

"Thank you," Jamie said politely, pulling away from his touch as soon as it was polite. He looked around. "Where is everyone?"

"Your mate is with my Queen," the Elder said, and Jamie's breath caught. Derek and Scott were together? Derek would have told Scott about TK; was Scott doing something with Derek to get revenge?

"No need to worry," the Elder said. "I keep my Queen under stricter control than your mate keeps you. They won't do anything together."

Jamie flushed, feeling humiliated. The Elder had seen him kiss TK, had seen his argument with Derek after. He must know that Derek and Scott had slept together in the past because it had happened while he was Derek's mate, which meant he had to have given permission. He wanted to break up Jamie and Scott's relationship and had given Derek permission just to get back at Jamie for killing Ashton. Why, then, was he reassuring Jamie now?

"This is a bad time for the Queens to be fighting," the Elder said, reaching out to lay his hand on Marisol's neck. The dragon pulled back quickly and the Elder's lips curved in amusement. "You have a lovely Queen," he added. Marisol cocked her head to study him. "Larger than any I've ever seen. She's young, too. She'll get larger over time."

"You already have a Queen," Jamie said sharply. "You won't be in my mating flight."

"I am quite satisfied with the Queen I have," the Elder said, to his relief. "I'm not interested in being your mate. At the moment."

Jamie tensed at the words, but the Elder grinned at him. "Who knows what the future will bring? You may want me in your mating flight someday."

"That will never happen," Jamie said icily. "Narné is the only dragon who will ever mate with Marisol."

"So you still want Scott as your mate? You kissed someone else," the Elder said, and Jamie felt heat flood over his cheeks. Why had he kissed TK, especially out in the open like that? Why had all of them been close enough to see it? Why hadn't he looked around before kissing him?

"Scott is the only mate I'll ever want," Jamie said firmly. "That will never change."

"You shouldn't toy with a mate's affections," the Elder said. "Queens are rarely monogamous, but their mates have the right to choose their partners for a reason. They are allowed to prevent threats to their power. Derek, for instance, is allowed to do whatever he wants with almost anyone on campus, provided he informs me first. But there are a few people he is not allowed to be intimate with. Scott is one of them."

"That hasn't always been true," Jamie said bitterly, thinking of how the Elder must have allowed Derek to seduce Scott.

"No, it hasn't," the Elder said. "At that point, it was in my interests to disrupt your relationship. But right now, it's in my interests to support you, and so he will not do anything with Scott."

"What changed?" Jamie asked, narrowing his eyes. Was the Elder doing him a favor? He didn't want to be in the Elder's debt.

"Despite what you may think about me, I put Tarragon society first," the Elder said. "If interfering with you gives Derek more power without harming you, I'll do it. But right now you're on the run from a dangerous threat and if you don't stay strong and focused, you could easily be overthrown. Margot is working to get rid of you permanently. And you're the only thing holding the worldwide Tarragon society together."

"What makes you say that?" Jamie asked, puzzled now. Everything he was saying was true, Jamie knew. It was why he spent so much time with Ethan coordinating with Gerard in Portland. Gerard needed to know what to say to the different nations whose allegiance was now to Jamie, because without Jamie there, there was a chance they would stop respecting Tarragon Academy and that would be deadly. Those of the Tarragon tribe only survived if they bonded with a dragon, and that could only happen at Tarragon Academy or on this new campus in Spokane. If the other nations stopped sending their children to the academy, they would die. But normally after a student graduated, they returned to their home nation and worked to support the academy even after graduation. The council was responsible for all sorts of secret projects. Jamie had discovered most of their endeavors but was still occasionally surprised by how much influence they had over world affairs. If their graduates lost their allegiance, then the entire Tarragon world would lose its power and Jamie would never let that happen. He didn't approve of a lot of what the council did behind the scenes but he respected its value.

"The entire Tarragon world lived in fear of Ashton," the Elder said. "Before that, they lived in fear of me. There must always be a single figure that they worship or everything will fall apart. If anyone else had killed Ashton, our society would not have survived because even though you're a Queen, no one would care about you. They have to know someone before they follow them."

"So why do they follow me, then?" Jamie asked. The Elder grinned.

"My dragon is unfortunately not connected to the other dragons so I missed out on it, but the invitation you sent to the other dragons on your first mating flight apparently made quite the impression."

Jamie ducked his head and looked away, humiliated again at the thought of the image he had sent out to the other dragons begging them to chase him and catch him. He had adapted to the idea that everyone he met had seen him like that and it had been a while since anyone had cornered him and tried to take advantage of him based on that image, but every once in a while something would happen to remind him that every single dragon and their partner, male and female, had seen him desperately needy and begging for release. The Elder chuckled.

"Every dragon knows you," he continued. "Every human knows you. It helps that you can speak to every dragon, and that

Marisol can speak to every human. But it's your mating flight that established you as the center of the Tarragon world. Ashton knew that; as soon as it happened, I'm sure he started acting against you. Fear is a powerful weapon, but desire is sometimes stronger. The world feared him, and they fear me, but they desire you. Both things require upkeep, though," he added. "If you vanish, no one will desire you anymore and Margot will attempt to take over completely. She'll fail. No one fears her, or even cares about her outside of the academy. You are the only one who can hold our society together. And so I will do my part in reestablishing your grip in Portland. Your dragon is here now; do you have plans for returning yet?"

"Not yet," Jamie admitted slowly. "I need the council's support. Well, enough of them that I can act. They may desire me, but they're not willing to risk losing their memories for me. If I were there, I could get them to do what I wanted. They would obey me in person. But I'm not there, and I can't go back until I'm sure I have their support."

"A dangerous situation," the Elder said. "Is there anything I can do to help?"

Jamie studied him. He seemed sincere. And he was bound to uphold Tarragon law and that meant protecting the first Queen, so he might actually be genuine in this offer of help. But there was very little he could do. He had said that the Tarragon world could be ruled by fear or desire and while Jamie controlled their desire – which he had to admit that he did – it wouldn't take much for the Elder to take charge and reinstate the kind of fear that Ashton had inspired. After all, the Elder had been Ashton's teacher. It would be easy for him. Even if there were something the Elder could do to help, he would be hesitant to ask because it might give the man more power. Jamie needed to stay in control. He was starting to slip in Portland because he wasn't there in person. He would not slip here.

"Queen," a voice said, and they turned to see Ethan approaching with Scott behind him. The Elder politely backed away and Scott cautiously embraced him. Jamie kissed his cheek and Scott relaxed slightly.

"Marisol is well?" Ethan inquired, and Marisol batted her eyes at him and tilted her head to invite him to stroke her. She would never ask for affection from the Elder but she was probably starved for attention and would demand quite a lot of it before she settled down. Ethan obediently rubbed her eye ridges and Jamie took Scott's hand. The Elder bowed to him.

"My Queen," he said, then headed in the direction of his apartment where Derek was probably waiting. Would he be angry at Derek over what had happened with TK? It was obvious Derek still loved Scott, after all. The Elder had warned against toying with a mate's affection; would he view Derek's actions as toying with him? He shivered and hoped not. He was still angry at Derek for what he had said, but he didn't want him hurt.

"Maybe we can talk in private," Scott suggested, and Jamie nodded.

"Marisol would love more attention," he said to Ethan. "But you can ignore her. She'll probably just fly around looking for people to pet her for a while. Is there any danger in that?"

"I'll have my dragon stay with her," Ethan said. "Narné can keep an eye on her as well. We'll make sure she gets attention while remaining safe."

"Thank you," Jamie said, and smiled cautiously to Scott. "Do you want to talk in our room?"

"I think we need to," he said, without a smile. Jamie nodded slowly and took a last look at Marisol preening as Ethan stroked her. She was finally here, and she was safe. He needed to be focused on reclaiming his position in Portland as the Elder had recommended but first, he needed to figure out his relationship with Scott. He loved Scott and didn't want anyone else, not really, but he had been drawn to kiss TK. Somehow, even with everything he had with Scott, he felt like he needed something else and that worried him. Scott ought to be everything. He shouldn't need anything else. But he did, and he didn't know why.

CHAPTER TWENTY-EIGHT

Cursed Ability

Derek twisted his hands together nervously as he sat at the kitchen table. He heard the door open and the familiar sound of the Elder coming in. He waited and soon the Elder appeared in the doorway, looking at him emotionlessly. He wasn't sure what to say. Was the Elder angry at him? The Elder knew he loved Scott; he had essentially confessed his feelings for Scott right after his mating flight. He allowed the Elder to dominate and teach him in bed because he wanted to dominate Scott, and the Elder had even given him permission to have sex with Scott before. Not this time, though. When Jamie and Scott had shown up unexpectedly at the beginning of the summer, the Elder had forbidden him from doing anything intimate with Scott. Had he broken that promise now? Was the Elder going to punish him because he couldn't hide his feelings for Scott?

"Why did you go to Scott instead of waiting for me?" the Elder asked softly, still standing in the doorway looking down at him. Derek gulped. It had been a mistake going straight to Scott. He saw that now. But they hadn't done anything.

"He needed to know," Derek said. "I wanted him to hear it from me."

"Did anything happen?"

"We hugged," Derek said cautiously, unsure whether or not that crossed any lines. "And we cried a little. I was probably as upset as he was."

"Why were you so upset?" the Elder asked, coming to sit next to him at the table. He took Derek's hand and stroked it. "Queens are allowed to be with other people. Why did it bother you so much to see Jamie with someone else?"

Derek looked away, remembering the rage that had swept over him, and the sense of injustice.

"When I saved Scott's memories, I saw his mind," Derek said slowly. "His soul. I saw how much he loved me. And he does love me. But now I knew there's no point trying anything with him, because I also saw how much he loves Jamie. His whole soul is built upon Jamie. Everything he does is for his mate. I hadn't realized that."

The Elder nodded, still stroking his hand, and Derek sighed.

"Scott lives for Jamie, and Jamie can't even stay true to him. I know that Jamie is angry and jealous about what I've done with Scott, but how can he act like that when he does the same with that student? Scott deserves someone who loves him the way he loves Jamie."

"You're still very much in love with him," the Elder observed, and Derek blushed. "And you haven't seen Jamie's mind. I suspect Jamie does love him the same way. But just as Scott can stray, so can Jamie."

"He betrayed Scott," Derek said in a low voice.

"No, he didn't," the Elder said, to his surprise. "If Scott really didn't want Jamie near that student, he would have forbidden it or at least restricted what they could do together. I'm always clear with you what you are and aren't allowed to do."

"Scott might not know to be that specific," Derek said. "You know how to be a Queen's mate. He doesn't."

"From what I understand, he's been taking lessons for two years," the Elder pointed out. "Learning to handle his Queen's bed would have been one of the first things they taught him."

Derek scowled. It was probably true. And he really doubted Jamie had actually slept with TK. They had just kissed. If even Derek had heard rumors about a relationship between them, then Scott certainly knew it was a risk. He would have done something to stop Jamie if he really cared. Maybe he didn't mind. But no, he had looked devastated when Derek had told him. Maybe he knew Jamie and TK were friendly but hadn't realized exactly how friendly and so hadn't thought to limit their relationship? He hadn't been shocked exactly, Derek didn't think, but he had been betrayed. He had to have known something, but hadn't expected Jamie would dare do something like that.

"Maybe Scott didn't think to limit it because he trusted Jamie," Derek said. "He loves Jamie, and he thought Jamie loved him, so maybe he didn't think there was a need to be clear."

"Perhaps," the Elder said. "That is possible. There are reasons why he wouldn't have forbidden Jamie even if he knew there was a threat. But Jamie didn't betray him, because he never forbid it."

"Jamie kissed another man," Derek said. "That's betrayal."

"How many men have you kissed?" the Elder asked, amused. "I would never be betrayed if you kissed someone unless it was one of the few people I've forbidden."

"You're different," Derek said. "I'm different. Jamie and Scott have always been true to each other. Everyone always talks about how devoted to each other they are, how they'll do anything for each other."

"And yet Scott slept with you," the Elder said, and Derek ducked his head. "Relationships are complex, especially for a Queen and his mate. You can't judge either of them for their actions, and you shouldn't try to interfere in something that should be strictly between them."

Derek stared at the table, at the Elder's hand stroking his.

These relationships were complex, he had to admit. In some ways he hated the Elder, his mate. The Elder had stolen his mating flight from Chris and then tried to get him killed and exiled him before he could even say goodbye. The Elder was a killer, and was just biding his time until he killed again. There were so many reasons to distrust and hate the Elder. And yet there was another side to the Elder that had been coming out more and more. He was forceful and domineering in the bedroom, but never hurt Derek. He never tried to push beyond Derek's limits even though it was within his rights to do so and even though Derek could tell he sometimes wanted it. He was always polite, and kind, and Derek had grown to enjoy spending time with him. Their relationship had moved from tolerance to friendship and that made everything a little easier. But it was undeniably complex.

Derek had assumed the relationship between Scott and Jamie was fairly simple. Scott was allowed to do what he wanted and love who he wanted, but his first love was always Jamie. And Jamie was true to him no matter what. That clearly wasn't the case, though. Jamie had other loves just as Scott did, or at least other flirtations. And if his flirting never went beyond a kiss, was it really a problem? He was intensely jealous of the fact that Jamie got to be with Scott and held his love, but maybe he shouldn't judge him so harshly. Maybe, as the Elder said, Jamie did love Scott. Maybe it was just an accident, or a mild crush, or something completely harmless. But he couldn't forget the look of betrayal on Scott's face. Innocent or not, Jamie's actions had hurt Scott and that couldn't be forgiven.

"Why are you defending Jamie, anyway?" Derek asked, unable to meet the Elder's eyes.

"Our society is weaker with our Queens fighting," the Elder said.

"So why aren't you taking my side in this? Why are you taking his side?"

"I'm not taking sides," the Elder said, sounding almost amused. "I'm simply explaining a possible explanation for what occurred that will help each of you understand the other. I want a good relationship between the two of you."

"Why? You hate him," Derek pointed out. The Elder had told him that when Derek had shared his feelings for Scott after the mating flight.

"He has something I need," the Elder said, and Derek huffed jealously.

"What could he possibly have that I don't?"

The Elder laughed and reached out to stroke Derek's cheek in a soothing gesture.

"I suppose it's not exactly him," the Elder said. "He has friends who have something I need, and the only way I can get to them is through him."

"What do you need?" Derek asked, puzzled. "What don't you have here?"

He might have assumed the Elder was talking about something related to killing dragons, but no one connected to Jamie would be involved in that. So what was he talking about?

The Elder was silent for several moments, looking towards the window. Then he sighed and smiled at Derek.

"You are my mate," he said. "My Queen. You trust me, as much as is reasonable. Can I trust you not to share what I tell you?"

"Of course," Derek said. "I don't share anything private between us."

"You have," the Elder said, and Derek was startled. Had he? Yes, he had, he realized. The Elder had told him that he wanted revenge on Jamie, and Derek had shared that information with Jamie. And later, when the dragon had been killed, Derek had shared intimate details of their relationship in order to reclaim his authority with Ethan and the rest of the council. He had shared some of the Elder's secrets, but he could also keep them quiet if necessary.

"As long as it doesn't hurt any people or dragons, I won't tell anyone," Derek promised.

"It doesn't," the Elder reassured him. "Though that is a good way to start. You know why dragons eat other living dragons, don't you?"

Derek shivered. "It revitalizes them and gives the dragon and their partner youth."

"Yes," the Elder said. "That's how Ashton was able to live for so long. But if he stopped, what would have happened to him?"

"Well, I guess he would grow old," Derek said, puzzled. "Right?"

"And after that?"

Derek drew a blank. "Um, I guess he'd die at some point. Is that what you mean?"

"Indeed," the Elder said seriously. "He would grow old and die. When our society started changing and eating dragons was no longer acceptable, I went into Mount Tarragon and left our world in Ashton's hands. I stopped killing and eating dragons at that point. Why didn't I die of old age in the centuries that followed?"

Derek blinked, having never considered that before. "You didn't go outside sometimes?" he asked, though he knew the Elder hadn't. Everyone had assumed the Elder was dead. He had passed into myth, into legend. No one had any clue he still existed until he showed up after Ashton's death and starting killing.

"My body aged," the Elder said in a distant voice. "Starvation and thirst wracked me. There was nothing in the mountain. My dragon suffered the same. And yet we didn't die. Do you know why?"

"No," Derek said, genuinely flummoxed. There was no possible way it could happen, but now that he thought about it, that must have happened. The Elder had been trapped in a mountain well over a hundred years with no food or drink. There was no way he could have survived even if old age hadn't been a factor. He shouldn't have even lasted a month.

"We all have gifts," the Elder said, stroking Derek's hand again. "Yours is traveling through the mist. An extremely useful gift. Mine is more a curse than a gift. You see, my dragon and I can't die."

Derek narrowed his eyes. "What do you mean, you can't die?"

"When society turned on me, they tried to kill me. They beheaded me, tore out my dragon's throat, and left us to the mountain. They thought we were dead. But we healed, and went into hiding. I've tried killing myself over the decades, but it never works. We're immune to death. But we age. We hunger. We need the flesh of living dragons to exist in bodies that aren't wracked by pain."

Derek shivered. He had never considered that the Elder had a real reason for killing dragons the way that he did. He had wondered why the Elder couldn't just stop killing now that he had a position of authority. It should have been easy enough. But if his body kept living no matter what, and only killing dragons gave him a body he could comfortably live in, then it really was inevitable that he would kill again. Would Derek allow it, knowing that was the reason? Maybe this was exactly what the council and his teachers had warned him about, he realized with a start. The Elder was spinning a tale to make him consider allowing the man to kill a dragon without consequences. He would not let that happen. No dragons would ever be killed again. No matter what.

"That is what Jamie's friends offer," the Elder said, and Derek tilted his head.

"You think you can kill them instead? I still won't allow that."

"No," the Elder said with a chuckle. "They offer a way for me to have a body that doesn't age. If I didn't have to constantly renew my body with dragon flesh, I would have no reason to kill dragons. Wouldn't you prefer that?"

"Of course," Derek said, puzzled. "But if there's something that would stop you from killing again, why don't you just ask Jamie? Wouldn't he give you anything if it meant you wouldn't kill again?"

"He doesn't trust me," the Elder said. "For good reason, I suppose. I wanted revenge on him and I've worked against him for too long for him to ever fully trust me. I need to find a way to manipulate him into helping me. If I help him against Margot, perhaps he'll return the favor. It's risky, but it might be the only way I can get what I need."

"You really want that?" Derek asked. "You really want to stop killing? You killed that criminal easily enough."

He shuddered at the thought of the Elder easily decapitating the body of the man who had tried to frame the Elder for the murder of a dragon. He didn't like to think of it but couldn't forget it even now.

"I have come to enjoy killing," the Elder said, and Derek shivered. "But only when it serves a purpose. That man violated Tarragon law and tried to blame me. He deserved death. If someone threatens or harms you, they probably deserve death. Tarragon law is harsh and I have lived by Tarragon law all of my life. It has softened in the last couple of centuries, but not much."

"So if you didn't have to kill dragons for youth, you wouldn't?" Derek asked. "But you might kill other people and their dragons?"

"I promised to uphold Tarragon law, and I will," the Elder said.

"Either I get help from Jamie's friends, or eventually I will have no choice but to kill another dragon."

Derek considered. He sounded absolutely sincere. It was true that Tarragon traditions were steeped in blood. Ashton had been ruthless and while Jamie seemed to be trying to pull back some of that, there was only so much he could do. The main crime that could never be forgiven was killing and eating a live dragon. As long as the Elder didn't do that, it was perfectly possible that he could continue killing people and be completely legal about it. Derek didn't like to think that his mate enjoyed killing, but if he were killing in defense of their laws and traditions, perhaps it wasn't as evil as it sounded. He would need to think about this more, in private, because his mind was whirling with new information right now.

"Do you want my help?" he asked. "I could talk to Jamie."

"The main thing you can do to help is to get back on good terms with Jamie," the Elder said, stroking his cheek again. "Don't ever bring any of this up. I'll figure it out on my own."

"All right," Derek said. The Elder's lips twitched into a smile.

"So you hugged Scott? That's right at the edge of what you're allowed. I might have to punish you."

Derek's heart skipped a beat. Punishment could be bad, but he had learned it could also be very good. And the Elder's smile indicated the latter. He cautiously matched the smile and the Elder pulled him into an embrace before kissing him soundly. As the Elder led him towards the bedroom and he trembled in anticipation, he had to push back the thoughts flooding through his mind. Right now, he just needed to worry about pleasing the Elder. There would be time to think about everything else later.

CHAPTER TWENTY-NINE

Possession

Scott glanced at Jamie's profile as they entered their apartment. He seemed deep in thought. Had he betrayed him? It was hard to imagine Jamie kissing someone else but he had. Why? It had only happened once, but it shouldn't have happened at all. He should have forbidden them from seeing each other the moment they got here. But Jamie hadn't even seemed to remember TK was here when they first arrived, and then Scott hadn't wanted to seem too jealous and alienate Jamie. He had trusted Jamie and Jamie had betrayed that trust.

Jamie shut the door and sat on the couch, and Scott sat next to him, unsure how to start. Should he start? Or should he let Jamie talk, since Jamie was the one who needed to apologize? There was a long moment of silence, then Jamie sighed and looked away.

"I'm sure you know what happened," Jamie said in a small voice.

"I'd rather hear it from you," Scott said, and Jamie shrugged uncomfortably, still looking away.

"I ran into TK and we started talking. He's just... I like being around him. I wasn't thinking. I just kissed him. I know I shouldn't have."

"Why did you do it?" Scott asked. Somehow it almost felt worse that it wasn't planned, that Jamie had done it on accident.

He was so attracted to TK that a kiss was a perfectly normal part of a conversation?

"I don't know," Jamie said, and to Scott's surprise, he saw tears in his eyes. Jamie looked over at him then, those green eyes filling up. Scott squeezed his hand.

"We've never really talked about this," Scott said slowly. "We sometimes skirt around the issue, but me and Derek, you and TK... we've never really addressed it."

Jamie sniffled. "I love you, Scott. Nothing will ever change that. I love you more than anything."

"And I love you," Scott said without hesitation. "But we seem to keep hurting each other. Ever since I nearly lost my memories, I haven't been drawn to Derek the same way. I don't think that will ever be an issue again, and I can't think of any circumstances where I would have to betray you as I have in the past. I'm sorry for everything I've done, Jamie," he added, because he realized he had never really apologized. "I know I've hurt you. Betrayed you. You've never complained but I know it's hurt. I don't ever want to hurt you again."

"When you were with Derek, I didn't understand," Jamie said slowly. "I couldn't imagine how you could love me and have feelings for someone else. When I met TK, I realized how it was possible. I care about him. I don't love him, but he makes me feel good and sometimes I need that."

"I don't make you feel good?" Scott asked, the words cutting through him.

"You do," Jamie said quickly. "You know you do. It's just... different with him. I'm sure it was different with Derek. But I don't love him. He's fun to be around. I don't know why I kissed him. It was a mistake. I know he has feelings for me and I led him on, because he's never going to be in my heart. My heart is devoted to you, Scott."

Scott took a shaky breath. That was some reassurance. But he didn't like to think of Jamie turning to someone else. It made him feel inadequate, as if his affection and love weren't enough. Jamie must have felt the same about Derek, he realized. Jamie and Derek had seemed to have put their differences behind them and Jamie didn't even seem to mind when Scott and Derek spent time together here. He was usually there for it, but Scott and Derek had been alone several times and Jamie didn't even seem to notice anymore. He had accepted Derek's relationship with Scott. Could Scott do the same for TK?

"It's dangerous to let him think something might happen between you," Scott said. "But I know you want to have friends. I want you to have friends. Just not romantic friends."

"I know," Jamie said, looking away again. "It was so nice to talk to him. He makes me laugh. If I could be friends with him, it would be great. But there's more between us, or there was."

Scott clenched his hands into fists. TK made him laugh? It had been a long time since he had heard Jamie's carefree laugh, he realized. Jamie had been so tense lately. Was that why Jamie had kissed him? TK had helped Jamie break free from his stress for a moment and Jamie had kissed him in thanks? And now Scott was pouring even more stress on him. Would Scott always be associated with tension in Jamie's mind? He wanted to be able to joke and laugh with Jamie. Once, that hadn't been a problem. And there had been times over the past summer when they had genuinely been carefree and light-hearted. They couldn't ignore the fact that they were in danger, though, not just from the Elder but from Margot, and it was always looming over them. Scott was the one in danger, specifically. Jamie could probably return on his own, since Margot wouldn't harm the Queen. If he took another mate, Margot probably wouldn't do anything against him at all. It was Scott she wanted to kill.

"I don't think I should see him again," Jamie continued thoughtfully. "He's fun, but I don't want to hurt you and I did."

"If you think you could be friends with him and nothing more," Scott started, not wanting to order Jamie to cut off a friendship, but Jamie shook his head.

"I don't know if that's possible," he said. "In time, maybe. But look how long it's taken for things to work out between you and Derek. I don't want to do that to you."

Scott's heart stung. He had hurt Jamie and instead of being angry, Jamie wanted to protect him from the same kind of hurt. He tentatively pulled Jamie into a hug.

"It's your choice, Jamie," he said. "I'm not going to restrict who you see. I trust you."

Jamie winced. "You shouldn't have," he whispered. "I betrayed you."

"It wasn't intentional."

"But I still did it."

"And I forgive you," Scott said, and to his surprise, he realized that he did. It was an accidental kiss and it didn't mean anything. Jamie was still his. He just had other emotions. Scott couldn't blame him for it. He understood the impulse to seek out other relationships even while being devoted to Jamie. They needed other people in their lives. And if Jamie were willing to cut off ties with TK, he wouldn't have to worry about anything.

"Thank you," Jamie whispered, clinging tightly to him. "We always seem to be fighting."

"Then let's change that," Scott said. "A few fights aren't bad, but let's promise to be more open in the future. It seems we're hurt the most when we do things without telling each other."

"I'll tell you everything," Jamie promised, his breath wisping across Scott's neck. He shifted so that he could kiss Jamie, and his boyfriend immediately locked lips with him passionately. He felt fire begin to build in his body and caressed Jamie through his clothes, wanting to feel his soft skin instead of the rough denim surrounding his ass. He stood up and led Jamie to the bedroom.

Jamie pulled at his shirt and he took it off, then slid Jamie's long-sleeved shirt over his head and kissed his neck, working his tongue across the skin hard enough to leave a mark. He rarely did that to Jamie but right now he wanted to mark him. He wanted everyone to know that Jamie belonged to him, and Jamie leaned into his tongue and encouraged him. Then Jamie finished undressing and went to the bed.

"I want you to claim me," he said in a husky voice. Scott's mouth went dry and he stumbled out of his shoes and pants, then lunged at Jamie and pushed him back into the mattress. Jamie laughed and it was a happy laugh, without any worries. So Scott could still give him this kind of freedom. Good. He would have to keep it up, because he wanted to completely erase those worry lines that often crinkled the corners of Jamie's eyes.

Jamie wrapped his arms around Scott and crooked his leg suggestively. Scott grinned and kissed him, letting his hand slide down to his ass. Jamie moaned under him and he let his fingers circle his opening. Normally they spend more time on foreplay but he could tell Jamie was more than ready and so was he. They both wanted this and while he probably should wait, he didn't want to. He positioned himself at Jamie's opening and stroked Jamie's hair back from his forehead, planting a kiss there.

"You're mine," he said, letting his jealousy and possessiveness rise to the surface as he entered Jamie and claimed him. Jamie *was* his, after all. His mate, his boyfriend, his love. Nothing would ever change that. No little kiss could affect the deep love between them. They were together, always, and as he plunged into Jamie's willing body, he felt the connection between their minds spark to life. It wasn't as good as it would be with their mating flight and he looked forward to that eagerly, but this was more than enough as he felt Jamie's pleasure echoing through him. Sometimes they kept parts of their minds closed off during sex. He rarely pushed for the reasons. He suspected Jamie was worried about things and didn't want him to worry, either, because that was usually why Scott did it. Right now, though, they were totally open with each other and he saw how absolutely unimportant TK was in Jamie's mind. There was only a whisper of him, and it was fading fast as Scott began thrusting into him.

In minutes, everything faded but the rhythm between them as Jamie gasped and moaned under him, writhing in time with his pulsing hips. Every thrust was echoed between them as Scott felt both his and Jamie's pleasure, the doubled sensations keeping him going even when he felt he was ready to explode. He wanted to feel this, needed to feel this, and they kept going forever, it seemed, until he could tell Jamie couldn't take any more. Jamie cried out as he came, and Scott thrust one more time, deep inside him, and his pleasure exploded into a million points as he cried out as well. They stayed locked together for a long time, their shared pleasure ringing through them, until finally, Scott pulled out and the connection between them fell apart. He collapsed next to Jamie and looked over at him.

Jamie laughed and stroked Scott's sweaty forehead.

"Maybe we should fight, if that's the result."

"I'm sure we can manage that on our own," Scott said with a grin. "We'll just have to try again later, won't we?"

Jamie agreed with a smile and nuzzled against him. Scott cradled him and felt deeply reassured by the feel of him in his arms. Things had never been perfect between him and Jamie, but from now on, he would never doubt his boyfriend again.

CHAPTER THIRTY

Hasty Departure

A light rain fell on the campus and Chris sighed. Normally August was fairly sunny in Portland. One of the few months when rain was a scarcity. But the past week had been filled with the kind of soft misting that he associated with fall and he wasn't ready for that yet. The Germans were pressing to see Jamie but he was managing, though he wondered how long that would last. He had just heard from another council member that Saudi Arabia was considering holding back their students from attending unless they offered proof that the Queen was safe. A dangerous precedent, and one Gerard had given him permission to tell Margot, so he had slipped over to the women's campus to let her know.

The path was muddy and he stepped carefully, since the path wasn't paved and the gravel often slid unexpectedly into puddles. It wasn't quite raining hard enough to justify an umbrella but he would likely be soaked by the time he arrived. It was getting dark and perhaps he should have waited for the morning, he considered. Margot might even be back in her apartment by now, though he knew she tended to work long hours at her office. He had come here before at this time during the summer, when the Germans had made an ultimatum about hearing from Jamie. They had backed down with Chris's reassurances, but Margot had helped him figure out what to say. This new information was just as important and risked just as much, so he knew she would want to hear right away.

As he walked, his mind went to Spokane, as it often did. It wouldn't be raining there, he knew. They had more traditional seasons there, with sunny days the entire summer. He hadn't been in Spokane long, but he had enjoyed it there. It was a little city and the mountains where the campus was were crisp and fresh. To be honest, much of why he had enjoyed it had been Derek. While he liked being a part of the campus's development, he hadn't been the Queen's mate and didn't have the kind of control and authority he should have had in assisting with executive decisions about the campus. Derek listened to him, of course, and always sought his advice, but he should have been the one in charge. And then, when the time finally came to claim his place as Derek's mate...

He clenched his hands into fists. The Elder had come and ruined everything. Well, the Elder had really been ruining everything for months before that, terrorizing the campus and killing young dragons. Much of Chris's time in Spokane had been dealing with that disaster, but he still enjoyed the place. Now he was banished, exiled, because he had lost his temper during the mating flight. Had been manipulated into losing his temper. He grit his teeth. It still hurt to think about. Next time would be different, he knew. The Elder would be arrogant and probably assume the flight would be easy since he was already Derek's mate. He wouldn't be expecting Chris to show up, and Chris would win. He would seduce Jettie and Derek far better than the Elder ever could. After all, Derek loved him. Derek would be susceptible to his seductions. He would succeed, and then he would take his rightful place as Derek's mate and the leader of Spokane. He sighed. He kept telling himself that this would happen, but there were so many obstacles. Still, Gerard and Margot believed in him and doubt would kill all of his chances, so he would hold firm to his vision of success and let the rest work itself out.

He approached the main campus where her office was and

looked around in surprise. Yasmina was nearby, though she normally preferred to spend her time away from campus. No one was really comfortable around her so she avoided the students as much as possible. Why was she here now? He couldn't see any way to avoid her if he wanted to talk to Margot, so he took a deep breath and came closer. As he did, the door opened and Margot strode out, anger written across her face. She noticed him immediately and he flinched at the rage in her eyes.

"I suppose you just found out and are here to tell me," she said as she came to face him aggressively.

"I didn't know you'd be upset about it," he said, and she hissed. He flinched. "It's just Saudi Arabia," he added almost desperately. "No other nations are following."

She paused. "Saudi Arabia?"

He nodded, and she looked at Yasmina, then at him again. "What about Saudi Arabia?"

"They might prevent their students from coming here unless we prove Jamie is safe," he said cautiously. Her eyes widened.

"How dare they," she said, but without the anger of before. "I'll deal with it when I return," she said, flicking her wrist dismissively. "They'll listen then."

"Return? Where are you going?"

Margot stared at him, that anger returning. He didn't know why she was leaving but she was angry about it. Had something happened nearby? No dragons had been killed, and none had even been injured, he could tell. Were her students in danger? What else would enrage her and make her leave? Maybe a nearby community was resisting the same way Saudi Arabia was. Maybe one of the women on the council was having similar issues and Margot was leaving to deal with it.

"I'll be back shortly," she said. "I trust Gerard doesn't need to hear about this."

"I understand," Chris said slowly.

"Good. Return to your campus and stay in your rooms until I return. Things will be different then."

"All right," he said, knowing better than to ask any questions. She turned to Yasmina and he hastily retreated and returned to his campus. As he entered the grounds, he saw Gerard talking to a councilmember. Margot had specifically warned him not to tell Gerard about her leaving. Did that mean she was going behind his back? If so, he had a responsibility to tell the man. After all, Gerard was his head of council, not Margot. She was threatening, but he actually had power over his position. He approached and the other councilmember eyed him dismissively, then returned to his conversation with Gerard. He was one of the few council-members who ranked higher than Chris and he knew he wasn't supposed to interrupt. But if Margot was leaving right now, this was pressing. What if Gerard needed to stop her? He took a few steps closer and cleared his throat. They both looked at him in surprise.

"Excuse me," Chris said cautiously. "I need to speak to Gerard. Immediately."

"Remember your place," the other councilmember said sharply, and Chris managed not to flinch. He would pay for this later, but he suspected it was important he tell Gerard about this while the man had time to stop whatever it was.

"Let me talk to him," Gerard said, staring at him curiously. "I'm sure it's important."

Chris gulped. If this wasn't important, both of them were going to punish him. The other councilmember sniffed and headed inside. The gentle rain wasn't quite enough to justify going under cover and they were so used to it here in Portland neither he nor Gerard headed for shelter. Gerard gestured for him to speak.

"I just saw Margot," he said, and Gerard's eyes narrowed. "She's

225

leaving. I don't know where she's going, but she was furious. She told me not to tell you, so I thought you should know."

"Did she say anything?" Gerard pressed. "Anything at all?"

"Just that she'll be back soon, and things will be different when she returns."

Gerard grabbed his arm and started heading towards the center of upper campus. He looked almost frightened.

"Can you tell where her dragon is heading?" he asked. "See if your dragon can tell, without letting her know."

Chris reached out to his dragon, who was paying attention to everything curiously. All dragons had a vague sense of each other, though they really only paid attention to their Queens. He felt Yaris reach out, then heard the answer and puzzled over it.

"She's heading towards Spokane," he said, and Gerard clenched his jaw and pulled Chris faster.

"Have your dragon come to the knoll," he said. "Now. No delays."

Chris obeyed, his heart racing. Somehow, going to Spokane was a threat. Was Derek in danger? Had the Elder done something and Margot was going to rescue him? Why was his dragon necessary, though?

"What's going on?" he asked, trying to stay calm even while the thought of Derek in danger flooded his body with cortisol.

"Jamie's in Spokane," Gerard said in a tight voice. "Marisol just arrived there today. Margot must have been tracking her. How dare she. We need to get there and protect Jamie."

"Protect him from what?" Chris asked. Derek wasn't in danger, which reassured him greatly, but somehow Jamie was? Was the Elder attacking him? Why was Jamie even in Spokane knowing the danger that the Elder posed?

"From her," Gerard said angrily. They reached the knoll. Yaris was a few minutes away. "The reason Jamie and Scott left was because Margot attacked them. She tried to erase Scott's memories. That's why they can't come back. Because she's here."

Chris stared at him in shock. Margot had attacked them? She was the reason they couldn't return? But that didn't make any sense. Did it? Why would Margot possibly attack the Queen? Why would she want to erase Scott's memories? And hadn't she always claimed that she couldn't manipulate the memories of people who had dragons? She had always said anyone with a dragon was safe, that it was only the ordinary humans who were susceptible. Had she lied all this time? Why? And why hurt the Queen and his mate?

"What happened?" Chris asked weakly. No wonder no one in the council had told him about this. Did they even know? They had to know, he realized. That was why they were so cautious around him, because they knew he reported things to her. She had manipulated him, he realized angrily. She had been using him to get information on Jamie and Scott without his knowledge. He had been searching for them to protect them and assumed she was too, but she had been trying to find them to hurt them.

"No one knows for sure," Gerard said. "It doesn't make sense that she would attack them, but Marisol projected the attack to all of the council's ranking dragons. We saw what she did."

"How long have you known where he was?"

"Ethan got in touch with me immediately," Gerard said grimly. "We've been trying to work something out. If Margot's heading there now… it's dangerous. Too dangerous. The Elder has been tolerating Jamie but if he joins up with Margot, he could easily eliminate Jamie and Scott, and become the first Queen's mate."

Chris's heart clenched. With Jamie gone, Derek would be in charge of all of Tarragon society and it would be simple for the

Elder to crush his spirit in order to gain absolute control. He suspected the Elder was treating Derek kindly right now because it was in his best interests to do so, but if the Elder had the opportunity to claim absolute power, he wouldn't hesitate to hurt Derek. Chris would do anything to prevent that.

Another councilmember rushed up as three dragons began circling down. Gerard filled the other man in on the situation quickly and they got on their dragons. Chris was a little reassured by the fact that the other councilmember didn't know Jamie was in Spokane; at least the entire council hadn't been lying to him all these months.

"Whatever happens, we have to protect Jamie and Scott," Gerard said as they lifted into the rainy sky. "Let's just hope we get there in time."

CHAPTER THIRTY-ONE

High Price

J amie was dozing against Scott, luxuriating in the feel of his mate against him in the afterglow of their union, when a message from Marisol shocked him to his core. Margot was coming on Yasmina. She had found him, and Yasmina's thoughts were of revenge. Yasmina was almost here, he realized. She had hidden her intentions from Marisol during her flight and would be here soon. He leapt out of bed and rushed for the door, stopped only by Scott, who forced him to dress. He threw on pants and a shirt without looking as Scott did the same and raced into the hall where he ran straight into the Elder, who was just leaving his room.

"What's wrong?" the Elder asked.

"Margot," Jamie said, and the Elder's eyes widened.

"Get your cats and bring them to the quad," the Elder ordered. "I'll lure her there. Have the council there as well. The cats will limit her powers enough for us to trap her and deal with her without fear of her ability."

Jamie's heart was racing but he paused at the Elder's words. He had planned on simply getting on Marisol and running away as fast as he could. But that would also be running away from the kittens, the only weapon against her that they had. He couldn't run.

"You'll help me?" Jamie asked the Elder, trying to listen for any deception.

"I promise," the Elder said. "I'm bound to obey Tarragon law and that means protecting my Queen with my life. She is the one being led into a trap, not you."

Jamie bit his lip. He instinctively mistrusted the Elder, but it was true. The Elder was bound by law to protect Jamie and he had even said that Jamie was necessary to keep the Tarragon world together. He had kept to his vow so far and if he broke it in front of the council, all of Tarragon society would turn against him. He might return to killing dragons, but with every dragon in the world seeking to kill him, he wouldn't last. The Elder knew that. He had to be telling the truth. Not even Scott was voicing doubts, Jamie realized in surprise. Scott must have reached the same conclusion about the Elder's intentions. Scott looked angry and frightened, but he wasn't demanding that they ignore the Elder.

"I'll send for the kittens," Jamie said. "The quad? Margot should be here in less than an hour. The council might not be able to assemble by then. It's the middle of the night."

"If you tell them you're in danger, they'll assemble as quickly as you command," the Elder said. "Less than an hour? I'll need twenty minutes to prepare, and then I'll be there. You should only go there after your cats are there. The cats need to be within sight of Margot at all times. She doesn't need to see them, but whoever has them needs to be able to see her."

Jamie nodded, then rushed out the door. Scott was quick to follow.

"Where are you going, Jamie?"

"To the forest," Jamie said. "I have to let them know to get the kittens."

"Who?"

But Jamie didn't answer. In his mind he was already searching for Rayne or any unicorn within range. Marisol was helping him but she was frightened. She was cowering in the apartment while Narné hovered outside protectively. She would need to be at the quad, he was sure. She and the Elder dragon were the only ones large enough to handle Yasmina. He kept searching as he ran, knowing he needed to get closer before he would be able to reach them. He and Scott entered the final strip of construction before the forest when he felt the flicker of a unicorn. Rayne. He let out a sigh of relief and stumbled to a halt, explaining his need to her. He felt silvery bells in his head and knew that Zari and possibly others from the unicorn tribe would bring Janna, Tiger, and the kittens to the quad. He indicated that they could stay hidden but needed to be close enough to see the woman who arrived, and he gave a mental image of Margot so they knew who to target. He felt Rayne's agreement and heaved a sigh of relief.

"Don't we have to get the kittens?" Scott asked, seemingly puzzled by their abrupt halt.

"No," Jamie said. "People are watching them, and they'll bring the kittens to the quad."

"Who?" Scott repeated.

"Friends," Jamie said evasively, hoping Scott didn't push because he didn't want to have to lie to his boyfriend right now. Not after they had just made up. Scott let the matter drop and wrapped an arm around his shoulder.

"I'll keep you safe, Jamie," he promised. "How soon will the kittens get there?"

"I don't know, but they'll let me know. Let's get a little closer to the quad."

As they walked, he summoned the council, contacting their dragons directly with the message that their Queen's life was at risk and no delay was allowed. By the time he and Scott were adjacent to the quad, they were surrounded by worried councilmembers. Ethan pushed through the crowd to face Jamie.

"The Elder told me what's happening," he said. "Don't get too close to her. We'll handle this. She'll be tried before the council. Since you're the target, you probably shouldn't be in charge, and I don't want to risk Derek, so I'll hold the trial. Does she need to be killed? We could strip her of her rank and exile her if necessary. The Elder assures me she'll agree to that to save her dragon's life."

Jamie considered. Margot would be a threat wherever she went but did she have to die? If she willing agreed to leave, then he suspected she would actually do it. She might go to another Tarragon community and take over, but he would make her exile known worldwide and she would never be able to gain any real power. The Elder had said that she didn't have the strength to unite the Tarragon world and he agreed. The Elder could do it, he was certain, but Margot would never be able to gain enough of a following to be dangerous once she was taken out of power.

"If she agrees to exile without rank, do that," Jamie said slowly. "But she has to agree to it willingly."

"I suspect some persuasion will have to be used," Ethan warned.

"Use whatever means necessary, but in the end she has to be choosing to do it. I don't want her backing out of it later."

"Understood," Ethan said. "The Elder said you had a weapon against her. Is it here yet?"

Jamie reached for Rayne and found her on the other side of the quad. She and the others were in position and Jamie nodded.

"We can go to the quad now. Margot should arrive shortly. Is the Elder here?"

"He's already there."

Jamie took a deep breath. He took Scott's hand and walked to the quad with the council at his back. Marisol and Narné perched on the administrative building next to the quad, and

Jamie thought he saw a flash of white between the trees lining the opposite end of the grassy area. The kittens were in position, then. The Elder was in the center of the quad but when Jamie approached, he gestured for everyone to stay to one side and came to join them.

"How soon until she arrives?"

"Less than ten minutes at the speed she's at," Jamie said, reaching for Yasmina. The dragon was furious that Jamie knew she was coming and it was pushing her to greater speeds, and Jamie caught a hint of other dragons behind her. "She's not alone," he added. "Some of the council is following."

"Are they on her side?"

Jamie squinted. It was Gerald's dragon, which honestly might go either way, but Chris was there too. He would never side with Margot when doing so might put Derek at risk. Where was Derek, he thought suddenly.

"No, they're not. Is Derek here?"

"He's nearby, but protected," the Elder said. "No need to involve him any more than necessary, but he needs to be a witness."

"In case something happens to me, you mean," Jamie said darkly. "He needs to take over for me."

"If you do as I say, you won't be hurt," the Elder said. "But both queens need to be able to say that Margot is giving up her power voluntarily."

He nodded. The Elder moved him and all the council back a little. He didn't go to the middle of the quad but he stood where he was visible to a dragon overhead. And soon enough, there was a dark shape approaching in the sky. She wasn't even bothering to hide herself from the city, Jamie realized. She would be obvious to anyone happening to look up.

"Jamie, instruct Yasmina to land here," the Elder said.

Jamie obeyed and flinched as Yasmina mentally snarled at him. But she would obey, because she knew this was where he was and she wanted him. In less than a minute, Yasmina hurtled to the ground and Margot leapt off. Yasmina took to the air again but Margot stood as if frozen, staring at the Elder.

"You," she hissed. "What is this?"

"You had to know this was coming, Margot," the Elder said. "Give up now."

She laughed. "Not even you can stop me, Elder. You've never been immune to me."

"Try me," the Elder challenged, and Margot's smile faded. Her eyes widened and she looked around, panicked.

"What is this? It can't be-" She snarled just as ferociously as Yasmina had. "Those damn cats. They'll be dead soon enough. Besides, I just need to touch you."

Jamie shivered. So her power still existed but she needed to be in physical contact to use it. She preferred being in physical contact, he knew, but normally she would have been able to exert her power in a larger area. He was grateful the kittens were powerful enough to negate that threat. But as she said, all she had to do was touch someone.

Yasmina flew towards the Elder menacingly and to Jamie's complete shock, he pulled out a gun. The entire council gasped and Yasmina halted midair, startled. No one in Tarragon society used guns. Everyone used swords. It had never even occurred to Jamie to use a gun, nor had it ever crossed his mind that the Elder would have a gun. How long had he had the gun? Why did he have it? Who was he planning on killing with it?

Three dragons approached and Gerald and Chris slid off their dragons, followed by another council member. They seemed stunned at the sight of the gun but Gerald recovered quickly. He strode to the Elder's side as Chris and the other edged away. Chris especially looked nervous as he was as likely to get killed by the Elder as Margot was. What was he even doing here?

"You've lost, Margot," the Elder said. "Let the council decide your fate. You know there aren't grounds for killing you."

"You think I'm going to do what the council says?" Margot asked in a mocking voice. "I control the council."

"Not anymore," Ethan said, stepping forward.

Margot eyed him nervously. She hadn't acknowledged the council that was standing at the edge of the quad and Jamie wondered if she had even noticed them before now. Her eyes went to him and she scowled.

"You don't control either council," Gerald added, stepping beside Ethan. Jamie was grateful he had kept in contact with Gerard all these months and kept the man on his side. "You came here to attack our Queen. That's grounds for removal."

"You can't remove me," Margot said. "I won't allow it."

"Think carefully," the Elder said. "Your dragon will pay the price if you refuse to submit to the council." He leaned forward and grinned. "You know I'm willing to help if your dragon needs to be killed."

She shivered and Yasmina flew slightly farther away. The Elder dragon was here, Jamie realized. It was still strange not being able to sense him but he was loosely circling Yasmina and her attempts to avoid him weren't working. She was trapped. Margot was trapped.

"Fine," Margot said, lifting her hands. "The council can decide my fate. If I believe it's fair, I'll go along with it. If not, I'll find a way to make you pay."

The Elder lowered his gun as Jamie and the council cautiously came forward. Margot glared at him but seemed willing to put up with the formalities of a council trial and as long as she cooperated, Jamie would ignore the Elder dragon growing increasingly more threatening towards Yasmina. He wasn't killing her and she needed the threat to know they were serious.

Ethan and Gerald glanced at each other, then at Scott and the Elder, probably trying to figure out who was supposed to run the meeting. Technically the council was headed by the Queen's mate, but the Elder hadn't been given that privilege without Derek's express permission and Scott was only the second Queen's mate. They were both heads of council but even though it was Ethan's campus, Gerald outranked him. Their eyes landed on Jamie and he gulped. Ethan had assured him that he wouldn't have to do this since he was the target, but with so many other people here to confuse the ranking, it seemed he would once again have to take on the task of disciplining a head of council. At least this time he wouldn't have to execute someone.

Jamie stepped forward when without warning, a shot rang out. Yasmina screamed in rage and Scott grabbed Jamie, yanking him backwards. Jamie stumbled to the ground and the Elder fired again. At what? Yasmina screamed again and plummeted to the ground. She was in agony and Jamie moaned and held his head as her cries pierced him. She was alone. Why was she alone?

CHAPTER THIRTY-TWO

Hidden Talent

D erek remained hidden towards the back of the council, able to see everything but completely protected. His eyes kept going to Chris, who was staying similarly hidden along with the other councilmember who had come from Portland. They were both behind Margot, helping to surround her. Why was Chris here? Had Chris come to protect him? He had forgotten how beautiful Chris was, he thought as he gazed at his former lover. Did Chris still love him? Did he still love Chris? Yes, he decided, feeling the warmth in his heart that couldn't be faked. He still loved him. But as the Elder strode out to face Margot, he realized he had feelings for the Elder as well and was terrified at the thought of Margot erasing his memories. Derek had been able to save Scott; would he be able to save the Elder as well?

He had been stunned when the Elder pulled a gun, but things seemed to settle down quickly. Margot was agreeing to a trial and it was unlikely she would be killed. It looked like Jamie would be handling the trial and he wouldn't kill her if he could help it. He was pretty sure her crimes, though serious, weren't enough to warrant death. As he turned to Jamie, he caught a glimpse of motion as Margot darted forward, and then a crack filled the night and Margot reeled backwards, blood splattering everywhere. Another crack and Margot's body collapsed as her dragon shrieked into the sky. Derek stared at the body. Margot was dead. His eyes traveled to the Elder, holding the gun calmly.

The Elder had shot her.

Yasmina screamed in rage, then her cries were abruptly cut short and he looked up to see the Elder dragon hurling her to the ground, blood dripping from his teeth. He had killed the dragon. But the Elder dragon didn't feed on her, and she hadn't died until after Margot was gone. No laws had been broken, he didn't think.

He stared between the bodies of the dragon and Margot, barely able to process what had happened. He saw Jamie crouched on the ground with Scott over him in a protective position and without thinking, he rushed to Jamie's side to comfort him. Jamie looked at him, eyes wide, and he saw his own horror and shock reflected in those emerald orbs. Scott stood between them and the Elder and while he was unarmed, he was clearly protecting them. Ethan and Gerard stepped between them as well.

The Elder tucked his gun in his belt and considered them.

"I apologize," he said without a trace of remorse in his voice. "She moved to attack you. I protect the Queen."

Jamie got to his feet and Derek stood as well, staring at his mate and unsure how to feel about this. It was true that Margot had moved towards Jamie, but would she have killed him?

"You planned on killing her," Jamie whispered. "It didn't matter what she did, you were going to kill her."

Derek shivered. Was that true? Had the Elder been prepared to kill Margot no matter what happened?

The Elder smiled mercilessly. "She was a threat to you. As I told you, I'm sworn to protect my Queen at all costs."

Derek trembled. So he had planned on it. It was so hard to forget that the Elder was a killer. Seeing him execute that man months ago had scarred him, but the Elder had been so sweet since then. It was hard to reconcile what seemed like diametrically opposed sides to his personality. But he had said that he enjoyed killing, Derek considered. And this was fairly justified.

"Elder," Jamie said, straightening and pushing to stand beside Scott, Ethan, and Gerard in facing the man. He sounded calm now. "Regardless of your intent, killing a member of the council is a grave crime. You did it in front of the entire Spokane council, who will now decide your fate."

Derek's breath caught. Was the Elder going to be killed for protecting Jamie? He knew that Jamie had probably been looking for ways to kill the Elder ever since the man had shown up. Had the Elder given Jamie that excuse? He trembled, unsure how to feel about this. On the one hand, the Elder was a killer who deserved to face justice for his actions. But he remembered what the Elder had said about why he killed, and the hope in his voice when he talked about escaping that fate. He would not let the Elder be killed like this. He took a step forward and the Elder caught his eye, shaking his head ever so slightly. Did the Elder really not want him standing up for him?

"Perhaps," the Elder said. "Or perhaps you'll pardon my crime, in addition to pardoning every murder of a human or dragon I've ever committed."

"Why would I possibly do that?" Jamie scoffed, and Derek wondered what his plan was. He had to have one. This seemed very calculated.

"Because you can't kill me, and if I decide I don't like your terms, I'll go back to killing all of you."

Derek's eyes widened. It was true that they couldn't kill the Elder. Beheading, hunger, thirst, and old age couldn't kill him, so it was unlikely anything else would, either. No one knew that, though, and the Elder hadn't wanted him to share it. Why was the Elder revealing this now? And was the rest of his statement true? If the council decided on a punishment he didn't like, would he break his promise and kill them? Would he kill Derek? He shivered. Did he have any love for Derek at all?

"Just because you have a gun and a large dragon doesn't mean we can't kill you," Jamie said skeptically.

"Do you know my dragon's ability?" the Elder asked with a grin. "Ashton and Margot did, and it's why they feared me. Shall I tell you?"

Everyone else looked confused and Derek stepped forward, but again the Elder shook his head slightly. He bit his lip. This was his mate being threatened, and he couldn't protect him?

"I'm going to draw my gun, but not to hurt you," the Elder said, then took his gun. He held out his other hand angled towards the ground and pointed the gun at his palm. He fired, the bullet bursting through his flesh and planting itself in the grass. The same way the bullet had torn through Margot's body, and Derek raised a hand to his mouth. The Elder winced in pain and he did as well, wanting to protect his mate. But he couldn't, because the Elder seemed to have a plan in all this and he didn't want to ruin it by interfering.

The Elder held up his hand. There was a gaping hole in the middle and Derek was surprised he wasn't in more pain. But as he watched, the hole began to shrink. He had guessed this would happen but it was still shocking to see the Elder healing before his eyes. He wondered how many times the Elder had done something like this, tried to kill himself while trapped in the mountain, but been forced into unending life.

"I'm immortal," the Elder said. "Nothing you do will kill me. If you want me to keep playing by your rules, I will. But you'll pardon me for every murder I've committed."

Jamie swallowed and seemed stunned. Everyone did. The Elder put away his gun and Derek wondered what Jamie would say.

"Why do you care if I pardon your crimes?" Jamie finally asked. "I'm already letting you live."

"I'm immortal," the Elder repeated. "Future Queens may not

be so forgiving. If you pardon everything I've done, then I won't have to worry about it in the future."

Derek didn't like the thought of future Queens, though he knew the Elder must be planning for that eventuality. The Elder would live long after he died, he thought with a shiver. Would he take another Queen? What if he took another Queen while Derek was still alive? Derek would grow old, after all, and maybe the Elder would want someone younger. No, he thought firmly. That would not happen. He wouldn't let it happen.

"There are conditions," Jamie said slowly. So he was considering it. That was good, Derek thought. He thought of what the Elder had said about Jamie's friends. Was he working towards that? Was he using this situation to manipulate Jamie the way he wanted?

"I would expect nothing less," the Elder said with a smirk.

Jamie looked at Ethan and Gerard, then at Derek and Scott, probably wanting to talk to all of them before making any decisions on this matter.

"Are you incapable of making your own decisions, Queen?" the Elder asked, and Jamie flushed in anger at the clearly mocking tone. Was the Elder trying to push Jamie into a bad agreement? Should Derek let that happen? Jamie was his Queen, after all, and a friend, though he still had some reservations. He didn't want Jamie manipulated but he did want the Elder freed from his need to kill. He would let this happen, he decided. He would trust the Elder.

"You'll continue to obey Tarragon law," Jamie said. "But you'll also swear that you won't try to influence the law. You'll obey it only, and you'll obey the spirit and not just the letter."

Derek relaxed slightly. That was a good requirement.

"You will treat all Queens with respect and will never physically or psychologically harm any of your mates, Queens or not,"

Jamie continued, and Derek was pleased that Jamie seemed to be considering him in this situation. Maybe Jamie had forgiven him after their argument earlier. He was starting to forgive Jamie. "You won't do anything that is considered a crime under Tarragon law, and you will never kill another human, dragon, or other creature."

The Elder smiled. "See? You didn't need them," he said, gesturing to Ethan and Gerard. "Those are strict terms, and I can do all but one. I can't guarantee that I won't kill another dragon unless you grant me a favor."

"What?" Jamie asked warily, because that was clearly the key promise being made. But Derek knew the Elder could never keep that promise without whatever favor he was about to ask. Jamie's friends had the power to stop the Elder from killing and Derek just hoped Jamie would grant this.

"I have immortality, but not eternal youth," the Elder said, and Derek could fear the bitterness and longing in that statement. "I need to kill dragons to stay young. But if you were to offer me something that could give me eternal youth, I would never need to kill another dragon."

"There's nothing that does that," Jamie said, sounding puzzled. Derek was, too. The Elder had never specified how Jamie's friends would help but this seemed impossible.

"You can't offer it to me directly, perhaps, but your friends can," the Elder said, and gestured to one side of the quad that was blocked by trees. Were the friends there? Had they come to support Jamie? Jamie looked surprised at the gesture, also looking into the trees. There was definitely someone or something there. He seemed thoughtful, and his eyes had the vacant look that indicated he was talking to his dragon. Then he looked back at the Elder.

"If you had eternal youth, you would agree to everything I've asked?"

"Yes," the Elder said without hesitation. "And as a gesture of goodwill, I won't participate in your mating flights unless you specifically request it, since I'm sure you meant to include that requirement."

Jamie blushed and Derek's eyes narrowed. Unless Jamie requested it? No. The Elder would never fly in Jamie's mating flight no matter what happened. What if Jamie accidentally sent out a request to every dragon the way he had for his first mating flight? Derek hadn't been linked to a dragon at the time but he knew every dragon in the world had felt it. If Jamie did that again, would the Elder join in? Even though the Elder belonged to Derek? He huffed jealously, then caught sight of Chris across the clearing. He had been assuming that the Elder would remain his mate, but what if Chris won? The Elder would want to be Queen's mate, he knew. If he didn't get Derek, would he go after Jamie? He would at least want the option. Maybe this wasn't as big a deal as he worried.

Jamie seemed deep in thought, though he wasn't glancing at anyone else for help now. This was up to him, the first Queen, and no one would interfere with whatever deal he made. It was a lot of pressure, Derek thought sympathetically. Jamie was only a year older than he was, after all, and he wouldn't want to be making this kind of choice. Whatever he did right now would have implications for years to come. Centuries, even, since the Elder was immortal.

"I'll only pardon you for murders you confess," Jamie said slowly. "Anything you don't tell me won't be covered."

"I've killed quite a few people over the centuries," the Elder said. "I've forgotten most of them."

"Your dragon will remember," Jamie said sharply. "Use your dragon to give me the information and for every murder that you tell me, I'll pardon it. I won't pardon anything else."

"And your friends?" the Elder asked, glancing again towards

the trees.

Jamie considered and again his eyes had that vacant look. Derek wondered who exactly these friends were that somehow knew how to grant eternal youth. He hoped that Jamie would agree to this, that his friends would agree. The Elder's eyes sparkled with hope, something he had never seen before.

We will grant you eternal youth in exchange for what our Queen has demanded, Marisol said so everyone could hear. Derek let out a sigh of relief and caught the victorious glint in the Elder's eye.

"One more thing," Jamie said. "I want to know your dragon's name."

"Is that your only other condition or are there more?" the Elder asked, but he asked in a polite tone. He was likely willing to agree to quite a lot for the promise of eternal youth. Why would Jamie need the dragon's name, though? The answer dawned on him and he looked at the Elder dragon consideringly. The Elder dragon was removed from all other dragons. Jamie couldn't sense him. But if he knew his name, he would be able to sense him and there was a good chance the dragon would be brought back into the fold of the other dragons. Did the Elder care about that? Maybe he would want it, Derek thought.

"That's it," Jamie said slowly, clearly uncertain of that statement. He probably knew he could get away with more right now but didn't know what else to ask. Ethan and Gerard didn't seem to have anything to add either, so this was probably a good deal for everyone. Especially the Elder. Derek had to hide a smile at the thought that the Elder would finally be free, and would never have to kill again.

"Do you accept?" Jamie asked.

The Elder stepped forward and extended his hand. "I do."

Jamie eyed his gun, then closed the distance between them and shook the man's hand. Derek let out a soft sigh and heard it echoed by the council around him. The Elder smiled.

"We have several pieces of agreement to work out before it goes into effect. To show my sincerity, I'll tell you my dragon's name and my crimes first, and then you can pardon me and your friends can give me youth."

"All right," Jamie said. "I assume it'll take time for you to list everything."

"With my dragon's help, not as much as you might think. My dragon is Nieve."

Jamie's eyes went blank and Derek knew he was already in communication with the creature. Nieve. It was a pretty name, he thought, and reached out to Jettie to share it with her. She was pleased to know the name of her mate and he could tell that she could sense the Elder dragon now, too. He was part of their society again and Jettie told him that the dragon was pleased, and happy he wouldn't have to kill again. She told him the Elder dragon didn't like killing, but liked old age worse and would do what it took to survive.

"He's not like you at all," Jamie observed, eyes fixed on Nieve. The Elder laughed.

"He complements me well. Are you ready to hear my crimes?"

"Here? Now?" Jamie asked, looking around. Derek was puzzled as well. Surely they should go to the council chamber at least. He suspected it would take hours if not days given the amount of murders the Elder must have committed to stay young all these centuries. But the Elder simply smiled.

"You said I should use my dragon's help, right?"

"Yes," Jamie said, sounding puzzled.

"Then there's no need to go anywhere. Hold on."

CHAPTER THIRTY-THREE

Overwhelmed

Scott didn't know what the Elder was going to say, what murders he was going to confess to, but he didn't like that it was happening in the open. There weren't any students around at the moment, as the council had cleared the area and it was so late at night, but what if a student came too close? This was going to take time, he was sure, and Jamie seemed equally wary. The Elder smiled, and then Jamie let out a stifled cry and fell to his knees, clutching his head.

"What did you do?" Scott cried, kneeling at Jamie's side. Jamie was tense and shaking, his hands scrabbling against his ears as if to block out some unheard noise. He was in pain and he could feel panic from Narné, from all of the dragons. Jamie was hurt and they were frightened.

"Nieve told him the people and dragons I've killed. All of them," the Elder said with a shrug. "You might want to have Marisol instruct the dragons not to panic. It may take a few hours for Jamie to process all of the information I just gave him, but he's in no danger."

"Of course he's in danger," Scott shouted, furious at the Elder, furious that they hadn't expected something like this. Jamie was completely helpless and in clear pain and the dragons were growing visibly distraught.

"Scott, order Marisol to calm the dragons," Ethan said, coming to his side and placing a hand on his shoulder. "The Elder can't be lying about this. Jamie will recover, but if the dragons continue like this, our society is at risk. Every dragon in the world is feeling this."

"You tell Marisol," Scott snapped.

"She isn't listening to anyone, but she'll listen to you," Ethan said. "Calm her down."

Reluctantly, Scott felt for Marisol. It was difficult communicating with her, since she wasn't Narné, and the instant he made contact, he felt her panic. Jamie's mind was overwhelmed and it was confusing Marisol because everything made sense to her. She didn't understand why it didn't make sense to Jamie and it was her fear, not Jamie's pain, that was upsetting the dragons. He soothed her and explained that so much information took a long time to sort out for humans. She didn't understand; how could Jamie not process things as quickly as she did? Scott continued to soothe her and in minutes she was calm, and he didn't feel panic emanating from Narné anymore. He asked Marisol to let the dragons across the world know that she and Jamie were safe and she obeyed.

He opened his eyes and everyone looked more relaxed. As he studied Jamie, he realized it wasn't that Jamie was in pain. He did simply look overwhelmed, as though too many voices were shouting at him all at once. Which was probably what it felt like. Derek hesitantly approached and knelt beside him, touching Jamie cautiously. Then Derek's eyes went to Chris, standing on the opposite side of the quad with the other councilmember from Portland. The Elder also looked at Chris, who flinched.

Then, to Scott's surprise, Chris smiled, a defiant grin aimed right at the Elder. His fear seemed to fade and the Elder grinned in response.

"I'm sure I'll see you in Derek's next mating flight," the Elder said. "You may remain on this campus if you like. You're not a threat."

"Don't underestimate me," Chris warned. "You're bound to obey Tarragon law even if you lose the mating flight."

"I won't lose," the Elder said. "But you're welcome to try."

Derek was looking between them nervously and Scott wondered how he felt about the two of them. He and the Elder had grown close despite everyone's best efforts to keep them apart, and since he hadn't seen Chris in so long, that relationship had faded. Who did Derek prefer to win? Did Derek even know? Derek would probably let the flight happen naturally, Scott thought, and take whatever mate he ended up with. Normally the dragon being chased had some say in their partner – though not always – but he suspected Jettie was going to be absolutely neutral about the two of them.

Scott stroked Jamie's head. He tried to hold Jamie's hands but Jamie pulled against him, still trying to block sounds that weren't there.

"I'm taking Jamie somewhere safer," Scott announced. "You'll remain with the council until he recovers."

He glanced in the direction he knew the kittens were in, though he couldn't actually see them. He wondered who these friends of Jamie were. Jamie had been so close about the forest and who had the kittens. Friends with the ability to grant eternal youth. Not humans, then, but what?

"Whoever has Janna and Tiger," he said loudly enough for them to hear, "I'm sure having them would help Jamie recover."

There was a moment of silence, and then a young black woman in a white outfit, almost like a uniform, approached. Janna was in her arms and Tiger trotted by her feet. She smiled cautiously at everyone and stared at the dragons in awe. Definitely not from Tarragon society, but who was she? He could tell everyone was wondering but he pushed it aside and scooped up

Jamie.

"You can use my office," a councilmember offered. "I have a couch."

It was one of the administrators so his office was right there, and Scott gratefully accepted. The councilmember led them into the building, Tiger and the girl trailing behind. It was a lush office and Scott was amazed the man hadn't been here for years. Not only was there a couch and a full bookshelf, the desk was littered with papers and various notes were stuck to the computer monitor and even though the semester hadn't started yet, it looked like it had always been his office. Scott laid Jamie on the couch. Jamie curled into a ball but when the girl placed Janna next to him, his tension lessened.

Janna butted against Jamie and he wrapped an arm around the cat, his hands finally stopped their incessant motions as he held her close. Tiger hopped up by Jamie's feet and started purring loudly, and Scott sat next to him and stroked his head. He hadn't realized how much he missed Tiger and as Tiger curled up on his lap, rather ignoring Jamie, he felt something relax deep inside him. Today had too much tension, but sitting here with his family, he knew they were safe. For the moment, at least.

The councilmember offered to walk the girl back to the quad to give Jamie and Scott privacy and she nervously agreed after Scott assured her that he would bring the cats back to their kittens. Although he would love to have his family on the campus, it was too dangerous having all of them so close to the dragons. While it didn't directly affect Narné's ability, his dragon let him know that other dragons were uncomfortable. The kittens would return to the forest but at least now Scott knew they were well taken care of.

He stroked Tiger and Jamie in a relaxing rhythm until finally, after what felt like forever, Jamie opened his eyes and held a hand to his head. He looked deeply shaken. Janna purred and he looked at her, but didn't smile. His eyes looked empty and Scott wondered what had happened. Slowly, Jamie sat up, keeping Janna on his lap and petting her. His eyes stayed on the cat until finally, minutes later, he looked at Scott.

"I saw all of it," Jamie said in a soft voice. "All the people he killed. All the dragons he killed. He showed me everything."

Scott's eyes narrowed. He hadn't actually thought of the implications of having Jamie hear about all of those murders, how it would devastate Jamie, and pouring that knowledge straight into his brain erased any filters that hearing it said aloud would provide. He hadn't heard about it; he had seen it. Killing Ashton had shaken Jamie for months. How long would it take for him to recover from this?

"It's all right," Jamie said, halting his petting of Janna to take Scott's arm and lean against him. "He was honest. He is honest. He wants this badly. He'll do what we want."

"Jamie," Scott began, though he didn't know what to say. What was there to say? They had to stay true to their part of the bargain. Scott sighed. "Did he hurt you? He promised not to hurt the Queen. If he did, then-"

"No, he didn't hurt me," Jamie said. "He surprised me, overwhelmed me, but he didn't hurt me. I'm sorry to make you worry."

"I'll always worry about you," Scott said, leaning to kiss Jamie's head. "Do you need more time to recover? The Elder said it would be a few hours but it's only been two."

"I'm fine," Jamie said. "I want to get this over with."

"How is he getting eternal youth?"

Jamie was silent, then met Scott's eyes. "I don't have their permission to tell you, Scott. I'm sorry. I hope someday I can, but I can't betray them after they've done so much for me."

Scott kissed him gently on the lips. He was disappointed, but he wouldn't push. Hopefully he would find out someday, and in the meantime he would research what could possibly give eternal youth. The fountain of youth, he supposed, but that didn't exist. Did it? Dragons weren't supposed to exist, so perhaps there was a fountain somewhere that people knew about and Jamie had somehow found them. The girl who had brought Janna and Tiger had looked quite young, after all. Maybe there was a fountain.

They got to their feet, both holding their cats. Jamie nuzzled against Janna with a soft smile.

"I missed you, baby," he said as he rubbed noses with her. "We'll be together again soon."

Tiger batted at Scott and he quickly started being more lovey-dovey with his kitty as well. They were so cute, always demanding attention and love. They were smart, too, far smarter than he would have expected from a cat. Not all cats were this perfect, he knew. Tiger and Janna were special. The best cats in the world.

They returned to the quad and were surprised to find it empty. Jamie looked to where the cats had been and waved, and the same girl approached.

"You're okay, Jamie?" she asked in a worried voice.

"Yeah," he said. He handed her Janna and Tiger squirmed out of Scott's arms to go to the girl's feet like before. "I'll be in touch about the rest. It'll probably be tomorrow night. Can that work?"

She eyed Scott before nodding, then headed back towards the trees. Jamie took Scott's arm.

"The others are in the council chamber," he said. "Or at least the ones we want are. Most of the council has dispersed."

"Where's Derek? And Chris?"

Jamie's brow crinkled and he had the absent look of one communicating with his dragon. He looked adorable and Scott was tempted to kiss him, but that might break his concentration.

"Derek's in the council chamber with the Elder," he said. "Mike is helping Chris get settled in. Chris is going to move back here. He and the Elder spoke a little. Mike thinks the situation is under control and now the Elder can't act against Chris."

Scott nodded. If Mike thought it was under control then it probably was. Mike more than anyone understood jealousy and if he thought Chris and the Elder could survive seeing each other every day, then the situation couldn't be as bad as Scott worried. They headed to the council chamber and found the two council heads and Derek with the Elder. Derek was sitting next to the Elder, their thighs pressed against each other. He would definitely be neutral in his mating flights and not automatically prefer Chris. Scott hoped he didn't come to prefer the Elder and wondered what Chris's reaction to that would be. Chris had been devastated when he lost Derek; if he realized that Derek truly belonged to the Elder, could he handle it? He would probably think of it as a challenge, Scott decided, thinking of the arrogant smile Chris had when he faced the Elder. He, like all of the council, were predators. If Derek's affection waned, he would just fight to get it back and the Elder had to know it.

"Elder," Jamie said solemnly. "You are pardoned for every murder you have committed before killing Margot, and for killing her and her dragon. You will never face punishment for them. You have your clean slate. Don't ruin it."

"I have no need, once the other part of our deal is complete," the Elder said, and he sounded pleased. "Thank you, Queen Jamie."

"We'll talk about the rest tomorrow night, when the moon rises," Jamie said. "Will you stay true to your agreement until then?"

"Of course," the Elder said. "There is one aspect of our deal you may want to reconsider, Jamie. I would be willing to remain with the current terms or change as you see fit."

"What is it?" Jamie asked warily.

"I'm bound to obey Tarragon law and its spirit, but right now you're making a considerable number of changes that go against the spirit of Tarragon law. I can either keep true to my promise and oppose you, or I can be your ally and support the changes you're making."

Scott was startled. It was true, Jamie was making a lot of changes that the council hated. He hadn't realized that the Elder would have every right to oppose Jamie and clearly Jamie hadn't realized it either. But if they altered the terms to make it dependent on a single Queen's wishes, that could easily backfire.

"The changes I'm making reflect the times we're living in," Jamie said slowly. "We live in a world that's growing more connected, so we can't leave people out. Our world values diversity, so we need to embrace those different from us and oppose intolerance. Humans have reached a point where survival isn't the main priority for most, and so it is our duty to use our privilege to help as many others as we can. You need to stay true to tradition but balance it with the changing needs of our world. If a Queen wishes to dramatically change Tarragon law and you feel that it threatens Tarragon society and sends us backwards as a society, then you should nonviolently oppose it. If you feel it will help our society advance, then you should embrace the change."

The Elder nodded and Ethan and Gerald looked pleased. Derek seemed impressed, as was Scott. That was a beautiful way to put it and also a clever way to get around the problem of having the Elder either follow current law too rigidly or obey the whims of whoever was Queen. There was still a lot of room for him to wreak chaos if he wanted, but it was the best set of guidelines Scott could imagine.

"Then I'll obey the spirit of Tarragon law as reflected by the ideals of the current world," the Elder said. "Since you must realize those are ideals only and not reality. Our world is just as cruel and divisive as ever, but you're right. We have advanced and our dreams have changed, even if our reality hasn't. I'll use that when deciding my approach, and I suspect I'll be your ally on any changes you make, since you seem to have thought out your changes more carefully than I realized."

"Thank you," Jamie said. "Are there any other problems you see with the demands I'm making of you?"

"An exemption for extraordinary circumstances would be nice," he said.

Jamie was silent for a long moment, clearly deep in thought. Then he sighed.

"You have to obey Tarragon law and its spirit, in the ways we just described. If the absolute only way to do that is to break some other part of what you've agreed to, then it will be allowed."

Scott was startled. The most obvious way the Elder could break his agreement was to kill someone, or kill a dragon, but Jamie was giving him permission if he deemed it necessary. Was that really wise? But only if it advanced Tarragon law, Scott considered. Perhaps it wasn't a bad amendment. Neither Ethan nor Gerald seemed to oppose it. The Elder smiled.

"You negotiate far better than I would have imagined, young Queen. But my own Queen and I need to speak in private."

Derek nodded. He was probably still in shock from seeing his mate kill someone and needed the Elder's reassurances. It had taken him weeks after the execution earlier in the summer. While Scott hated that he was turning to the Elder for comfort, it was necessary that Derek maintain a good relationship until the next mating flight. As Derek and the Elder stood to leave, Derek came to his side and kissed his cheek.

"Keep Jamie out of trouble, okay?" he asked softly, smiling that irresistible smile of his. Scott smiled back, pleased that it seemed the Queens weren't fighting anymore, then blushed as he looked at Jamie. But Jamie didn't look upset or jealous of the kiss and the whispered words. He just looked thoughtful.

When they had left, Jamie spoke to Ethan and Gerald for quite a while to sort out what needed to happen on both campuses. The Portland women's campus had lost its head, after all, and while there were several women who could potentially take over, none of them really stood out. Ashton had maintained a strict hierarchy within the men's council so after his death, everyone already knew exactly where the power fell, but Margot had kept everyone at around the same level. Age would most likely determine it, and status as a pet, since Margot, like Ashton, had kept pets and given them preferential treatment. As they spoke, Scott realized that both Ethan and Gerald must have been Ashton's pets in the same way Mike had been. It was an odd realization about such powerful men, but then again, Mike was powerful in his own way.

Finally, Jamie led him back to their room where their pleasure had been spoiled what seemed like days ago. Jamie flopped on the bed, staring at the ceiling. Scott cuddled next to him and Jamie curved against his body.

"I'm so tired," Jamie said. "My head is still spinning."

"Just sleep," Scott said, kissing his forehead. "I'll protect you. You're safe."

As Jamie's eyes shut, Scott realized that it was actually true. For the first time in a very long time, they were safe. Margot was gone, the Elder was no longer an active threat, and their relationship was solid enough that Jamie hadn't been jealous of Derek at all. Of course, it wasn't Jamie's jealousy that had been a problem since arriving here, but Derek had never kissed him in front of Jamie either. Their relationship, for once, seemed absolutely steady and there were no outside threats that he could think of. Janna and Tiger weren't here, but they would be soon. They were safe, protected by powerful and mysterious friends. And the kittens would have a new home here in Spokane.

Scott shut his eyes and rested against Jamie. For once, he could imagine a future with him and Jamie living and laughing and loving in peace. He smiled and nestled against his lover, finally content.

CHAPTER THIRTY-FOUR

Young Hope

J amie was careful not to wake Scott as he unwound himself and got out of bed. It was dark and the moon was rising. The day had passed smoothly and it was time for the final part of the agreement, and the part he had the least control over. If for some reason the unicorns backed out of this, then everything else would fall apart. He had pardoned the Elder and couldn't go back on that even if this didn't work.

The Elder was waiting in the hall as he quietly let himself out and shut the door. He didn't want Scott to wake up and find him gone even though Scott would know where he was. The Elder smiled at him and for the first time, it seemed sincere. He seemed almost hopeful. His dragon only killed to survive; did the Elder secretly regret the deaths he had caused as well? Jamie could only hope that were the case. Without a word, Jamie led the Elder to the woods. The Elder didn't question him but once they were surrounded by trees, he did question himself. Normally the mist led him where he needed to go but there was no mist yet. He kept walking, waiting for the mist to roll in and guide his steps, but none did.

Was it because the Elder was with him? The mist always protected him; did he not need protection with the Elder at his side, or was this an indication that the mist and the mountain didn't want him to go through with this? Had the unicorns changed their minds and so the mist wouldn't take him to the right place?

They had been walking without any hint of mist for several minutes when a branch snapped nearby and Jamie froze. There were dangerous creatures here, after all, bears and cougars who would attack humans unlucky enough to stumble on their path.

But it was Zuri who walked out to their path. She looked a little uncertain but gestured for them to follow. As they walked, she glanced at the Elder.

"What do you know about us?" she asked.

"The unicorn tribe has been in Spokane for over a thousand years," the Elder said, and Zuri's eyes widened. "While I've never spoken to any of you before, I'm well aware of your presence."

"But no one else in your society knows?" she asked, sounding worried.

"Two others knew. They are now both dead."

Jamie was surprised. That meant that Ashton and Margot had known, since they had to be the two people he was taking about.

"You're sure they didn't tell anyone?" Jamie asked.

"They knew to keep it to themselves. They stumbled upon knowledge of the tribe the same way I did, though researching eternal youth. The dragons do not allow humans to speak about other tribes."

That was true; Marisol would never forgive Jamie if he mentioned the unicorns or any of the other creatures she had accidentally indicated. Ashton and Margot, whatever their flaws, obeyed their dragons. They wouldn't have told anyone, but people might have found out the same way they had. Jamie would have to keep an eye on it. He remembered once in class he had asked if unicorns were real, if other creatures were real, and he had been ridiculed. At the time, he had assumed the teacher had dismissed the question because it was ridiculous, but maybe the man's dragon had told him that was the only appropriate response. What if there were other people who wondered about the other tribes? Well, that couldn't be a new phenomenon and if the other creatures were currently safe, they would probably remain that way.

They finally reached a clearing. Rayne was waiting with two other unicorns and the Elder gasped. Even Jamie was stunned at their combined beauty. Their horns glittered in the moonlight and there was a glow around them. A sense of contentment washed over him. With these incredible creatures around, he was safe. No one or nothing could hurt him.

"Step forward," Zuri said to the Elder. "Now, you're not a virgin so this will probably hurt a lot, but they have to touch you to give you youth. Don't fight them, even if you think you're dying."

"I can't die," the Elder said, but he sounded breathless. He was in awe of the unicorns just as Jamie was.

"Immortal creatures can kill each other," Zuri said. "They can kill you if they want."

The Elder appeared shocked at that, but then Rayne approached and lowered her horn to his heart. He seemed to brace himself and then Rayne lunged forward, piercing his chest with her horn. The Elder screamed. The second unicorn plunged its horn through the Elder's body, then the third unicorn, until the Elder's body dangled between the three horns. If the unicorns weren't exuding such peace, Jamie might have vomited at the sudden violence and the way the Elder's body seemed to be barely held together by skin and horns. A light began glowing, flushing across his skin, and in unison the three unicorns pulled their horns out of his body. He collapsed, but the light grew brighter and brighter.

Jamie shielded his eyes until the light faded and when he could see again, the Elder was sitting on the ground staring at his body in shock. He looked younger than he had moments ago, and healthier. He ran his hands over each other with a look of stunned pleasure on his face, then he leapt to his feet.

"Don't touch them," Zuri warned, and it seemed like the warning was needed because the Elder visibly stopped himself from lunging at the unicorns.

"I need to thank them," the Elder said. "You don't know what this means. You don't know how thankful I am."

"They know," Zuri said.

The three unicorns faded into the trees and Jamie felt a sense of loss. He would never see them again, he realized. He would still see the kittens, still see Zuri, but he knew without question that he would never again see a unicorn and the loss hit him deeply. Zuri escorted them back to campus without a word and the Elder was beaming. It was hard to match the excited young man next to Jamie with the bitter monster he had been only hours before. Maybe this change was more than just youth. Maybe this really was his chance to free himself from murder and sin. And maybe Zuri's words about immortals killing each other had offered him another escape, Jamie considered. After all, true immortality seemed more like a curse than a gift and perhaps the knowledge that he could end his life would help him live more fully and appreciate life in all its forms. Whatever had changed, Jamie knew from watching him that the Elder would never again be a threat to Jamie or anyone in Tarragon society.

Derek and Scott were both waiting in the hall talking to each other when Jamie and the Elder approached and though the two were quite close, Jamie didn't feel even a bit of jealousy. Well, maybe a bit. But not the jealousy that would have consumed him before he and Scott had sorted things out. Derek seemed stunned by the changes in the Elder, approaching him slowly and stroking his cheek. Jamie wondered idly if the Elder would start using his real name now that the title of the Elder no longer fit, and he wondered what that name might be. Then the Elder kissed Derek passionately, surprising Jamie. He knew they were lovers, obviously, but Derek and the Elder were scrupulous about keeping displays of affection in private. Scott took Jamie's hand and led him into their bedroom, shutting the door before sweeping him into their own kiss, a far more intimate and tender affair.

"I hope you tell me about it someday, Jamie," Scott said. "You look more peaceful than I've ever seen you."

Jamie smiled and inhaled the dandelion scent of his boyfriend, his lover, his mate.

"I am peaceful," he said. "Everything's finally right in the world, and I'm in your arms. This is all I've ever wanted."

As Scott led him to the bed, he realized how absolutely true that was. All his life he had wanted love and a family. Someone to protect him. After his father died, he had been self-destructive and abused, neglected by his remaining family and spiraling into fear and loneliness. From the moment he first saw Scott, he had fallen in love. He remembered the first weeks of their relationship as they slowly got to know each other, and then his stumbling coming out as he admitted how much he loved Scott. At that point he had thought he loved Scott, but now he knew how deep their love truly went. They had been through so much, had so many fights and betrayals and they had hated and resented each other for so many reasons, but through all of it, their love won out. And now, with everything right in the world, they had each other. It was everything he had ever wanted, and more.

ABOUT THE AUTHOR

Elizabeth James

Elizabeth James hails from Portland, Oregon and spent many hours of her childhood tucked away in the Gold Room of Powell's Books, reading science fiction and fantasy masterpieces and hidden treasures. She writes romance with strong elements of science fiction and fantasy as a result, focusing on LGBT characters.

THRALL OF DARKNESS

Thrall of Darkness was founded because there is a shortage of good, quality literature featuring gay protagonists that does not reduce gay characters to stereotypes or dismiss them as secondary characters. Every story seeks to challenge the status quo by focusing on gay characters and combining drama, action, and sex into an addicting blend of fun-filled narrative.

You can find more information on Thrall of Darkness
novels and short stories at thrallofdarkness.com.

BOOKS BY THIS AUTHOR

Demon Season

Taylor just wanted to bond with a regular demon during his first demon season, but instead he ends up with the prince of demons, an incubus! He fights through his fears of intimacy while battling past enemies as he and his demon come to a new understanding.

A Vampire's Desire

Kairos takes a job in an ancient vampire house knowing nothing about them and their society, and immediately falls in love with his boss, a powerful but cold vampire. As he tries to get closer, threats from a rival house threaten to tear them apart. Kairos pursues his boss's heart while struggling to protect himself and the ones he loves, and he wonders if he made the right choice entering vampire society.

Dragon Tamer

Luke has heard dragons all his life and when a dragon summons him to raise her dragonlings, he runs away to help her. But the world he enters is fraught with danger and he knows little of the outside world. As the dragons begin dying off and dragon tamers like him become scarce, a rival tribe kidnaps him and everything he knows is thrown into question.

Sagent

Gabriel is a sagent, a sex agent, at the start of his career, but he is already scarred by his previous agency. When he is sent on a dangerous mission to the underbelly of Destiny, everything starts to fall apart. Isolated from his agency and not knowing where to go, Gabriel must choose between returning to safety and Destiny, or staying and forging his own path.

First Prince

Wren is the beautiful yet rebellious first prince of Fontain, forced to move to the Imperial Palace as part of a treaty. Upon arriving, he receives a frigid welcome and realizes his stay will be fraught with danger. When he finds romance in an unexpected place, he realizes that his life may not be as dire as he imagined and pleasure can be found where it is least expected.

Prisoner Of Love

When Prince Tristan is captured in battle, he fully expects to be tortured and killed. But the torture turns to erotic pleasure as he learns that his enemy, Prince Ryan, is in love with him and has been planning his capture with meticulous care for years. Will Tristan hold firm to his principles, or will Ryan's forceful seduction overpower his senses?

Dark Offering

Nightmares are a nightly occurrence on the planet of Ylse, and they're strong enough to lure humans to be fed on by the creatures who haunt the night. Jarl is charged with risking the night to feed the colony. He comes across one of the creatures offering peace. Is the creature sincere or is this just a new way to lure the humans to their deaths on this inhospitable planet?

Bride Of Albis

Sam and his small crew of space-faring traders have their usual routine permanently shattered when they are kidnapped by pirates. Sam makes a deal with the head of the pirates: he will be sold as a slave in exchange for the freedom of his crew. But when he discovers that the pirate lied and sold his crew as well, he vows vengeance.

Seeking More

Seeking More is a collection of eight contemporary gay romance stories that range from the deeply emotional to action-packed, from hapless MFA students to couples on the brink of a new relationship. Each story is focused not only on steamy romance, of which there is plenty, but also on character development and an emotional connection between reader and character.

Eve Of Eternity

Sabine is a young woman searching for her identity while fleeing the powerful man trying to steal her heart and mind. She's almost under his control when she is kidnapped by a man with conflicting loyalties and a mysterious past who claims to kidnap her in order to rescue her. Will she break free from the men around her?

Treacherous A Dragon's Love

In the middle of the final battle against the great dragon Arostrath, a woman appears bound in golden chains. The King claims her as his reward but the youngest son has an unusual fondness for her that could cast the kingdom into ruin. Will his love for the beautiful and strange woman destroy the kingdom, or does her mystery hide the answer to all of their prayers?